**Based on the real diaries of pioneer women
and including a historical forward by the author**

They camped nearby for the night, and by mid-morning of the next day, the company came to the fork in the road that was called the "Parting of the Ways." Some wagons would head northwest to Oregon, and the others would head southwest to California. America had decided to continue on to California Territory, despite the war.

All the women had tears in their voices when they said good-bye....

THE

OVERLAND

TRAIL

WENDI LEE

A TOM DOHERTY ASSOCIATES BOOK

NEW YORK

This is a work of fiction. All the characters and events portrayed in this book are either products of the author's imagination or are used fictitiously.

THE OVERLAND TRAIL

Copyright © 1996 by Wendi Lee

Cover art by Albert Bierstadt, *The Oregon Trail*, Courtesy of The Butler Institute of American Art

A Forge Book
Published by Tom Doherty Associates, Inc.
175 Fifth Avenue
New York, NY 10010

Forge® is a registered trademark of Tom Doherty Associates, Inc.

ISBN: 0-812-55528-7
Library of Congress Card Catalog Number: 96-1411

First edition: June 1996
First mass market edition: August 1997

Printed in the United States of America

0 9 8 7 6 5 4 3 2 1

In memory of
Sarah Winnemucca Hopkins,
an interpreter and a diplomat
who tried to bridge the gap
between white men and the Paiute nation,
and
Jane Gould
and all the anonymous women
who traversed the Overland Trail
and carved out a life in the West.

ACKNOWLEDGMENTS

The following people were instrumental in helping my research of the material that led to the writing of this book: Mary Kay Lane, Terri Willits, Sierra Adare, Natalia Aponte, Barbara Puechner, Linda Quinton, Karen Lovell, Charles and Cathy Shouse, Matt Clemens, Kathy Ptacek, the Women Writing the West, and, of course, my wonderful husband, Terry Beatty.

I couldn't have written this book without their support.

FOREWORD

Very few women are mentioned in history books, and the women who inhabit the mythical West of fiction and movies tend to be stereotypical: someone's wife or mother, a prostitute or saloon girl. In America Hollis, the heroine of *The Overland Trail*, I've tried to create a character based on the *real* women who traveled west in the mid-1800s by using the actual diaries of the women who made the journey.

The year America traveled, 1846, was the year of the doomed Donner party, and it was three years before gold was discovered at Sutter's Mill. Most of the women who traveled west went with their husbands, but many died along the way, often leaving widowers with children to raise in a strange land with no one to help them.

It was common practice for women to give birth along the trail. Waiting until a baby was born before going on the journey wasn't an option for many families. But the fact is that those women who traveled the Overland Trail, better known back then as the Emigrant Trail, were more than an appendage to a man. A good number of these women left loved ones behind to settle a forbidding land.

There were many dangers for the emigrants to face besides hostile Indians, wild animals, and Mother Nature. For instance, cooking around the campfire could become a hazard on the prairie when the winds whipped up suddenly. If a woman wearing a dress was standing downwind, her skirt could easily catch fire and she could burn to death before anyone could find a bucket of water. Most women would wear their husbands' pants for safety, but sometimes they just didn't think it would happen to them.

Some perils were more insidious because the signs weren't as prominent as a rattlesnake bite or a war shout. During my research, I came across an account of a woman who had a fight with her husband and refused to go on. Her children were placed in other wagons as the train moved on, and when the husband couldn't convince her to continue, he left her behind as well. The account does not go on to tell what happened to this woman—did she finally decide to catch up with them or did she go back east? It is a dramatic moment, whether in fiction or real life.

On the brighter side, emigrants used any excuse to break out the musical instruments. Weddings were as good a reason as any. Marriage was not looked at in the same way as it is today. Men and women often got married more for companionship than romance or passion. Many men and women "sparked," or courted, while journeying to the Territories and, somewhere along the way, decided to marry. When a preacher was available, whether in the wagon train itself or at one of the forts visited, the couple would say their vows.

I used numerous Overland Trail diaries and spent hours of research to evoke America Hollis's arduous journey. Among the most memorable women was Jane Gould, who made the trek in 1862 with her husband, Albert, their two sons, and Albert's sister and brother-in-law. Jane's wagon train survived a cattle stampede and an encounter with hostile Indians.

Jane was the more durable one of the couple—Albert was ill for most of the journey, and a year after their move to California, he died. But Jane married again and had another son with her second husband.

One of the other interesting women diarists was Mary Louisa Black, who was sick with choleralike symptoms for most of the way. She was a woman of strong Northern sympathies and treated all races equally, even teaching her slaves (her husband was raised in the tradition of the South) to read alongside her own daughter. I took America's attitude toward slavery from Mary Louisa.

Researching the aspects of cooking was a treat for me—when food was plentiful, there was a lot more variety than one might imagine. Jackrabbits, buffalo, and deer were easy to come by in the early years of emigration. But even then, it could be tough to find meat on occasion. And when that happened, cooks often got creative, boiling beans with whatever wild vegetables and roots could be found, and if there was a little bacon and red onion to add for flavor, all the better.

Ash cake was a common bread. Emigrants used two parts cornmeal to one part buttermilk or water, one-third part fat, and a healthy pinch of baking soda. The ingredients were mixed together with enough water to make a thick dough. A hole was made in the ashes of a hot fire and the ash cake was placed in the center. Once it had a crust, the baking bread was covered with ashes until it was done.

Fried sweet potatoes or yams were a treat for the early emigrants and for Indians. Sweet potatoes were peeled and cut into thick slices, then fried on both sides in hot fat in a skillet. Three healthy pinches of brown sugar and three parts milk were then added and the dish simmered until the sweet potatoes were tender.

Nothing was wasted by the Indians. There is even a recipe for soup made from meat skins. Meat skins (any kind) were roasted until brown, then boiled in a kettle of water with salt until the water had the right flavor. Cornmeal was added and the soup simmered until it was done.

When I began to research the Paiute, I found it difficult because there was so little information on this tribe, except for the Ghost Dance religion that found new life in 1889 with Paiute prophet Wovoka and eventually led to the tragedy at Wounded Knee.

I have to confess that I took a slight liberty by including Sarah Winnemucca as a minor character in this book, along with her sister Mary, and her grandfather, Chief Truckee. I gained some insight into the Paiute (or the "Diggers," as they were called by the emigrants) from reading about Sarah Winnemucca, who was born in 1844.

But I still am not sure how or when Sarah and her sister Mary got their Christian names.

There are two scenarios: Sarah's grandfather, Chief Truckee, encountered his first white men when Sarah was about two years old. It may have happened that the white men gave these girls their names as children. Sarah later went to live with a trader's family to learn English, and it may have been that she was given the name Sarah then. In any case, she learned enough English to become a translator for the U.S. Army.

Popular with white people, Sarah became celebrated for bringing an end to the Bannock Uprising. Soon afterward, she gave lectures to liberals on the east coast who wanted to hear about the wrongs done to her people. Still, she never spent too much time away from her tribe, and Sarah always felt the bitter sting of injustice done to her people.

In her book, *Life Among the Paiutes*, Sarah talks of her first encounter with white people, the Paiute's customs and moralities, and the Bannock War, among other things.

One of the greatest things I learned about the men and women who settled the West in the 1800s was that they were not so different from the average man or woman of today—they wanted what we all want in the end: to feel a sense of accomplishment. And there is no greater achievement than taming the unknown, be it a land or an idea.

$\mathcal{P}$ R O L O G U E

The sunlight fell over America like delicate lace. She opened her eyes to find out where she was, but a ray of light blinded her. Using one hand to shield the light, she took in her immediate surroundings. She had originally assumed that she was in one of the wagons and that they had stopped for the midday rest.

Lifting herself onto one elbow took immense effort, as if the energy had been sucked out of her, but she discovered that what made the lacelike pattern of light and dark was a woven wall of poles and dried grass. If she let her head fall to one side, she could see a small opening held up by two branches stuck in the ground a few feet apart and tied together where they met at an angle. With her free hand, America felt the ground beneath her. It was a hard-packed sand floor. When she moved, a grass mat crackled underneath her. It was then that she realized she was no longer with the wagon train. A hollow feeling worked its way into the pit of her stomach.

America's body ached, not from physical pain, but from the agony of loss. It came back to her like a dam bursting.

"My baby," she whispered. An involuntary moan escaped from her lips and she choked back a sob. Surely the baby was nearby. America pushed down the rising panic with her logic.

She remembered the birth—the first sight of the tiny, red, wrinkled body that emerged from her just before she slipped into unconsciousness. She had had enough time to note that it was a girl. She hadn't had time to name the baby, but she had been in sight of the Sierra Mountains. Sierra was a good name. She would name her new daughter Sierra when they were reunited. It wouldn't be long now. There was a rustle as a slender figure slipped into America's shelter. It was a woman, dark-skinned from the sun, hair falling in her face. She wore no shirtwaist, and her small breasts hung free. A plaited grass apron encircled her waist.

America's first instinct was to look away for modesty's sake, but then she realized that this was an Indian woman and that their customs were different from the white man's. A low, velvety voice called out. Although she had closed her eyes, America understood that this woman had come to check on her. In her trancelike state, America thought that she knew what this woman was saying. She was calling out, beckoning other tribe members to come into the brush-covered shelter.

She addressed the woman. Her voice came out cracked and unused. "My baby. Where is my baby?"

The young woman cocked her head, clearly not understanding. America sat up slowly, carefully. Her bones strained with the sudden movement. She must have been sick for a long time. She pointed to her belly, then made a rocking motion, as if she were cradling a baby in her arms.

The woman nodded her understanding.

"My baby," America asked, "where?"

The woman shook her head, pointing to America's belly, then gestured around her and made the same rocking motion with her arms. She shook her head. "Baby."

Another woman entered the shelter, an older woman, her face wizened by the desert sun. The younger woman turned to her and began to talk in her language. The older woman's eyes slid back toward America, studying her. Then she gave a short, decisive nod and approached America. She made the same motions as the younger woman said, "Baby, no. No baby."

"No," she muttered to herself, "that can't be true." America suppressed a sob, but couldn't stop the salty tears that ran freely down her face and settled in the corners of her mouth. A low moan escaped, a soft keening that kept rising and falling.

The other women sat back, watching her with curiosity and sadness. America thought that despite the language barrier, these women understood what had happened to her.

Her baby, her baby. Sierra was gone. Will was gone. *Please let me die, too,* America silently begged before she lay back down on her grass mat and slipped back into blissful unconsciousness.

PART 1

CHAPTER 1

Today was May 13, the day America Hollis was leaving Independence, Missouri, heading west to a new land and a new life. Even though she had spent several weeks traveling by Conestoga wagon and riverboat, she felt that the real journey was just beginning now that they had joined the wagon train. The trek from Philadelphia had been a Sunday drive compared with what she and her husband, Will, would encounter from here on out.

It had rained lightly the night before, which America thought accounted for the hissing snakes in her dreams. The dirt and grass road they followed out of town smelled fresh, as though the land had been scrubbed clean for their departure. While Will drove their three teams of horses, America swayed to the creak and groan of the wagon, which she had christened Betsy after the song, "Sweet Betsy From Pike."

She tucked a stray lock of fine blond hair beneath her bonnet, then turned for one last experience of the sights, smells, and sounds of this prairie town. Small booths of merchants that sold everything from fried fish to fishing nets to bolts of gingham and silk were set up along the pier; people bustled along the dusty streets preparing for the journey, or selling to those who were leaving.

When they had arrived here a few days ago, America felt reckless and free, as though she had landed in some exotic port halfway around the world. She was enchanted by the rugged beauty of this town on the edge of the Territories and could see immediately that the gateway to the West was far different from the polished city she had lived in during all of her twenty-one years.

Although she knew it was too late, America turned to Will and said once again, "This land is so beautiful, I would be most content to stay in this place."

He scanned the horizon silently and nodded. "Aye, it is. But I do not think I could settle here. The way west is open to those who want to tame it."

America sighed and studied Will's profile. Although most of her friends considered him mysterious and hand-some, America had always found him to be taciturn. Now, she focused on his physical features whenever she tried to find something she could like about her new husband.

His eyes were so pale blue that sometimes it seemed that the sun shone right through them. His dark brown hair curled over his paper collar, his shoulders were broad, his posture straight. As time went on, she knew she would find more and more to admire about this intelligent, kind, and gentle man.

"You look unwell today," Will remarked, showing a surprising concern for his wife. "Is it the child?"

America winced whenever he referred to her unborn

baby as *the* child, but knew that she would eventually adjust to his attitude.

"No," she responded, "we're both fine." She hesitated, unsure if she should tell him what was on her mind.

"Forgive me," she finally said, deciding that she needed to share her fears with him, "but I was just wondering if, when we settle in the Territory, I will ever see my parents again."

She looked away. A burning sensation prickled at the back of her eyes and she blinked several times to keep the hot, wet tears from flowing. When she had herself under control, she looked up and saw the startled look in his eyes. "No, I'm not having second thoughts," she quickly added, "but I do wonder."

He smiled at her. "I am sure we will see them again. There is talk of the Iron Horse out west, of laying tracks into the Territory. And until that time, I promise I will send you back east from time to time to visit."

By all rights, America should not have been missing her parents, but she still loved them, regardless of the harsh way she had been treated after confessing her pregnancy to them.

"You have brought shame to this family," her father, the honorable Judge Frederick DeVries, had declared, his muttonchop-covered jowls quivering in rage. America's mother had said nothing, but had collapsed upon the velvet settee, a monogrammed linen and lace handkerchief dabbing her eyes.

"You shall marry immediately, before anyone else becomes aware of your scandalous behavior," her father commanded, as if he were handing down a life sentence in his courtroom.

To America, marrying immediately *would* be a life sentence. She reached her arms out to her mother, whose tiny eyes hardened as if America had become pregnant just to cause them dishonor. She retreated and blinked back her tears, knowing her father would tolerate no show of weakness from her. Especially now.

"How am I to find a husband so soon?" America asked, finally trusting her voice enough to speak.

Her father glared at her still-flat stomach with disdain. "It is your poor judgment that has gotten you into this disgraceful predicament. I will choose a husband for you."

America had other ideas, but nodded to her parents and retired to her bedroom to contemplate her options. There was only one man from their social circle whom she would consider marrying, and he was gone. She couldn't abide any of the rest of the young high society men who had vied for her hand.

The following morning, her mother had ordered America to accompany her on a trip across town.

"What is this place, Mother?" America asked nervously as their coach stopped in front of a dumpy, nondescript brick building in a wretched section of town.

"You are fully aware that an unwed mother in our society is unheard of. If you do not wish to marry, then you must go into this building and get rid of that child."

America was shocked. She knew that she would have

to pay the price for giving herself to a man before marriage, but this was asking too much. "No," she said, refusing to get out of the coach.

"Why must you be so stubborn?" her mother asked, stamping her foot. "You have no business embarrassing us."

She raised her chin. "I *want* this child, Mother. I will not have an abortion. If I can't have Jan, at least I'll have a part of him." America returned home to consider her choices.

Many young women of her age considered Will Hollis to be a desirable suitor, with his dark looks and his Harvard education. But that is where his suitability ended. Coming back to Philadelphia with his law degree firmly in hand, Will hadn't been content to work for his father's law firm. Instead, he had been more interested in the mysterious West, the uncharted territory that had opened up in the last few years to people who were eager to forge a new life.

"Will Hollis!" her mother had exclaimed the night America informed her parents that she had chosen her own fiancé. "How could you consider marrying that man? All he ever speaks of is joining the trek west. I will not stand by and watch my only daughter joined in marriage to a man who will take you away from your family."

America was perplexed. "But I thought you wanted me to leave town."

"Of course we do, dear," her mother explained, as if America were still five years old. "Your father has been searching New York for a suitable husband for you. That way, you could be married and gone before anyone discovered your condition. Then, when you returned for visits, none of our friends would know exactly how old the child was."

"I'm sorry if I've ruined your plans, but my mind is made up. Will Hollis has proposed and I've accepted."

When she had let Will know of her interest in him, he had stepped into the void that Jan De Smet had left upon his death, and quickly proposed. America was well aware of how drastic a step she had taken, but did not want to embarrass her parents any more than she already had.

Finally, her parents capitulated and agreed to attend the small wedding, although her mother cried and her father sat silent and stone-faced throughout the ceremony. On her wedding night, as Will and America lay stiffly side by side in their marriage bed, she wondered how she had come to be married to this stranger.

Will turned to her in the darkness. He did not touch her, but spoke with fiery purpose. "To think that there is a whole other part of this continent that hasn't been fully explored. Think of it, America. What would you do? Would you go there?"

"Yes," she answered. "It sounds like the greatest adventure a person could have." It wasn't the adventure that she would have chosen for herself, but she was determined to make the best of her situation.

Will would come home with the newspaper every day and search it for stories and letters about people who were already out in the Oregon Territory. He prepared himself by making lists of what they would need and how much it would cost. Through relatives and friends, he contacted a group of people who were also emigrating west and they all agreed to meet in Independence, Missouri, in mid-May.

America also made preparations, seeking out information from her friends who corresponded with sisters and brothers who went west, and she would relay this information to Will when he arrived home for supper. She was surprised to discover that the idea of traveling into unknown territories excited her. She even borrowed one of her father's navigation books to see if she could find the constellations and understand how they moved across the great night sky.

And so it was that she found herself preparing for the day when she and her bridegroom would board their Conestoga and make their way to Independence, Missouri, where they would meet the rest of the wagon train. They carefully planned their journey, which they had learned would take between four and six months, depending on the weather, the state of the wagons and the emigrants, and whether they encountered hostile Indians along the way.

As the time to leave drew near, there were so many considerations to be made about the journey that America would sometimes find it overwhelming. When they finally reached their destination, they would need to build a cabin or house while Will set up his law practice. They would also have a new baby, which would require a whole new set of responsibilities. America wondered if Will would be a good father and a good provider. Her greatest fear was that Will would reject her child in favor of the children that would come later.

She often thought about the unborn child and the others that would fill their house someday. Children was a subject they hadn't talked about, but there were plenty of things that had been left unsaid before their quick marriage. In fact, they hadn't even been intimate yet.

She had ridden a wave of emotions: one moment she had felt fear rising, only to be washed away by giddiness at the thought of the great unknown adventure to come. There had been so many things to do, so many beloved friends and relatives to call on and to whom she must say her farewells. Would she ever see them again? The distance she was to travel with her new husband was so vast, so unfathomable, she just couldn't predict.

America studied the people walking past their wagon as they lumbered out of town. Most of them had left their homes, too, for a new life. But they seemed so plain. Was it the land that produced this drab, washed-out look, or was survival that much harder out here?

She noted that their clothes were well-worn and she was suddenly aware of her own finery—the delicate pink silk and ivory lace, the deep blue satin with the gold brocade trim, and the emerald green velvet gowns, the linen shirtwaists, and fine wool skirts that were all tucked away in her trunk. But what America was most proud of was the deep blue woolen cottage cloak that she had chosen. It would keep her warm during those cold days over the mountainous region of the Emigrant Trail.

The dress she wore on this beautiful May day was a gray serge tailored in the latest fashion. Before America and Will left for Independence, her mother had insisted on having her dressmaker sew several dresses for America to take with her. She wondered what her wardrobe would look like by the time she reached the Oregon Territory, then chided herself for her shallowness.

In a way, though, she was pleased that she was at last pondering something other than the tragedy of her life. For the last few months, she had been living in a fog, grieving the death of her unborn child's father. Jan De Smet had been as in love with her as she had been with him. They had been courting for over a year, and it was clear to, and heartily approved by, both families that he was ready to ask for her hand.

Jan came from a wealthy merchant family, and it went without saying that he would take over the import business when his father retired. He was sent over to Great Britain to buy Scottish woolens, but when his ship didn't reach England, word was received by his family that he was dead. America had had no time to grieve.

And now was not the time, either, she told herself, as she looked over to her new husband. She must not look behind her, but focus ahead, on the trail that led to her future.

"You're thinking of him again, aren't you?"

America blushed, wondering if she had accidentally

spoken aloud, or if somehow Will had read her mind.

He smiled. "We may have been strangers when we married, but I have since learned to read your face." He paused. "I know I was not your first choice, America, but I promise that I will take care of you."

She drew in a sharp breath, unaware until now that Will had feelings for her. "Thank you."

America turned her gaze from Will back to the trail. While she may have been used to the swaying and creaking of Betsy, she was having a harder time adjusting to the wide expanse of prairie that seemed to go on and on. In her mother's carefully tended garden, a profusion of well-bred tulips and daffodils would be blooming right now. Looking out over the never-ending grasslands, she spotted a number of blooming wildflowers popping up here and there. Some grew in clumps, but others pushed up out of the soil alone, as though they relished their solitude.

Once again, Will must have read the look on America's face as he said, "I promise you will have a garden filled with exotic flowers when we find our place out there."

She turned and saw admiration in his pale blue eyes. Tears welled in her own eyes and she turned away, ostensibly to look at the prairie unfolding before them.

CHAPTER 2

When America had first set eyes on Betsy back in Pennsylvania, the Conestoga's body had been painted a bright blue with Pennsylvania Dutch trimmings of red, white, and yellow flowers. Even the wagon jack was gaily painted in the same manner. After almost a month of sun and dust, Betsy's bright blue paint had turned dull and some of the trimmings had been rubbed off by the horses scratching the sides of their faces against the hard surface.

Betsy was filled to the brim with trunks, food, supplies, tools, and shoes for the horses. One of the trunks held the couple's summer and winter suits and frocks, and some practical items like the patchwork quilt that Will's mother had made for them, the box of herbal medicines, and the three-legged skillet.

The other trunk held some of America's treasures, a small sample of civilization that she would bring with her into the new Territory—her blue-and-white Delft china, her Swiss mantle clock with the delicate French porcelain columns that decorated either side of the glass pendulum casing. It also contained Will's law books and his family Bible, the one his parents had given to them as a wedding gift.

During the trip from Philadelphia to Independence, they had been able to find accommodations almost every night. The few times that sleeping quarters were unavailable, they had slept inside their wagon. Now there wasn't an inch of space available.

Yesterday, Will and the owner of the general store had loaded the wagon with the recommended fifty pounds of flour, half a bushel of beans, one hundred and fifty pounds of bacon, ten pounds of rice, and twenty pounds each of sugar and coffee for the trip.

"Where will we sleep?" America had asked when the job was completed.

He frowned and shook his head. "As the supplies dwindle, there may be room for you in the wagon. Until then, we will have to sleep under it. If you need to rest when we are moving, we can fix up a space on the staple sacks."

America was doubtful as she looked at the brimming wagon. She'd never slept outside before. Will saw it as an adventure, but all she could think of were all the dangers that she'd read about—the rattlesnakes, the coyotes, the cougars, and bears. And the Indians.

It seemed that they were everywhere. She recalled with dread the stories she'd heard and read, about the scalpings and the attacks on wagon trains that led to the deaths of the men and the capture of the women and children. She shuddered at the thought of being held hostage by a tribe of savages, then immediately felt ashamed for such a thought. After all, hadn't she just defended the Indians to that intolerable Moore couple?

The night before, after supper in the boarding house, their landlady had led her boarders to the parlor.

"I must apologize for not introducing you to each other before now, but suppertime is not meant to be a social occasion," Mrs. Withers began with severity. "This is Mr. and Mrs. Isaac Moore of Virginia. Mr. Moore is a preacher and they are going west on missionary work."

Mrs. Moore was a short, squat, older woman with a permanent frown and bad table manners. America also noticed the bruise on the woman's cheek, as if someone had hit her with a fist. Her husband was short and scrawny with a crooked nose and a poor excuse for a beard. He made America nervous whenever he turned his pebble-hard eyes on her.

With an expression of distaste, the hostess turned to the other young woman. "And this is Miss Welborne of Salem, Massachusetts. She is going west to marry."

Then Mrs. Withers introduced America to the others.

"Mrs. Hollis and her husband are from—where, dear?"

"Philadelphia," America replied with a smile, wishing that Will had not needed to tend to their wagon and miss the evening meal, which they insisted on calling "supper" out here. It was one of the many new customs she would have to get used to, she supposed. "My husband is a lawyer and we will settle in the Oregon Territory."

"Philadelphia, eh?" Mr. Moore asked, his eyes gleaming.

Mrs. Withers must have sensed that the discussion was about to become heated. She got up. "I have pies baking in the oven for tomorrow night's supper. Please excuse me." She hurried out of the room.

Mr. Moore barely acknowledged the landlady's departure before he turned back to America and barked, "What does your husband plan to do, represent the buffalo in a lawsuit? Perhaps he will represent the redskins in a suit against the United States government."

Isaac Moore's manner greatly offended America, and although she hadn't thought about the subject much, she had listened to Will whenever he discussed matters regarding the rights, or lack thereof, of Indians—a subject of endless fascination to him.

"Perhaps he *will* represent the Indians, Mr. Moore," America said in a sharper manner than she had intended. She softened her next words. "The Lord knows they need all the help they can get."

Isaac Moore stared at America and gave a dismissive snort. Mrs. Moore's eyes bulged and her mouth was set in a thin, tight line.

"I agree with you wholeheartedly, Mrs. Hollis," said Miss Welborne. "I have read about the Indians' plight and it seems that our government has done nothing but make empty promises to the poor creatures." She turned to Mrs. Moore, who apparently didn't have a first name, and asked, "What do you think, Mrs. Moore?"

The timid woman opened her mouth to speak. "Well, I think—"

"She has no opinion, Miss Welborne," Isaac Moore rudely blurted out. He snorted again, adding, "Women should be seen and not heard on such subjects, Miss Welborne."

Miss Welborne smiled at him and said calmly, "I believe that phrase is used for children, Mr. Moore, not women." She gave a pointed look to Mrs. Moore, who blinked rapidly and stood up, looking like a frightened mouse who had just been accosted by a very aggressive cat.

After the Moores left the room, America turned to the plump young woman who appeared to be about her own age. Her cheeks reminded America of polished red apples in baskets at a farmer's market and the woman's abundant red-gold hair was pinned up in soft waves. Her brown dress was of a simple cut with white lace collar and cuffs. She wore a cameo at her throat.

"So you're going out to Oregon to marry, Miss Welborne?" America asked. She was curious about the repugnant look that Mrs. Withers had given this woman, as if she were saying that Miss Welborne was going out west to become a prostitute. The possibility flitted briefly through America's thoughts before she dismissed it. The woman was too well dressed and too refined.

"Please call me Catherine."

"And my given name is America."

"What an unusual name. It's very beautiful. How did you come by it?" Catherine asked.

America smiled. "My parents combined the names Amity and Erica. Since they emigrated from the Netherlands, it seemed appropriate that their first born daughter should be named America."

They laughed.

"This man you will marry, is he already settled in the Oregon Territory?" America asked.

"I haven't yet met him," Catherine explained, looking down at her hands. "You see, I'm what the newspapers out east call a mail-order bride."

America had heard of the phrase, and of the practice. She didn't have any views on it one way or the other, but there were many people who thought poorly of the idea. There was an overwhelming number of men out in the Territories, and the need for women was great.

"That sounds exciting."

"I read an advertisement in a Boston newspaper about a year ago, and responded." Catherine seemed to be looking for any hint of disapproval on America's part, but seemed satisfied that her new friend was passing no judgment. "You see, I reached the age of twenty-five in January, and have not yet married. My parents are both dead and I have no siblings."

"How did you support yourself in Boston?"

Catherine gave a wry smile. "I worked in a large store, selling ladies' unmentionables." She put on a solemn expression and addressed an imaginary customer. "Yes, madam, that *is* the largest size corset we have available. Perhaps you should have one custom made."

America laughed and Catherine broke out into a smile.

"I can imagine that you were not attached to your position," America said.

"An understatement," Catherine replied. "No, I had

read about the Emigrant Trail and the idea of going west intrigued me."

"But you will have an unknown man waiting for you at the end of the journey," America pointed out. As if she was not married to a stranger, herself.

Catherine shrugged. "I know him as well as I would have known any suitor in Boston. I have a letter from him, and I have responded favorably."

"What is he like?"

"He's a widower, seventeen years older than me, and has five children, three who are grown and married. He owns a general store in a town in California Territory called Grass Valley. His name is Throup Chase." Catherine cocked her head to the side. "But what about you? How many months have you been with child?"

America had grimaced and her hand had gone protectively over her slightly swollen belly. "Four months."

Catherine's eyebrows had raised. "Then you may very well bear your child on the Emigrant Trail."

As America jostled down the road in the wagon, she thought to herself, *I very well may.*

"Do you see any water ahead?" Will asked, breaking into her thoughts.

America lifted her head high and took a deep breath. "We must be nearing a river," she replied, smelling the thick dankness in the air. She had begun to rely on her sense of smell to predict when they would come to water. It had become almost a game to her, trying to find the scent before coming upon it.

Just before her growling stomach signaled that it must be close to lunchtime, America caught a glimpse of glittering blue water about a mile away. A few minutes later, Tal Bowen rode up to their wagon on his bay horse. He was a stocky young man of about America's age. His fair hair was worn long and one lock flopped in his eyes as he removed his hat. America noticed that he was trying to grow a beard, but it was so sparse that she would be surprised if he kept it more than a week.

"We'll noon here," he announced. "You can bring your wagon up to the river closer to the bank if you like. We're planning a picnic so that everybody in the wagon train can get acquainted."

"Is this where we'll be stopping for the day?" America asked, anxious to stretch her legs after a long morning's ride.

"Oh no, ma'am," Tal said. "After lunch we'll have to ford the river. There's another watering hole seven miles from here. We'll camp there tonight."

It was at the picnic gathering that America finally had a chance to meet the wagon master, Captain Terwilliger. She was just delivering her contribution to its place on a makeshift table laden with the last kitchen-cooked food they would see for months when Will tugged at her elbow.

"There he is." He pointed the captain out to America from across the crowd. Terwilliger was a commanding presence in his military frock coat, devoid of its medals and braids since he had retired from the army. His slouch hat was not military issue, but dusty, worn, and torn from many trips made back and forth from the very edge of the Territories to the Oregon Territory. Mr. Terwilliger caught Will's eye and moved across the gathering toward them, a companion following in his wake.

The captain had recently shaved, but America could tell that he was the sort of man who didn't go in for shaving often. She wondered if he remained clean-shaven in towns as big as Independence, only to degenerate to scraggly beard as the trip wore on. She fervently hoped that Will would maintain his clean-shaven appearance, in spite of the long trip to come.

Next to Terwilliger was a scrawny man in faded denims and a flannel cotton shirt of some indeterminate color. The man's eyes were hidden by a permanent squint and his skin was folded into wrinkles as if it was too large for his skull. A thin blanket of colorless hair was brushed back from his hairline and his beard and mustache were untrimmed.

"Captain, this is my wife, America Hollis."

Terwilliger turned and appraised America before solemnly offering his hand. "How do you do, madam? I hope that you will be able to endure the journey without too much difficulty."

"I intend to, Captain," America replied.

Terwilliger sized her up and nodded, as if he believed she could do it. "Besides Dr. Bauer and his wife, there is one midwife in your division. I will make sure her wagon will be close to yours."

"Thank you, sir," America replied. She was aware that

too few doctors ever made the trek west. When a doctor did decide to go west, it was not from lack of work, but because he had adventure in his soul. She secretly felt relieved at her good fortune.

The captain indicated the other man. "This is our pilot, Mr. Pike."

"Pleased to meetcha, ma'am," Pike replied. She noticed that he held a scrunched-up hat in his hand.

"And what does the pilot do, Mr. Pike?" America asked.

Pike's face flushed and he bobbed his head before answering. "I scout ahead for good places to camp and for good watering holes. I been doing this for a few years, ma'am."

Before she could say anything, Terwilliger spoke up. "Pike will make sure the animals are watered right and get enough to eat. Those with horses will have grain for their animals, but you will still need to let them graze on good grass, same as cattle."

"And is good grass plentiful this time of year?" she asked.

Pike and Terwilliger exchanged looks. Clearly they weren't used to a woman asking such technical questions. Pike finally spoke up. "Well, to tell you the truth, ma'am, it will get hard as we get farther into the summer months. But even yellow grass is better than no grass."

America excused herself, then piled her plate with food. She strolled to the riverbank, found a stool by a weeping willow, and listened to the conversations around her. Sitting there quietly eating, she learned a good deal of information about the trip, including the fact that there were twenty-four wagons making the journey.

As she finished the last of her biscuit, Captain Terwilliger called for everyone's attention. "As you know, the train has already been divided into twelve wagons each. My assistant, Talmadge Bowen, is leading the second half of the train."

Tal Bowen stood to one side and bobbed his head when introduced.

Terwilliger continued. "Each section will be divided further into platoons of four wagons. Even though Tal and I are in charge, the wagons in each platoon will ultimately be responsible for each other. If one wagon has a problem, say a wheel breaks or a horse needs shoeing, the other three wagons are obliged to help. If someone in your platoon gets sick, the other families are expected to help in any way they can."

When the captain had finished his speech, America saw Will join the representatives from each wagon who would be choosing platoon assignments. She turned to look out over the sparkling, slow-moving water.

"May I sit with you?"

America looked up to see Catherine standing over her with two glasses of lemonade in her hands. She extended one to America.

"You looked thirsty."

America took it gratefully. "Thank you. It's so nice to see you again. Sit down, please." She motioned to a soft grassy spot next to her. "I'm sorry I can't offer you a comfortable chair."

Catherine sank onto the ground and arranged her heavy skirts around her feet.

"Who are you traveling with?" America asked.

Catherine grimaced. "I have two other traveling companions, women who are affianced to someone out west as well. Our fiancés have rented a wagon from Mr. Terwilliger to take us west."

America took a sip of the sweet and tart lemonade. She wished that she had some ice to make it cold, but this wasn't Philadelphia, and there would be no iceman to bring relief on summer days out here.

The two women exchanged pleasantries while they finished their lemonade; then America rose to look for Will. She found him in conversation with a family.

"Come, America," he said, motioning her to the group. "This is the Hayes family, and they will be in our platoon."

Gil and Celeste Hayes were an older couple. Gil was a large, bearded man who told them that he was a blacksmith from New York.

"Good luck for us," Will joked, "when one of our horses throws a shoe, he'll be there to oversee that the shoe goes on the right hoof."

Despite her delicate name, Celeste had obviously worked alongside her husband when the need arose in their blacksmith shop back in Yonkers. She was strong and capable with long black hair liberally threaded with gray, and looked like the sort of woman America would like to have beside her when the birth pains began. America knew the subject was too delicate to discuss here, but she hoped Celeste was the midwife Mr. Terwilliger had referred to earlier.

"Why have you left the east coast?" America asked as she helped Celeste carry dirty dishes to the river for rinsing, while the men showed off their horses to each other.

Celeste shrugged. "Too many forges, not enough business. Gil wants to go to an area where horses outnumber the people."

"Do you have any children?" America asked, aware of her own child inside her as she bent over the water.

Celeste called to some children playing in the rushes, and two left the group to run toward her.

"This is my son, George." He was a reticent boy of sixteen who resembled his father, already muscular from wielding a hammer and tongs.

"And this is Mary Elizabeth; she's ten."

America thought the girl had the look of a consumption patient. She was a slender child whose white skin and large delft blue eyes reminded America of the delicate English porcelain shepherdess figurine that graced the mantelpiece back in her parents' home.

She also reminded America of herself as a child. Her mother had never let her play outside, insisting that she stay out of the sun to retain the milky whiteness of her complexion. And her own eyes, a deep, indigo blue, reflected this girl's, who stood quietly under America's gaze.

When the dishes were finished, America excused herself to find Catherine so she could meet her traveling mates. When she approached their wagon, Catherine ran toward her.

"America, have you heard? We're to be in the same platoon."

She was pleased that Catherine Welborne would be traveling nearby. It was a relief for America to have a friend to talk to on this long, arduous journey.

Calling two other women over, Catherine made proper introductions. "America Hollis, I'd like you to meet Addie Schreck."

"It's a pleasure to meet you," she responded to the sensible-looking woman who appeared to be in her early thirties.

"And this is Flavia Townsend," Catherine said, indicating a very pretty woman in her mid-twenties.

"And where are the two of you headed?" she asked.

Flavia spoke up. "Addie and I are bound for towns in the Oregon Territory."

After America had taken her leave, she found Will at the wagon of another family.

"America, this is Reverend Tarleton Sanford, his wife Muriel, and their son Lem."

She paused to study this family. Muriel was a dour-faced woman who looked as if life had turned out to be a big disappointment to her. Her husband, a portly, red-faced man, held firmly onto a Bible in both hands as though it were a shield. Lem, who looked to be about thirteen, was a slight boy who stared at the ground during the entire conversation.

America assumed she would slowly get to know the people from each of the wagons over the coming months, but it appeared that Muriel Sanford had other ideas.

"We're headed to the California Territory to settle down. I'll raise the boy there while my husband preaches on Sundays. The rest of the week, of course, he'll be put to work raising fruit trees."

America nodded and turned to leave, but Mrs. Sanford continued. "Lem will be able to help Tarleton with the farm chores, but I wish I had me a daughter to help with the household chores. That is one of the great disappointments of my life, that we were not able to conceive and birth another child."

America secretly believed that it was a blessing that another child had not been born to have to endure this awful woman's care, but she kept her opinion to herself.

Reverend Sanford then cut in with his own plans for the future. "I am heading west to teach the heathens about God. I will walk amongst the taverns and saloons of the godless gold-mining towns and teach Christian charity and preach the word of the Lord God, Our Savior."

"And just who do you consider to be heathens?" Will asked.

The good reverend did not answer the question, but frowned at Will. "Have you been saved yet, my son?"

Will's brow darkened. "I believe in God, if that answers your question."

America smiled her approval, proud of the way her husband had spoken up. Each day she seemed to discover a new character trait that made her more and more glad that she had married this man. She only hoped that he felt the same.

CHAPTER 3

Despite his lip service about Christian charity, the reverend proved to be a good deal less charitable if it meant setting his own needs aside. The lineup for the wagon train had been decided at the picnic simply by drawing straws. When it was completed, Reverend Sanford wasted no time in expressing displeasure with his place in the train.

"I cannot be in the last platoon," he complained to the captain after the picks had been made. "I must be in the front of this wagon train to lead these children into God's promised land."

The captain stood firm. "Fair is fair, Reverend. That's the place you drew, so you'll be in the last platoon."

Even though America and Will had gotten the shortest straw and would, therefore, be the last wagon in the last platoon, she said nothing. The captain was right; it was a fair drawing.

However, Catherine spoke up when she learned of their place. "She's with child," she pointed out, appealing to the others in their platoon. "If my companions wouldn't mind, we could bring up the rear."

The other brides, however, expressed uneasiness with the idea of trading places with the Hollises. "I read that wild Indians usually attack the wagon with the lone women in it, and if we are last, we will be inviting attack," said Addie.

"Indians!" said Flavia, whose face flushed at the thought. "We can't be at the end of the train. We don't know how to defend ourselves."

America knew that all three women were from big cities back east and was sure they were neither willing nor able to shoot a gun. Until quite recently, she had not been willing, either.

The day before they had left Independence, as they shopped for supplies, Will had pulled her into a gun shop that smelled like bear grease and gunpowder. She stood by unobtrusively and watched as he tested a few flintlocks, hefting them for weight and balance, and finally selected one. Then he turned to her. "We'll buy a pistol for you as well."

America took a step back. "Me? I—I don't know how to shoot one of those things." Although she hesitated, a part of her was intrigued.

He seemed to be suppressing a grin. "Then it's high time you learned."

As he looked over the guns and chose a lightweight caplock pistol for her, the gunsmith spoke. "You folks goin' with that train leavin' tomorrow?"

America nodded, then looked on as the gunsmith talked Will into buying a Bowie knife, too.

"Wouldn't go west without one, young man. All Westerners need one." He had glanced over at America. "Handy item for cuttin' bacon slabs and stirrin' boilin' rice when you can't find the kitchen tools."

America studied the three mail-order brides. No, she could not see any of them shooting a gun, or stirring rice with a Bowie knife, either, for that matter.

Gil Hayes looked apologetic as he spoke. "I would be happy to be last in line, Mrs. Hollis, but Mary Elizabeth has breathing problems sometimes, and we need to be as close to the doctor as possible. I hope you understand."

"Of course I do, Mr. Hayes. You should stay in the front of our platoon. But thank you kindly for thinking of us."

Everyone turned to the Sanfords, who had remained silent after the reverend's initial outburst.

"God has decreed that this young couple will be last," intoned the Reverend Sanford in a pious manner.

"What about you, Reverend? Couldn't you bring up the rear?" Catherine asked.

"I cannot make that sacrifice, dear lady," the reverend said, shaking his head regretfully. "I will be needed by this flock, and being last in line will make my journey to comfort tormented souls all the more difficult."

"But she's with child," Celeste pointed out. "She shouldn't be at the end of the train. You are better equipped to bring up the rear."

Instead of answering Celeste, the reverend turned to glare at her husband. "Sir, your wife does not know her place. I will not bring up the line, and that is the end of it."

For emphasis, Muriel Sanford nodded grimly, her arms crossed, as if she considered the matter closed. Their son, Lem, seemed unsure and spoke up. "But Father, we are second to last anyway. What difference will it make if you have to travel one more wagon length?"

"You keep quiet, boy," Muriel Sanford said harshly.

The reverend stepped toward Lem, quivering with fury. He lifted his hand as if to strike his son, then seemed to think better of it, as if he suddenly remembered that he was in the company of strangers.

Will began to speak, but America put a hand on his arm. "It's fine, Will. We just won't allow the train to move out of our sight."

The tension dissipated, and the families made their way back to their wagons. Catherine shook her head, a look of disgust on her face. "I am about to voice an unchristian thought—I can only hope that if the Indians do attack, the Sanford are the first to go."

America glanced over at the reverend and his wife. Mrs. Sanford took up the reins while her husband sat beside her in the jump seat of their wagon, reading from the Good Book and puffing on a pipe. Lem was crouched in the back on a flour barrel, with a look of misery on his face. America immediately thought about her friend's harsh words— Lem didn't deserve the same fate as his parents.

Catherine stood by while Will helped America climb onto Betsy. They all watched as the Sanfords rode past.

America had always enjoyed the smell of good pipe tobacco, but the reverend's tobacco left a foul stench in its
wake.

"Catherine, I think the Indians would pass him by, as
well as his wife, the sour creature." Although America immediately felt guilty for saying such a terrible thing,
Catherine chuckled and moved back to her wagon.

That evening, after a long afternoon's ride, each family
retired quickly to their own wagons for a quiet supper.

America worked on a piece of embroidery in the wan-
ing light. "I do hope this isn't an indication of how camp
will be every night," she said. "I enjoy the community
meals and had hoped to become friends with some of
these people."

Will smiled at her over the campfire. "They are probably just feeling a bit nervous about their first night on the
trail. I am sure that by the end of this trek, you will be
wishing for some quiet time to yourself."

America nodded and went back to her needlework, a
piece of sturdy, deep blue velvet on which she was em-
broidering a simple Pennsylvania Dutch tulip design in
white, yellow, red, and light blue. It would eventually become a pillow that would be displayed on a settee in their
parlor.

She brushed her fingertips over the silk threads and
thought about the house she and Will had talked about
one day building. It would be a two-story wooden house
with a parlor and library in front, a dining room just beyond the parlor, and a kitchen at the back of the house.

The upstairs would have three bedrooms and a linen closet. There would be a back staircase from the kitchen to the upstairs for a maid or for kitchen help.

America looked out at the dark emptiness that spread out around her. How different this primitive existence was from her old life back east. And how different her new life would be once they were settled in a town in the Oregon Territory.

When Will got up to check the horses, America set the embroidery project back into her satchel. Her hand closed around a small jewelry box at the bottom of the bag. She opened the box, took out a gold and garnet ring, and held it up to the firelight. It was the ring that Jan had given her as a token of his love—just before he set sail.

Closing her eyes, she tried to calm her racing heart. Hot tears pricked at the corners of her eyes, but she wouldn't let them flow. Crying wouldn't help her situation. She slipped the garnet ring onto her finger and studied it. She'd have to put it back in the jewelry box before Will came back, but for now, it felt warm and comforting on her finger.

Later that night, when America climbed into her blankets under the wagon, she could feel the breeze brushing gently over her face. So this was what it was like to sleep under the stars. Lying still, she could hear every night noise—the hooting of an owl, the rustle of the wind in the cottonwood that stood on the riverbank, the chuffing of the horses. She had wondered if the noise of the prairie would be magnified a thousand times, or would be as quiet as death. She had not expected this lullaby of nature.

America turned to watch her husband in his sleep, his breathing even, his face untroubled by what lay ahead of them. Shifting her weight slightly, she felt Will turn over in his sleep. His arm draped around her waist and she tensed, holding her breath for a moment. In the three months that they had been married, he had not once tried to become intimate with her.

Since their wedding night, Will had been a perfect gentleman, always attentive when she needed him. There had been no utterances of love from either of them, and she had assumed that he had married her because he wanted a bride to take west with him, not because he loved her. The fact that she was pregnant by another man was always unspoken between them.

She knew he didn't love her now, but hoped that in time he would learn to have some deep affection for her. And she hoped that she could fall in love with him someday, too. But for now, her heart still felt as cold and barren as the north wind. She drifted off to a sleep filled with troubled dreams of howling coyotes, poisonous snakes, and silent, deadly Indians.

The next day, the company nooned during the hottest hours, and America was pleased that they were camped in such a lovely spot. Willow trees bent gracefully toward the wide, flat, shallow river. Some of the men fished while the women built a campfire and prepared a meal that would possibly include trout later on. At America's suggestion, the women in the platoon agreed to build a community campfire and work together to cook their meals.

America had just finished making four loaves of bread that were baking over the fire when Mary Elizabeth came running into the camp, clutching a bunch of pink, blue, yellow, and white hollyhocks in her hand.

"Look what I found, Mother!"

Celeste stopped stirring the rice. "Let's make hollyhock dolls."

With a big smile and sparkling eyes, Mary Elizabeth nodded. "We can have a tea party!"

America was mystified. She had heard of hollyhock dolls, but had never made them. Born to privilege, she had been given dainty porcelain dolls with soft bodies that she had to be careful with, and one rag doll for play.

Celeste must have noticed her expression, because she took America by the hand and said, "Come on. We'll show you how to make one." She looked pointedly at America's middle and smiled. "You will need the practice for your own children."

Leaving Catherine and Addie to watch over the loaves of bread and the rice, the mother and daughter took America to a field of tall grass and sat down. Celeste showed America how it was done while Mary Elizabeth flattened an area of the grass to make a dollhouse.

Using the petals of one hollyhock for the gown and the peeled back bud of another for the head, the two women and the girl made twelve dolls in all. When they were finished, the dolls were set up in the ballroom to twirl around and show off their colorful gowns.

Mary Elizabeth was setting her dolls up for tea when George came over. "Father has caught some trout," he said, then looked at Mrs. Hollis. "I'm afraid Mr. Hollis didn't catch any, but we're willing to share." He grinned, and America couldn't help thinking what a handsome man he would be someday.

After a fine midday meal of rice, baked trout, and bread, the wagon train rested a few more hours while one of the wagons up ahead made some repairs. America was beginning to think that they would be camping here for the night when Mr. Bowen came down the line just before sunset.

"I want everybody to light a lantern and hang it on the back of your wagon," he ordered. "That way, the wagon behind you will have a signal to drive by after dark."

"We can't afford to waste the camphene," Muriel Sanford complained loudly, standing in front of the small bucket on the side of their wagon that held the fuel.

"There's plenty to go around, Mrs. Sanford," Bowen said in an impatient tone. "We'll be passing a few more towns in the next two weeks, and you can buy more camphene to replace it. Remember, part of your duty is to help your platoon along."

He looked over at America, smiled grimly, and touched his fingers to his hat in greeting to her. He then turned his horse around and galloped back to the head of his division.

Mrs. Sanford followed his gaze and glared at the Hollis wagon as if it were America's fault that she had to waste camphene. America smiled to herself. If the Sanfords had agreed to be last, Muriel wouldn't have had to use any of their precious camphene.

It was well after dark when they arrived at a large grove of trees by the Little Blue River. This river, America remembered from studying a map back in her parents' house, joined up with the Platte River several hundred miles northwest in Nebraska Territory.

Will built a fire for the women to cook over, and America made a stew with jerky and beans. Just as the group sat down to eat, a woman and her two young daughters came into camp with large baskets on their arms. Celeste Hayes greeted them.

"We saw your wagons from our farmhouse up the hill," the woman explained, indicating a northerly direction, "and thought you might like some fresh eggs and bread."

Unlike most of the emigrants who would be traveling with them, Will and America had not brought cows or chickens along. Since they were not farmers, nor did they intend to farm once they were in the Territories, Will had said there was no sense in buying an animal or a bird for the journey. Now that they'd spent eight weeks journeying to Independence and had more than once begged a farmer for milk or eggs, they could see that a cow and a chicken would have been useful.

The women within hearing distance gathered round and began bartering for the fresh food. When the farm wife, who introduced herself as Mrs. McGreer, set eyes on America, she handed six eggs and two loaves to her.

"You're eating for two," she said with a smile.

America gratefully took the food while Will handed Mrs. McGreer some coins. America knew that she would need to let out her clothes soon—at four months, her waist was beginning to expand and she would soon be unable to fasten her skirts and shirtwaists.

Just after supper, Tal Bowen rode back into their camp. America, Catherine, and Celeste Hayes were rinsing their skillets, plates, and utensils in a bucket of water from the river.

Gil and George Hayes were examining the shoes on their oxen, Mary Elizabeth was working on a sampler, and Will was feeding the team of horses. Catherine's companions, Flavia and Addie, had gone for a nature walk along the river, and the Sanford boy was chasing and tormenting frogs. The reverend had left to "do his Good Works," as his wife explained earlier, and she was getting their wagon ready to bed down for the night.

"Greetings, Mr. Bowen," Catherine said.

He touched his hat briefly and dismounted. "Ma'ams," he returned, his eyes sweeping all three women at once in greeting.

"What brings you out here, Mr. Bowen?" Celeste asked pleasantly. "Do you have news to share?"

Bowen had taken off his hat almost as an afterthought, as if he wasn't used to being in the presence of women. He ducked his head. "Yes. The captain wants everyone to know that you should make the most of the next week. As we get farther away from Independence, we'll have to start cooking in the daytime. No fires after dark."

America had stopped scrubbing her three-legged skillet and looked up. "Why is that?"

There was no hesitation in his answer. "We're in Indian country, Mrs. Hollis."

Will joined the discussion. "But aren't the Indians considered friendly this far east?"

Bowen seemed to be sizing up Will before giving his answer. "Well, that's true, Mr. Hollis, the Omaha and the Kaw are holding with the treaty, but there's been some hostility farther west with the Cheyenne."

"But aren't we too far north and east for the Cheyenne to travel?" asked Catherine. She'd stopped washing up her utensils as well and her face seemed to have drained of color.

"It's not uncommon for a Cheyenne war party to head up this way. The last wagon train to pass through here sent word back to Independence that they had to fight off a group of Cheyenne warriors. That was less than a month ago."

America watched everyone's faces. Gil Hayes's eyes immediately went to his daughter. Celeste's chin was determinedly set, her mouth a straight line. Mrs. Sanford stood wiping her hands on the front of her skirt, and Will looked distracted and troubled.

She wondered if anyone in their platoon would abandon their plans to go west. America was aware that it was not uncommon for emigrants to become discouraged by rumors and half-truths, and she hoped that no one would panic and turn back.

"Well, thank you, Mr. Bowen, for your instructions. And kindly refrain from telling us the details of that skirmish a month ago," Catherine said in a clipped tone of voice. "As you are most certainly aware, an adventure such as you just described can be exaggerated when a member of the party is unavailable to question."

Bowen's eyes bulged. "Are you calling me a liar, ma'am?"

The onlookers seemed to draw in closer, watching this drama play itself out between Catherine Welborne and Tal Bowen.

"Of course not, Mr. Bowen," she replied more kindly. "I'm just pointing out that when an incident is described in a letter or by word of mouth, the details can be changed in the repeated telling of the incident."

America suppressed a smile. "I think what Miss Welborne is trying to say, Mr. Bowen, is that we all appreciate your honesty, but I'm certain you don't want to alarm anyone unnecessarily."

Bowen's face paled. "No, ma'am. That was never my intention. All I was suggesting was that everyone needs to take precautions from here on out. And when we tell you no fires at night, please abide by our decision. That's all I was saying." He jammed his hat back on his head and mounted his horse.

America's first impression of Bowen had been that he

was still more boy than man, but the serious look in his eyes startled her and she realized that she had misjudged him, dismissed him because of his youth.

He spoke again from atop his horse. "You all just have to realize that we will encounter Indians along the way from here on, and some will be friendly, and some won't. And sometimes, it's hard to tell. Just don't turn your back on 'em."

CHAPTER 4

The camp remained silent through the rest of cleanup, and when America looked up at her companions, she could see the pensive looks on their faces. Each person appeared to be plagued by the same misgivings that were racing through her. What had she gotten herself into by agreeing to accompany Will on this journey?

It was far too late to turn back, so America dismissed the doubts from her mind and sought out Catherine to work on their quilt. They were still cutting squares of cloth when Flavia and Addie returned from their walk. Catherine filled them in on Tal Bowen's visit.

"Mr. Bowen was just trying to help, Catherine," Addie said in a high, nervous voice, her cheeks flushing.

Catherine stopped cutting for a moment and stared at her companion. "You're right, Addie," she finally said in a thoughtful manner. America met Catherine's eyes and they smiled. "Yes, he was just trying to help. I shouldn't have said anything."

Addie looked up at the two of them and her eyelashes fluttered for a moment. Then she lowered her eyes again and compared one square with another. A moment later, she cleared her throat and said, "I apologize if I sounded emotional a moment ago, Catherine. But Mr. Bowen *has* made this journey before."

The sweet, clear sound of a flute drifted through the campsite, and America was grateful for the intrusion on their uncomfortable conversation.

"Come on," Catherine urged, setting down her scissors. "Let's go find out who's playing the music."

"Oh, I don't know," Addie replied as she began to stitch the fabric. "It's late and we have a long day of traveling tomorrow. A good night's rest tempts me more than music."

Flavia disagreed. "We shall have plenty of time to rest soon enough. If what Mr. Bowen said is true about the campfires, I imagine playing music after dark will soon be banned as well." Without looking at Addie, she added, "Mr. Bowen will probably be there."

Addie pricked her finger with a needle. "Ow!" She glared at Flavia and sucked her finger.

Catherine turned to America. "What about you, Amy?" She had taken to using the shortened name, and America found it comfortable. Her mother would have had one of her spells if she ever heard her daughter called by such a name.

"I'd like to go. It would be an opportunity to meet some of the other people in our division, and even if I can't dance, I can enjoy the music." America stood up as if it were decided. Then she thought of Will. "I'll go ask Will. Maybe he'd like to go as well."

She walked back two wagons and found her husband smoking a pipe with Gil and George Hayes. Celeste was nearby looking after her young daughter, both of them working on a sampler. The group looked up when she came into their encampment.

"Where have you been?" Will asked in a contentious tone. "Don't tell me—you've been with Catherine again, haven't you?"

America wasn't used to having to account for her whereabouts. In Philadelphia, it was true that she often had to let her parents know where she was going to be, but there had never been that sense of being watched. At least until the news of her pregnancy. When she and Will had been traveling in their wagon to Missouri, he had never questioned her whereabouts when they stopped in a town for the night and went separately to re-stock their supplies.

Ever since they left Independence, however, Will had been more watchful of her. Although she might have enjoyed such attentions from Jan, she found it tedious and annoying coming from this stranger, her husband.

America fought down the feeling of exasperation that rose up in her breast. "I've been talking with Catherine, Flavia, and Addie. We've started to make a quilt. Why do you ask?"

Will frowned and shook his head. "I was just—curious." He broke into a grin and added, "You are my wife, after all."

Even Celeste seemed aware of the tension between the two of them, and she broke in. "George plays a fine fiddle. Maybe we should join the people making music downriver."

Putting aside the sampler and tamping out their pipes, the group set out for the evening's entertainment, George clutching his battered fiddle and bow, Mary Elizabeth by his side, skipping with excitement.

The flute player turned out to be the captain. America was surprised that a gruff old army man would play such a delicate instrument, but then many things she had encountered so far on this trip were not as she had expected them to be.

Several couples had gathered on a flat, grassy area in a grove of cottonwoods by the river and were dancing to a tune that America didn't recognize. The captain ended the tune amid clapping and laughter, several people calling out the names of other tunes as requests.

Terwilliger noticed America's group on the edge of the site and gestured for them to join in. "Ah! A fiddle player. Well, come here, young man. What tunes do you know?"

"How about 'When Bob Got Throwed'?" George suggested shyly.

The captain nodded and George began sawing the strings of his old fiddle. The audience clapped in time to the lively melody, and Terwilliger added sprightly notes from the flute to the tune. Suddenly, Tal Bowen stepped up, doffed his hat, and began singing.

> *"That time when Bob got throwed,*
> *I thought I sure would bust;*
> *I liked to died a-laffin'*
> *to see him chewing dust."*

Bowen sang in a pleasant tenor, and soon others joined in on the second verse.

> *"He crawled on that pinto bronc*
> *and hit him with a quirt;*
> *the next thing that he knew,*
> *he was wallerin' in the dirt."*

There was laughter from the gathering crowd as Bowen and company launched into the third verse. Gil grabbed Celeste and whirled her into the dancing circle, and several other men raised their eyebrows as a way of inquiry before taking their eager partners onto the grassy flat. America noticed Catherine and Flavia were dancing with two elderly bachelor brothers from another platoon.

Will touched her elbow during the interlude and America looked up, startled. "Would you care to dance, Mrs. Hollis?"

"I—do you think it's all right?" America looked out at the dancers enviously, and thought of her condition. She felt fine, but she'd seen the looks people had given her, the worry in everyone's eyes when they looked down at her belly. Will smiled. "Of course it's all right. You're my wife."

"So you keep reminding me," she said in a wry tone as she slipped her hand into his and held on for dear life as they schottïsched into the center to the next verse.

> *"'Twarn't more than a week ago*
> *that I myself got throwed,*
> *but that was from a meaner horse*
> *than old Bob ever rode."*

Her head felt light from spinning around and she felt creaky limbs and stretching muscles that hadn't been used in a long time.

"Stop! Stop this blasphemous behavior." Terwilliger looked up from the flute, George's fiddle played out a long scratchy note before dying, and everyone stared at Sanford as he stalked into the center of the dancers. The reverend stood on the edge of the crowd, shaking in fury. His eyes were bulging as he brandished a fist at the dancers and musicians.

"How dare you dance to a heathen song," he intoned, turning his wrath upon America and Will. "And you, you should know better. This is sinful, a woman with child caught in heathen dancing." Sanford turned his face toward the sky, his arms stretched upward in a supplicating gesture. "Lord forgive them for they know not what they do—"

Will broke away from America, strode over to Sanford, and grabbed him by his shirt. "Reverend, if you don't mind my saying so, you're interfering with everyone's pleasure tonight. Why don't you sit over here?" He hauled the sputtering reverend to an empty stool and sat him down in a decisive manner.

"It's the devil's work," Reverend Sanford continued as he jumped back to his feet and shook his fist impotently. "This music and dancing will turn you all into pillars of salt. Heathens—all of you!"

The emigrants began to murmur among themselves, a feeling of unease flowing throughout the campsite. Captain Terwilliger put down his flute and gazed steadily at the man. "Well then, Reverend, why don't I give you enough time to make yourself scarce before I begin piping another devil's tune?"

He addressed the crowd, silencing them. "And as for the rest of you, if you want to go with him, that's your decision. But for those of us who know what lies ahead, there won't be many more nights like this."

He brought the flute back to his mouth and picked up where he left off on "When Bob Got Throwed." George's fiddling joined in, bringing the crowd's spirits back up.

Will nudged America and nodded in the direction of the reverend. Several people followed him out of the camp, including Isaac Moore. His wife hung back and Mr. Moore grabbed her by the elbow and herded her roughly away. "Aren't those the people who stayed at the boarding house with us?" Will asked.

"Mr. and Mrs. Moore," America replied. "They're from Virginia, and he's some kind of lay preacher, too. And that couple over there, the Sorensons, are German Lutheran," she added. "Lutherans don't dance because they believe it's too risqué."

Will raised his eyebrows in what could only be intended to be a lascivious manner. "Since we're not Lutheran, shall we dance?"

America laughed. She couldn't help herself as Will led her in a lively hop-step. "When Bob Got Throwed" gave way to "Buffalo Gals," then "Oh! Susanna." Tal Bowen continued to sing, occasionally accompanied by others. Addie joined him in a duet for "Sweet Betsy From Pike," and as Will and America waltzed close by, she could see angry tears forming in Addie's eyes during the last verse.

"Long Ike and Sweet Betsy got married, of course,
  But Ike getting jealous obtained a divorce;
  And Betsy, well satisfied, said with a shout,
  'Good-bye, you big lummox; I'm glad you backed out.'"

America had learned from Catherine that Addie was married out east, but that her husband had left her. After finally securing a divorce, she contracted with a man in the Oregon Territory to be his bride. Although she had never discussed the matter directly with Addie, America knew how the other woman must have felt. Once a woman suffered scandal in her town, the only way out was to leave the area and start a new life elsewhere.

Already, America was beginning to see that people treated her differently here. In Philadelphia, once the news was out about her pregnancy, and after her hurried marriage, she couldn't help but notice the sly looks and the whispered conversations that stopped when she entered a room. Here, away from her hometown, people weren't aware of the scandal, of the way she had conducted herself by giving herself to the man she had loved.

America studied Will by the light of the fire and found herself, for the first time, attracted to him. He caught her eye and she blushed at his sly smile. Beneath the physical attraction, though, she could feel twinges of affection for this man she was finally getting to know. He had proved himself time and again on this trip to be a man of fine character. He was a hard worker, yet gentle with people, especially America herself.

It was during a slow waltz that she began to feel sleepy, and she moved closer to Will.

"Would you like to go back to our wagon?" he murmured in her ear. "Do you need to rest?"

"Not yet," she replied with a yawn. "Maybe we can sit here on the side and just listen to the music."

"I am sorry I sounded so quarrelsome earlier tonight when you came by the Hayes wagon," Will said. "I guess I have been a little envious of the time you spend with Catherine."

America wasn't angry anymore and she rested her head comfortably on his shoulder. "You're forgiven. Just remember that you've been spending time with Gil Hayes and I haven't said anything about that."

He laughed. "That's true. But it would be nice if you spent time with Celeste as well. She seems rather nice."

"She is. We spent a good portion of this afternoon playing with hollyhock dolls."

Will drew away so he could look at her. She explained about the dolls and Mary Elizabeth. A big grin spread over his face. "It sounds like you had fun." The grin died, to be replaced by a more somber look. "I have to confess something to you, America."

She waited.

"When we first started out from Pennsylvania, I was worried about you."

She cocked her head slightly. "Why?"

He took a moment before continuing. "I saw something in you when we first met, a spark of life that I had not found in the other girls I had met in your social circle. But I knew that you had come from a privileged background, more privileged than my own. And I have been worried that the trek west might be too much for you."

America tilted her face up toward his, keeping her expression impassive. "And what do you think now?" she asked.

He traced her jawline lightly with one calloused finger. "I think you have more backbone than most of the men here."

She smiled at him and their eyes locked for a long minute before she brought her head to rest on his shoulder once more. They sat on a blanket by the fire until George's fingers were too raw to continue fiddling and the captain was too dry to pucker up and blow.

The mail-order brides had long gone, and the Hayeses

waited patiently for George, who was talking excitedly to Terwilliger about some new song called "Jim Crack Corn" that he wanted them to practice together sometime. Gil effortlessly carried his pale, tired daughter in his strong arms, while Celeste stroked Mary Elizabeth's pale hair.

When America tried to stand, she discovered that she had been sitting so long that the circulation in her limbs had been cut off. Her feet tingled when she tried to walk, and she laughed at her wobbly efforts.

Will grabbed her elbow. "Are you all right?"

She leaned against him and shook one foot, then the other, before taking a few steps. "I'm fine. It'll take a moment for that funny feeling to go away."

"Your feet went to sleep?"

America raised her eyebrows, never having heard that expression. "Sleep," she said thoughtfully. "That's exactly what it feels like." They started back toward their wagon. "Mmmm, sleep sounds like a good idea."

When they got back to camp, Will pulled blankets out of the wagon and made a bed for them under the stars. He stood up and looked at America.

"I can separate the blankets, if you would prefer it," he suggested, just as he did every night.

Ever since their marriage, Will had made every effort to make it clear that America was under no obligation to sleep with him. She looked at him, suddenly shy, but needing to know his feelings for her.

"I was wondering, Will," she took a deep breath, "when you agreed to marry me, did you have feelings for me?"

He took a step back and ran his hand through his dark hair. "I—I was enamoured. I *am* enamoured of you," he corrected himself, then looked away. "Even though I am well aware of the fact that you are in love with someone else and that we are only married because of—our child."

"That's the first time you've called it our child." She reached out a hand hesitantly and touched his shoulder. Her soul soared at the bonding that had just occurred between them, whether her husband was aware of it or not.

A sad smile touched Will's lips. "I only wish it were mine. But I will love our baby as if it were." He paused a moment. "Do you think it will be a girl or a boy?"

She shook her head. "As long as the baby is healthy, it doesn't matter to me. Does it matter to you?"

After another moment of hesitation, Will shook his head, too. It had worried her in the past when he had expressed a desire for a boy. She often wondered how he would react if it was a girl—would he lose interest in this baby?

But with their journey now realized, America had been wondering if Will was too worried about what he called her "delicate condition" to care what gender the baby was. She found it odd that men thought of most women with child as fragile and unhealthy, as if pregnancy were a sickness. It was one of the few areas in which she and Will disagreed. However, now he was speaking openly and sharing his worries that the journey would be too hard on her and the baby.

America felt as if a great burden had been lifted off her

heart. For months, they had been polite strangers, and now they were talking about something more intimate than feeding the horses or building the fire. She knew that he didn't love her now, but hoped that he would learn to love her. And for the first time, she felt that she could fall in love with him someday. This evening she felt well on her way.

"I am sorry that we hadn't more time to get to know one another," she said, her cheeks burning. They were both well aware that it had been her decision to sleep separately thus far. "I can only hope that you will find affection for me the way I am learning to care for you." There, she'd said it.

Will stood still a moment more, not saying anything. "I, too, care for you, America," he finally answered.

She caught her breath and stepped closer to him. It wasn't everything she hoped for, but it was a start. Jan was becoming a memory and she must look to the future she would share with the man standing in front of her.

Will looked into her eyes. He reached out to brush her cheek with one finger as if she were a piece of delicate bone china. "And I believe that our feelings will grow into love if we just give them time."

America caught his hand in hers and pressed it to her face, continuing to gaze boldly at him. He held her gaze. "Yes," she whispered, "I believe it, too."

Hesitant at first, then drawn to each other like a magnet is drawn to iron, they kissed. It was not like the chaste, dutiful kisses they had shared in the past, at the ceremony, on their wedding night or any of the other nights thereafter; it was a kiss full of promise and desire.

She ran her hands tentatively up the back of his muscular neck, then entwined her fingers in his thick, black hair. She felt the stubble of his beard brush against her cheek as Will's kisses became more fervent, moving to her face, her neck, her hands. Her breath came in quick, shallow gasps as a flame of desire surged up in her. It had been so long since she'd felt this way. His long, slender hands stroked her fine, straight blond hair and she moaned.

In an ardent embrace, America and Will sank to their knees onto the blankets. Will began to undo her dress, his hands moving clumsily over the buttons. Soon America lay on the blankets, clad only in her shift, shivering slightly in the cool night air. She reached out a hand and laid it on Will's bare chest, moving her hand up to his face. He reached for her, one hand cupping the back of her neck and the other hand wrapping around her waist, pulling her toward his unclothed body.

Afterward, lying back on their makeshift bed, she could hear both their hearts wildly beating under the starlit night. Tonight she would not dream of coyotes or Indians, but of Will.

CHAPTER 5

Over the next three weeks on the trail, America began to think of Will as not only her husband, but her closest friend. They worked well together, with Will teaching her how to hitch and unhitch the horses, and how to shoot to defend herself.

They had to be careful to ration the gunpowder and shot, but after she had practiced with the unloaded caplock, he did load it a few times for her to use. She found it hard to get used to squeezing the trigger and feeling it jump in her hand as if it were alive. But after a few more shots, Will reloading it each time, she became more proficient.

America had never wanted to learn to shoot a pistol. It was not expected of Philadelphia women of a certain society, and, in fact, was considered a vulgar talent. She had read about the unreliability of pistols, and had heard that they could even explode in one's hand. That worried her, especially now that she was with child. But she also knew that it was imperative to know how to shoot out on the Plains if they ever encountered a war party and had to defend themselves.

"Shouldn't I know how to load the pistol?" she asked one day after target practice. They were nooning by Sugar Creek, about a week away from the Great Platte River Road.

Will gave America a dubious look. "I am not sure that's a good idea."

"Why," she teased, "because I'm a woman?"

Will's brow darkened. "You know me better than that, America." But his eyes involuntarily flickered to her waistline, and she knew what he was thinking.

She laughed. "Yes, I understand. But what if I don't hit my target in the first shot?"

He frowned. "Well, if it is a jackrabbit or prairie dog you are trying to hit, it will be gone before you can reload. If you miss an attacker, you will probably be dead before you get the chance to reload."

America had noticed that Will would become pig-headed about certain ideas, and he always meant well for her, but she had found ways around this peculiarity of his. She had discovered that maintaining a calm exterior and deliberate reason always worked with a lawyer. "But what if we're under attack and I'm pinned down with the rest of the wagon train? You don't want to stop defending our encampment to teach me how to reload, do you?"

She watched Will as he considered her logic. Suddenly the look on his face changed and she knew that she had won.

"You are right," he said as she showed her how to pour in the powder, tamp it down, and add the gunshot.

"Always remember that your best shot is up close," Will warned her. "It will be very difficult to keep from pulling the trigger if a war-painted Dog soldier is running toward you with his tomahawk raised, but you will get your best shot if you wait."

America could feel her heart speed up at the thought. They had yet to come across Indians, even though they were well into Indian Territory. It had been six years since all the major northeastern tribes—the Kickapoo, the Shawnee, and the Delaware—and the southeastern tribes—the Cherokee, Chickasaw, Creek, Seminole, and Choctaw—had been relocated to the Kansas and Oklahoma Territories. There were still some Indians near the Emigrant Trail here in Nebraska Territory, although America had been told by the captain and Tal that they were friendly.

That night, as she wrote in her journal, she made sure to include all the information she had learned about shooting and loading a pistol. Before leaving Philadelphia, America had purchased a blank book in which she could write the details of their trip. She learned that many of the emigrant wagon trains trekking west used some of the more detailed journals as guidebooks. These journals told future travelers where to find fresh water supplies, good grazing grass for the animals, and the best places to stop along the way for nooning and camping overnight.

In fact, the captain was now using a guidebook kept by one of the women from his last journey west. America had learned that although the pilot, Pike, was scouting ahead, he had to know in which direction the last wagon train had gone, and if there had been grass and water there.

America was determined to create such a book for the wagon trains that would follow the trail next year. It gave her something to do, and she felt it was her duty for those who chose to follow her out to the Territories.

Unfortunately, some of the incidents she wrote of in her journal were painful, but needed telling just the same. One day while the wagon train was nooning, America and Catherine took a walk. Catherine was just describing a shell brooch she had lost when, as they neared a clump of bushes, America heard a soft mewling sound. She stopped. "Do you hear that?" she asked her companion.

"Hear what?"

"Shh," America said, "there it is again. Do you hear it now?"

Catherine nodded and the two women stared toward the bushes. At first America thought it might be a wounded animal, until the whimpering took on a distinctive human sound.

"Shall we investigate?" America asked, taking a tentative step forward.

Catherine put a hand on her arm. "You're getting so heavy with child," she explained, "you'll need a little more time to get away if it's dangerous."

America smiled at the image of herself running in this condition, then watched as Catherine parted the bushes. Mrs. Moore lay on the ground, curled up in a bundle, her face battered and bruised. When the stout woman saw them, she turned away.

America watched Catherine's face soften for a moment, then harden. They bent down and gently helped Mrs. Moore up to her feet.

"Who did this to you?" she asked the injured woman. One of the woman's arms was bent at an unnatural angle and with horror America realized that the arm was broken.

Mrs. Moore was still shaking, and Catherine blurted out what they already knew. "That son of a bitch left her here to die." The moment the words left her mouth, she widened her eyes and covered her mouth. If the situation hadn't been so serious, her vulgar language might have been something America and Catherine could have a laugh over.

"Mrs. Moore," America said again, "can you tell me who did this to you?"

The voice that emerged was thin and shaky, and sounded badly in need of water. "Elva. My name is Elva."

"Elva, we're going to take care of you." America turned to Catherine. "Let's get her to the doctor's wagon." Together, they supported Elva Moore into the encampment and left her with Eliza and Theodore Bauer. Catherine disappeared while America went in search of Tal Bowen or Captain Terwilliger. She found Bowen and told him what had happened.

"But you can't be sure it was her husband?" he asked in a dubious tone.

"Of course it was Isaac Moore! I've seen bruises on her face before." If she wasn't such a lady, she might have hit something herself, she was so angry.

Bowen shook his head. "I'm sorry, but there's nothing we can do about it."

Just then, they heard the crack of a bullwhip and a man's scream coming from the other end of the campsite. America and Bowen raced over to find Catherine wielding the whip. She was aiming it at Isaac Moore, who cowered at the back of his wagon. When he saw Bowen, he attempted to escape, but Catherine cracked the whip again, just inches from his face.

Moore covered his mottled, purple face with his hands. "Get this bitch away from me. She's deranged."

Bowen started to move toward Catherine, but her whip stopped him. Her face was contorted with fury and her eyes glittered. With her back turned toward Bowen, Moore took a step toward her, but she turned around fast enough and stopped him in his tracks.

"Don't come near me, sir," she commanded, "and if you know what's good for you, you won't go near your wife again, either."

Other emigrants had started to gather at the sound of the commotion, although most of them stood well back. Terwilliger made his way through the crowd.

"What's going on here?" he demanded.

"It seems that Mr. Moore is getting a taste of his own medicine," America replied. Some of the women in the growing crowd laughed uncomfortably. America explained the situation to the wagon master.

Terwilliger nodded irritably. "I think we'd all feel better if you'd talk some sense into your friend, Mrs. Hollis."

America stood silently, staring at Catherine and Mr. Moore.

"What's keeping you?" Terwilliger asked in an exasperated voice. "Go on." He made a shooing gesture to America. In response, she crossed her arms and stood her ground.

"Why should I help him?" she asked in a calm tone that belied the rage boiling within her.

Terwilliger stared at America. "He's being assaulted, Mrs. Hollis," he explained in a slow, patient voice.

She gazed coolly at him. "So was his wife. Mr. Bowen told me nothing could be done about it."

"She's his wife, dear lady. That's his right!" Terwilliger exploded.

America smiled blandly. "Beating a woman is acceptable, but a woman beating a man is not? I don't see how this can be any different."

"Mrs. Hollis," Terwilliger began, his finger pointing at her, his mustache and eyebrows quivering. He paused a moment before answering her, then said in a triumphant tone, "Miss Welborne is not married to Mr. Moore, so she has no right to beat him."

America knew deep inside that marriage should make

no difference when it came to assault, but she was well aware that most of society thought otherwise. Since an eye for an eye didn't seem to be the answer, she'd have to try another approach.

"Mr. Terwilliger, we have to work together, and knowing that there is a man in our company who is beating his wife and nothing is being done to resolve the situation makes me fear for myself and my unborn child." America looked around and saw several other women in the company nodding in agreement. A few of them murmured their assents.

"Why would the Moores' private life even concern you, Mrs. Hollis?" Terwilliger countered.

She gaped at him. "I was one of the women who found Elva Moore. It *does* concern me. If you do nothing to ensure her safety, I have to wonder if you will do nothing in a more serious situation that endangers all of us."

Now America could hear men joining in the conflict, voicing their concerns.

"Yes, Mr. Terwilliger," Gil Hayes added, stepping forward, "Mrs. Hollis has a point."

Crack! "Ow! You bitch!" Crack! Moore began to whimper.

"All right, then," Mr. Terwilliger conceded testily. "We'll see what we can do for Mrs. Moore."

When the crowd had dispersed, America approached Catherine. She could see that her friend was trembling. "Catherine, please put the whip down. This isn't going to solve anything. The captain promised that he will deal with Mr. Moore. Elva will be safe."

She stopped and waited. Her friend's shoulders slumped and she held the whip in her hand as if it was too heavy for her. America came forward to take it gently out of Catherine's hand.

"How can they do this, America?" Catherine asked in a small voice as America led her back to the brides' wagon. "How can a woman allow a man to do something like that to her? Does he think of her as no better than an animal? Would he do that to his own horse?"

"Some do," America murmured, wrapping her arms around the still-trembling woman. When they arrived at the wagon, she made Catherine lie down, tucking several blankets over her. Then she heated up a mug of broth for her brave friend.

"I'd rather have a shot of whiskey," Catherine said with a weak smile. She blew on the hot broth before taking a sip.

America thought a moment, then said, "Dr. Bauer probably has a flask in his wagon, if you'd like me to get you some."

"Mr. Terwilliger, more likely," Catherine grumbled.

America covered her friend's hand and squeezed. "What made you take such drastic action, and where did you learn to wield a bullwhip like that?"

Catherine laughed at America's question. "Well, answering the last part first, my uncle taught me when I was a little girl." Her expression grew solemn. "My father used to beat my mother, until she finally got up the courage to leave him. That's why I worked back in Boston. I had to help my mother make ends meet. We had run away from my father in Richmond when I was fifteen. He was a brutal man, and my mother had the scars to prove it."

"Why did she wait until you were fifteen to leave him?" America asked.

"Because that was when he started beating me and my sisters." Catherine took another sip of her cooling broth and smiled a little. "I guess that's why, when we came across Elva Moore today, I just couldn't help myself. I saw Isaac Moore, I saw the bullwhip, and to be honest, I don't remember much of the rest."

After leaving Catherine, America went back to the doctor's wagon to find out how Elva was doing. Eliza Bauer told her that the woman would be moved in temporarily with the mail-order brides and that Addie Schreck had agreed to look after both Elva and Catherine.

That night, America recounted what had happened to Will, who had been out hunting and dressing black jackrabbits for their supper.

"Do you think Mrs. Moore will go back to her husband?" he asked.

America shrugged. "I don't know. But I'm worried about Catherine. She's going to marry a man she doesn't know very well. What if he turns out to be like her father?"

Will was silent for a minute, then said, "It seems Catherine can fend for herself."

They laughed to cut the tension, but it was a question that kept America awake half the night.

The next day, Terwilliger called on Will to represent Catherine. "We have to settle this," he said. "We can't have women taking a bullwhip to any man who offends them. Isaac Moore wants Miss Welborne to be suitably punished for her crime."

America stopped stirring the soup and came up behind Will. "What about Mr. Moore's behavior? Won't he be punished for beating his wife?"

The wagon master looked troubled. "Mrs. Hollis, as you are undoubtedly aware, when a woman becomes a man's wife, she essentially becomes his property. You know full well that married women have no rights."

After he left, America stomped around the campsite, fuming and clattering her spoon against the soup pot. Whenever Will tried to talk to her, she snapped at him. He finally came up behind her.

"America, please talk to me."

"Why should I?" She turned around abruptly to face him, waving the soupspoon in his face. "I'm only a possession of yours and possessions should know their place."

Will put his hands up in defense. "Did I ever say or do anything that made you think that I believed that?"

All the fire went out of her and her shoulders deflated in frustration. "I'm sorry, Will. You have been nothing but kind, loving, and respectful toward me. But it upsets me that Catherine will be punished while that beast gets away with what he did to his wife."

Will looked thoughtful. "Maybe not. Let me see what I can do." He went off to the back of the wagon and rummaged through one of their trunks until he found his law books. After studying for a bit, he left to talk to other members of the wagon train, not returning for almost two hours. America would catch glimpses of him in deep conversation with various men in the company, and finally, she saw him talking to Terwilliger and Isaac Moore. From Moore's physical appearance, America thought that he looked unhappy and tense, and not at all agreeable to whatever Will was saying. Eventually, Will came back with a big smile on his face.

She was eager to hear his news. "Well? Tell me before I burst!"

"Isaac Moore has agreed to drop his complaint against Catherine Welborne, and further, he will refrain from striking his wife while on this journey."

America was stunned. She knew that she had married a lawyer, but she hadn't known what he was capable of doing. "How did you manage that?"

Will shrugged, but failed to maintain his unconcerned facade for long, his face breaking into a grin. "Simply by pointing out to Mr. Moore that if he insisted on pursuing this complaint against Catherine Welborne, whose behavior even *he* admitted had been cause for provocation, then I would have to file a complaint on behalf of the rest of the company."

"For what?"

"Disturbing the peace and harmony of our community," Will replied. "The other men agreed to it before I talked to Mr. Moore." Taking America by the shoulders, Will turned serious. "America, not all men are like Isaac Moore. Please tell this to Catherine. The other men I talked to were angry and disgusted with him. Furthermore, they were appalled at the mere idea of beating their wives." He kissed her lightly on the forehead.

America threw her arms around her husband and kissed his cheek. "Oh, you are surely the best lawyer in the country."

Will returned her affection with another kiss, this time on her lips. "I believe I am, at that."

America left to relate Will's cleverness to Catherine and Elva. Both women smiled wanly. She had expected a more favorable response from one or both of them, and was disappointed. Catherine seemed to read America's bewilderment and reached out to squeeze her friend's hand.

"Oh, America, that is wonderful news, but," she looked over at Elva, "Elva still has to go back to him."

"Go back to him? Why?" America looked over at Elva Moore's broken arm in a sling and shook her head. "You don't have to go back, Elva. Catherine, Addie, and Flavia would be happy to let you stay here, or you could come stay with Will and me. We'd be happy to take you in."

Elva tried to smile through her split lip, then stopped trying and shook her head. "Thank you for your kind offer, America, but I have to go back. I love Isaac."

America couldn't believe what she was hearing, but after she left the wagon and thought about it for a while, it made a kind of pathetic sense. She wondered how she would have reacted if Jan had lived and they had married. If he had begun beating her, would she have left him? Maybe.

America counted herself lucky. She had married a stranger who turned out to be a handsome, intelligent man who respected her. America shuddered at the thought that she could so easily be in Elva's place.

$\mathscr{C}$ H A P T E R   6

America spent a good deal of time with the women in the wagons near hers, working on the quilt, cooking, watching the children, and walking beside the wagons along the Emigrant Trail's prairie grasses. Catherine had become Elva Moore's protectress, and could be found most of the time with the older woman. This did not hinder their friendship, however, as America grew to enjoy Mrs. Moore's company, as well.

Catherine's presence had a sizeable effect on Isaac Moore. He stayed clear of his own wife whenever Catherine was around. When they nooned, Isaac always found excuses to leave the encampment, spending a good deal of time out hunting with his mule. He became a good provider for the company, usually bringing back several rabbits, a deer, or an elk.

One afternoon America realized that she hadn't seen Elva since the night before. She increased her walking pace until she had caught up with Catherine's wagon. "Where is Elva this afternoon?"

Catherine shook her head grimly. "I stopped by to see her at lunch. She refused to leave her bed."

"But why?"

"She said that she's tired and wants to sleep."

America frowned. "Is she ill?"

Catherine shook her head and looked down. "She just didn't want to get up this morning."

"It sounds to me like she has melancholy," America said. "Shouldn't the doctor have a look at her?"

Catherine looked at America, her eyes bright with unshed tears, and tried to smile. "Mr. Moore already had Dr. Bauer check her. America, I don't know how else to help her."

In the following days, Elva didn't get better. She shuffled around her campfire, doing the most perfunctory of chores, but kept mostly to herself. She began to lose weight and there were dark circles under her eyes. America noticed that Isaac slept outside under the wagon each night while Elva slept inside with the canvas cover closed, even on the hottest nights. Catherine and America both offered to help, but were curtly rebuffed each time.

The men were more vigilant when Elva and Isaac were together in public, yet everyone in the company was appreciative of Moore's hunting contributions of fresh game into the community stewpot.

There were, in fact, some less sensitive people who saw the humor in it. America overheard one man say, "Looks like Isaac finally found a useful purpose for that mean temper of his. Instead of beating his wife, he goes out and kills creatures."

The following week, the wagon train nooned just short of the Platte River. The knee-high prairie grass was beginning to turn golden yellow as the heat of summer became more intense, but the river grass was still green with life. America was beginning to believe that the dust and heat would never leave her skin or her lungs. She could feel the dust of the trail sinking into her skin. It was packed beneath her fingernails and no matter how long or hard she scrubbed her hands in a pail of water, they would never be clean and white and soft again like they had been in Philadelphia.

When Celeste suggested that the women go down to the river to wash some clothes, and perhaps wash themselves as well, America didn't have to think long about her answer. Addie and Catherine came along, and they even managed to coax Elva into joining them, if just to distract her. Most of Elva's washing would have to be done by the other women.

The stream they used was a small tributary that broke off of the Blue River. Addie had just made a lighthearted comment about hanging the clothes to dry on strings that stretched from one wagon to the other when they heard a yell. They looked up to see Isaac Moore sprinting toward them. He was half dressed, wearing only his pants with suspenders flapping behind him.

"Indians! They attacked me," he yelled, waving his arms as if the Indians were an angry swarm of bees surrounding him. "Elva! Get back to the wagon."

America peered beyond him and saw not a single red-skin in pursuit. Still, she followed her companions as they briskly rinsed and wrung out their clothing.

Elva sat stock still, peering straight at the spot where her husband had emerged. Helping Elva to her feet, the women walked quickly back to the encampment. Moore was already there, talking wildly with his hands.

"They were there and they took my gun, my pistol, my mule, and my clothes," Moore said breathlessly. "And they're coming this way, too."

Terwilliger stood with his arms crossed. "Now, calm down, Mr. Moore. What do you mean, they're coming this way? I don't see anyone behind you. What were you doing out alone?"

Moore blinked as if he'd just been struck by the wagon master. "What do you mean, what was I doing out there? I was huntin' for food—a jackrabbit, a deer, something for dinner other than beans and bacon."

Terwilliger nodded. With great admiration, America realized that the captain had asked the question not because he cared what Moore was doing out there, but to get the man to calm down slightly and speak more coherently. "Describe these Indians to me," Terwilliger said.

Moore flung his hands in the air. With no shirt on, his paunchy belly and flabby arms gleamed white in the sun. "Describe 'em? They was Injuns, that's what they was. Why ain't you out there huntin' 'em down?"

Amid the excitement, America found it amusing that

Moore's English was deteriorating, his accent becoming more pronounced.

Tal Bowen stood a little in back of the wagon master, gripping a flintlock. There was anger and determination in his eyes. "What Captain Terwilliger wants to know is if there were women and children among the Indians you met."

America looked around for Will and found him walking toward her. He had a grim look on his face and his gun and powder flask in his hands.

Moore made a visible effort to calm down. "No, no women or children. Wait! There was one woman."

Terwilliger turned to Bowen and murmured, "Probably a medicine woman."

"And they had paint on their faces," Moore continued. "War paint. They was something fierce to behold."

The captain turned to Tal. Pike had joined them, catching the last part of Moore's description. There was a hurried discussion.

America looked around and found the women and men talking excitedly. Flavia, Addie, and the Hayes men had joined Catherine and Celeste. The Sanfords, who had become very familiar with the Moores, had gathered round Elva Moore and brought her over to her husband.

"At times like this," intoned the Reverend Sanford, "a man needs his helpmate by his side."

A dazed Elva dutifully took her husband's arm. America wondered if Mrs. Sanford ever talked. She didn't think she'd heard her utter more than a dozen words since the day they had met at the picnic. America noted that the Reverend Sanford carried a flintlock and a harsh expression. A shiver ran up her spine at the possibility of fighting off a war party. She hadn't encountered Indians yet, but she'd read accounts of raids on wagon trains and lone frontier homes out on the prairie.

"What's going on?" Will murmured. "I heard the commotion."

Before she could answer, Terwilliger held his hands up. She noticed that the level of tension and talk had risen considerably in the last few minutes.

"Now hold your horses, folks," Terwilliger said in a loud voice. "No one will be saddling up just yet. I think only Pike and me will go out there."

He turned to Bowen, who had approached leading his own blood bay and Terwilliger's roan. Pike was already mounted on his broomtail paint, ready to ride. America studied the scout, admiring the comfortable way he sat in his saddle. She had ridden horses whenever she and her parents went visiting friends and family that lived outside of Philadelphia, but she had never felt comfortable in a saddle.

"Tal, you're in charge for now. Make sure no one leaves this camp." The captain threw a warning glance at the reverend for good measure, then mounted his horse.

When Terwilliger had gone with Pike, Sanford stepped forward and addressed the rest of the men. "I'll go to hell and back to bring those redskins to justice," he said, shaking the Bible that he always carried. "Who will go with me?"

America watched Tal study Sanford for a moment. "Reverend, I do believe the women need a man to protect them and to quote a few words from the Good Book."

"Sir," Sanford replied, shifting his eyes to Isaac Moore, who had been given a shirt to cover up his bare chest, "I believe my good friend Isaac Moore would be more than willing to keep these women and children safe."

Sanford started to move toward his horse, a dun gelding, but Tal stepped into his path, carrying his pistol loosely in his hand.

"Reverend, I'd be much obliged if you stayed here. We'll need some men to defend the wagons if Pike and the captain don't make it back. In fact," he turned to look at the assembly of men ready to ignore the wagon master's orders and trail the war party on their own, "I believe that if it was all a misunderstanding between these Indians and Mr. Moore in the first place—"

Moore was trembling with rage at the insinuation. "Misunderstanding! It was no misunderstanding, sir. They stripped me of everything, including my dignity."

Tal cast a cool glance at Moore before continuing. "As I was saying, if this turns out to be a misunderstanding, we'd like to keep this encounter as friendly as possible."

"Now just hold on there, Mr. Bowen—" Sanford said, but got no further.

America suddenly felt cold as she looked toward the direction Terwilliger and Pike had gone. She hoped it was all a misunderstanding as Tal Bowen had suggested. Someone touched her shoulder and she turned to face Celeste. George stood a little apart from them, and Mary Elizabeth sat by their wagon, playing with a cornhusk doll that Celeste had made for her only the other day. Gil was showing Will how to whittle.

"I think we need to get on with our daily chores, same as usual," Celeste suggested. America agreed and they went back to their wagons where Celeste already had a fire going. Pooling their supplies, they decided on a rabbit soup, seasoned with root vegetables and a red onion that Mary Elizabeth had found on the trail.

"I don't know if we'll be able to let out that dress anymore, America," Celeste said, eyeing her friend's growing figure critically as they tended the dinner.

America laughed. "It's getting harder for me to fasten the waists.

"Some of us can take our old dresses and make a couple of new ones for you."

America had grown closer to Celeste over the past few weeks. Celeste reminded America of the older sister she had always wanted. She was able to talk to Celeste about things that Catherine hadn't experienced yet—her fears of pregnancy, of the actual birth, and taking care of a newborn.

"Oh, don't worry," Celeste had told her. "I've given birth twice, and there wasn't a doctor or midwife within ten miles either time. I'll be right by your side when your time comes."

Even though Celeste was not the midwife Mr. Terwilliger had mentioned, her reassurances touched America's heart and eased her own doubts about having her baby on the Emigrant Trail.

America peered at the soup. It was bubbling now, and thickening nicely. Even though she'd been eating the same menu most of the time on the trail, the aroma of the red onion mixed in with the rabbit, carrots, and potatoes made her hungry.

"Do you think the men are all right?" she asked Celeste.

The older woman stopped kneading the bread to flour her hands again. "Don't you worry about those Indians, America. Reverend Sanford needs a large dose of humility to keep him from inciting panic in others. Gil and I lived near the Kickapoo back in Illinois a short time before making our way west this year, and they were always friendly."

"You think the reverend was exaggerating?" America had moved over to Celeste's worktable to talk more intimately. The wagons had been pulled into a loose square, six wagons per side, and the animals not in use had been picketed inside in the center. The nearness of the other wagons, America sometimes thought, was too close for shared confidences. Celeste threw America a wry grin. Her long salt-and-pepper hair had been pulled back into a loose braid that hung over her left shoulder.

"I think the good reverend has more wind than a bull at green corn time."

America giggled at her sudden vision of Reverend Sanford, complete with bull horns, out in the middle of a cornfield.

Catherine wandered into their camp. "Mmm, that smells wonderful."

After glancing at Celeste for silent approval, America suggested to Catherine that she join them for supper.

"I have some macaroni," Catherine offered. "My sister made it for me before I undertook this journey."

"Why don't you go back to your wagon and get it," Celeste suggested. "I can watch the soup while I put the bread in to bake, and we can let America rest." She plopped the mound of dough into her cast-iron Dutch oven and clamped the lid on before hoisting it over the open fire.

America tried to keep from thinking about the Indians that the search party were sure to have encountered by now. She'd caught a glimpse of the Moores as they made their way back to their wagon—Elva's arm was healing fast—and it was difficult not to hear the good Reverend Sanford's booming voice reading from the book of Job.

America went back to her wagon. In the next few days, the wagon train would be approaching Fort Kearny at the fork where the Little Blue River met the Platte River. It would be an opportunity to send another letter to her parents, letting them know that she and Will were well.

Inside, she had made a little space to sit by stacking sugar and bean sacks against one side of the buckboard. The round top of an empty barrel served as her lap desk. Earlier that day they had stopped for their nooning in a

meadow where a cool breeze continued to blow and colorful wildflowers were scattered across the field. To take
advantage of the nice day, Will had stripped the canvas
cover off the wagon, so America had plenty of light to see
what she was writing.

She had just put pen to paper to tell her mother and father of Mr. Moore's adventure, when she heard a commotion coming from the far end of the encampment where
Terwilliger and Pike had departed.

CHAPTER 7

Even though America was anxious to find out what had happened with the Indians, she carefully put away her writing implements, cleaning out the pen to keep the leftover ink from drying in the nib. She may run across Indians many times during her journey, but this pen and ink was her only means of communicating with her family.

When she reached the edge of the encampment, Catherine and Celeste were already there. The men were in front, but had started to back up. Looking over their heads, America could make out Terwilliger and Pike dismounting.

An agitated murmur rippled throughout the emigrants. Moore and his wife were up front, and the reverend was trying to push his way through the crowd. He gave America a hard shove and, with a startled cry, she stumbled to the right. Before she had a chance to say anything, Bowen clamped his hand on the reverend's shoulder.

"Reverend, I think you'd better listen to what the captain has to say from back here."

"Well, I've never been treated like this in my entire life," Reverend Sanford said in a huff.

"And neither have I," America snapped. It took a lot to rouse her. "The next time you decide to shove a woman to the side without so much as an 'excuse me,' be careful that she doesn't have a cast-iron skillet in her hand, or you may find yourself wearing it."

The reverend blinked a couple of times, but said nothing as America turned away from him to listen to what Terwilliger had to say.

"Good people," the captain began, "these Indians, the Cheyenne, have come here to make amends."

Will had found America and pulled her out of the crowd and around the outside of the wagons. From there she had a perfect view of the Indians. Two of them, an old woman and an older warrior, had stepped forward with Pike and Terwilliger while their braves stood in the background holding the reins of their horses.

America had never seen people like these before. Just as in the accounts she had read, the Indians had dark skin, a reddish brown color that gleamed in the sunlight. And the way they were dressed brought a flush to America's face.

The men, the braves, were bare-chested with the exception of colorful bone bead-and-feather necklaces. Some of the warriors were clothed in leather breeches and others in only a loincloth that barely covered them from their waist to their knees. Their hair was long and worn either braided or wrapped with feathers and beads.

The chief, the man who had stepped forward with Terwilliger and the woman, wore a fringed leather shirt with ceremonial decorations and many feathers and beads in his carefully dressed hair.

The woman was dressed much the same way as the chief, except that her clothing had few decorations. She also wore a small, intricately decorated pouch at her side. America wondered if she was a medicine woman. Her face was a map of wrinkles and it appeared as if she had few teeth left. In her hand, she held the reins of a mule that looked remarkably like the one Isaac Moore owned.

America studied their faces and found these Indians to be handsome people, dignified despite the fact that many white men called them savages. She had a desire to know more about them. Perhaps if this meeting went well, she could talk to Mr. Pike and learn more about the Cheyenne.

The chief spoke while Pike translated. "This is Medicine Knife, chief of the tribe you see here. He has come here to return some items to Mr. Moore."

The wagon master called out, "Mr. Moore, will you step forward?"

America caught sight of the scrawny, pale man making his way through the crowd on shaky legs.

The chief spoke again, looking directly at Mr. Moore. Pike translated, keeping his voice bland. "He says that he would like to give you back your pistol. It's unloaded, so don't try to use it just now. And here is your mule."

The woman came forward, leading the mule, and handed the reins to Moore. America got the impression that the woman found the whole incident amusing.

The chief spoke again. "He says that if you hadn't waved that pistol around in such a dangerous manner when they encountered you, they would never have taken it away from you. As for the mule, the chief is puzzled about why you gave it to them. He cannot accept it as a gift."

America thought she detected a twinkle in the chief's eye, but she couldn't be certain.

Moore was flushed red by now, but he still managed to speak. "What about my clothes—where are they?"

Pike translated the question to the chief, who looked at his medicine woman. They both shook their heads, mystified expressions on their faces, and in a halting manner, the chief replied by way of Pike. "We do not know what happened to his clothes. As soon as we disarmed him to keep him from hurting himself or us, he gave us the mule and his flintlock."

Terwilliger hefted the flintlock for the emigrants to see that it had been returned.

Pike finished the translation. "Then he began throwing his clothes off as he ran back toward your encampment."

There was silence for a minute; then a hushed muttering rose up from the crowd, becoming louder, until America recognized it as laughter. Men and women alike chuckled and smiled at the story, the relief evident in their faces.

Where was the reverend in all this and why wasn't he making trouble? She looked around and found him glowering in the back, Tal Bowen by his side. Bowen caught her eye and winked. She nodded, satisfied that this first meeting with the Indians wouldn't turn into a tragedy or an embarrassment.

Moore stood there, head bowed, his wife by his side, taking in the humiliation. Terwilliger seemed to notice and clapped him on the back.

"From now on, Mr. Moore, if it's all right with you, we'll just call you 'Injun' Moore."

Moore appeared insulted until Chief Medicine Knife stepped forward and offered an intricately decorated pipe to him. "You must carry this pipe with you at all times and when you encounter my brothers on your journey, show it to them and smoke with them as a sign of peace."

As Moore turned it over in his hand, examining the carved stone pipe, his face cleared and he nodded in relief and acceptance. America could see the red paint, the feathers and beads and intricate carvings on it from where she stood and she wished she could get a closer look.

Pike muttered something to Moore and then spoke to the chief. The captain turned and announced to the rest of the emigrants that the men would gather and smoke the peace pipe to seal their friendship with the Cheyenne.

America felt left out as she watched Will join the men just beyond the wagon circle. The rest of the women had gone reluctantly back to their chores, but she had been given an order from Celeste and Catherine to rest in her wagon.

She attempted to finish the letter to her parents, but was too restless. They wouldn't reach another fort where she could leave the letter, for at least another three days. Instead, she decided to take a walk. Looking around with guilt, knowing she shouldn't go for a walk by herself, America snuck away from the campsite and headed for the river, downstream from where she had done her washing and encountered a panicked Isaac Moore earlier.

There was a clump of cottonwoods and horse chestnuts by the Blue River, and she thought she saw a few sugarplum bushes blooming a lacy white in the distance. She wondered if the fruit was ripe enough to pick. As America strolled toward the small stand of trees, a hawk caught her eye with his antics, diving and gliding on the gentle breeze. She let a feeling of peaceful solitude wash over her.

The shadbushes turned out to bear fruit too green to pick, so she walked back to the banks of the Little Blue, where she hunted for pretty stones to add to the small pile of rocks that she had collected on her journey from Pennsylvania. The stones were small enough to carry with her as a symbol of the changes she was going through as she and Will made their way west.

She heard a small sound behind her and jumped in fear. Had some less friendly Indians followed her out here? Looking around warily, it took a moment to pick out the medicine woman from her surroundings. The dull tanned hide she wore blended in with the trees, and the woman moved slowly and surely.

"Oh! You startled me," America said. She felt foolish for talking, because this woman probably didn't understand her at all, but thought it would be even more impolite if she just stood and stared.

Then America smiled and nodded, and the woman smiled back. At least they could communicate in the universal language. The woman took a step toward America and patted her own belly as her eyes rested pointedly on America's shape. America blushed and nodded.

The woman dug an empty leather pouch out of a hidden pocket in her skirt and extended it toward America, who took it hesitantly. The Indian woman made gestures to indicate that America should put her pebbles in the bag, then gestured for her to follow. America complied.

After they walked a short distance, the woman stopped and pointed to the bank of the river. America came up and stooped over the ground, noting that there was only a small, empty turtle shell where the medicine woman pointed. The woman grunted and tapped America's shoulder and she finally understood—the woman wanted her to put the turtle shell in the bag.

She did, and they resumed walking. Farther along the riverbank the woman stopped again, pointing this time to a small, delicate shell that lay with the pearly side up, gleaming white in the sun. America put that in the bag as well. She had no idea what this pouch was for, but she continued to follow the medicine woman, gathering up weeds and flowers and grass until the woman turned around and they headed back toward the encampment in companionable silence.

When they were in sight of the wagons, America turned and offered the bag to the medicine woman, but she just smiled, touched America's belly again, and walked toward the Cheyenne braves who waited patiently for her. America walked back to the encampment, lost in her own thoughts. It was only when she encountered Pike that she realized that the Indians were leaving.

"Oh! Mr. Pike, maybe you can answer my question."

Pike raised his eyebrows when she extended the pouch and told her story. Then he smiled. "Mrs. Hollis, you have had a rare experience. That medicine woman has helped you gather a medicine bundle for your childbirth."

"A medicine bundle?"

"The Indians don't worship God like the white men do," he explained. "They have their own gods and they believe that there's healing power in nature. The medicine bundle is for you to carry with you until your child is born." He gave her a sideways glance. "Of course, you being a Christian woman and all, well, I can understand if you don't believe in all that."

America thought about what Pike told her. According to him, it was an honor to be given a medicine bundle, and to have a medicine woman pay this much attention to her. And she had to admit that she was excited by what he'd imparted to her. "I think I will keep this, Mr. Pike, as a reminder of my first meeting with the Indians."

He showed her how to wear it around her neck and told her to drop it inside her shirtwaist so that the others wouldn't see it and question it.

"Especially that crazy as a loon Reverend Sanford," Pike said, reading her mind.

They shared a muffled laugh before America thanked

him and headed back to her wagon. On her way, she passed "Injun" Moore, who was still showing his peace pipe off to some of the boys who hadn't been old enough to join the pipe smoking ceremony. He caught her eye, now proud of his new nickname.

"Mrs. Hollis! Did you see what the Injuns gave me?" he asked, excitement sparkling in his eyes.

As she examined it closer and exclaimed over how beautiful it was, America couldn't help remembering the dour little man she had met back in Independence at the boarding house. This experience seemed to have changed him for the better. She hoped the effect was lasting.

"Godless heathens!" a voice pronounced from behind her. America turned around to face the Reverend Sanford. "And you, Mrs. Hollis! I saw you walking with that pagan Indian woman on the riverbank. Mark my words, no good will come from shunning the word of God and glorying in the devilish rituals of those savages." He opened his Bible and began to intone a passage from Leviticus. " 'I will set my face against anyone who consults mediums and wizards instead of me, and I will cut that person off from his people' . . ."

"Excuse me, Reverend," America interrupted him. "I must be getting back to Will. He'll want to know where I've been." She turned her back to the reverend and briskly walked away. Mr. Moore stood there, peace pipe in hand, looking torn by indecision. She hoped he would keep the pipe and ignore the reverend's ignorant rantings.

CHAPTER 8

Each day the wagon train covered between sixteen and twenty miles of smooth hilly land as they moved across the Great Plains. The day they arrived at the Platte River was a milestone. Although they had traveled two hundred miles since leaving Independence, America and many others felt as if the Emigrant Trail and the westward journey really began with the Platte.

The wagon master ordered the emigrants to build their fires in the daytime when they nooned, and to do a full day's cooking at one time. While the men hunted for game and the women cooked the meal, the children were put to work gathering dried buffalo chips for fuel. The days grew longer as June came and went, and they kept on the move from sunup until sundown. Sometimes Will and America ate their supper while sitting in the jump seat, taking turns holding the reins of their team of horses. The supplies started to dwindle, and farmhouses became few and far between.

Then the day came when they passed the first grave.

"Slow down, Will," America said. She'd been walking

to stretch her legs and she bent over the crude stick in the ground with the broken board that was nailed to it.

HERE LIES EMMALINE FOLEY
BELOVED WIFE AND MOTHER
MAY 9, 1846

Will stopped the wagon and jumped off. "Who is it?" He took off the dusty slouch hat that shaded his face from the searing summer sun.

"Emmaline Foley died less than two months ago." America squatted over the shallow grave and fingered her medicine bundle. "I wonder how she died."

Will wiped his brow with a dirty rag that he kept in his back pocket. He squinted ahead. "We'd better get going. The rest of the wagon train is moving on without us. We don't want to be caught too far behind." He let himself up into the jump seat and waited for her.

"Wait." America ran over to a clump of red and yellow paintbrush. She picked the best of them and laid the bunch on Emmaline Foley's grave. "I wonder how old her children are," she said softly to herself.

They passed seven more graves before Terwilliger stopped by the Platte to camp that night. America drew some water from the river and tasted it. "Ugh!" She spat the water out, but the taste of alkaline still lingered. Looking around, America noticed that the grass was thin from the last wagon train that had come through a month earlier.

Will returned from meeting with Terwilliger. "The captain says that Pike has gone out to scout for good grass and a water hole with better water. Until then, we should use the Platte water as little as possible." He hesitated, then added, "And he says that he thinks the wagon train ahead of us had some people die of cholera. When Pike came back from scouting up ahead, he said there were even more graves and personal belongings that had been left by the side of the trail. He advises us not to touch them or take anything with us, no matter how tempting."

America looked around. The sun was beginning to set, and she could feel the tension tightening around the group of emigrants. Now she knew why—an epidemic of cholera would set anyone on edge.

"Can I go play with Hedy and Claramae?" she heard Mary Elizabeth ask her mother.

"No."

"Why can't I?" the ten-year-old asked in a plaintive tone.

"You just can't," Celeste said. "I need you to help me take stock of our supplies and darn some stockings."

"But I did that last night," Mary Elizabeth said. "It's George's—"

Celeste turned on her daughter and grabbed her shoulders. "You just can't go play, Mary. Not now." Tears streamed down her daughter's cheeks and she bowed her head. Celeste held Mary Elizabeth and kissed the top of her head, whispering, "I'm sorry, sweetheart."

She searched for Catherine and found her busy on the

quilt. Their pattern was called Wild Geese and the squares looked like a flock of geese heading south on a field of muslin.

"This will be beautiful when it's finished, don't you think?" America asked. Catherine didn't respond. "You're worried about the cholera, too, aren't you?"

Catherine gave America a strange look. "Who wouldn't be? Sometimes I think I'll never make it to Oregon."

America caught her friend's hand up in her own. "Don't say that," she admonished. "We'll be there by October. You'll see."

The trek continued through July. The sun burned down on them all day long, making it unpleasant to cook over a fire. With the wind blowing up at any moment, there was the constant threat that their skirts would whip up over the flames and catch fire. Most of the women had already solved the problem by borrowing their husbands' pants to wear while cooking over the open campfires. In the past three weeks alone, four dresses that had scorch marks on the skirts had been donated to America so she could make a couple of new dresses for her expanding waistline.

When the men went hunting, sometimes the game was plentiful, but most of the time they were lucky to come back with a few prairie dogs or sage hens. Several cattle died from drinking bad water or eating locoweed. Occasionally an ox or a horse would die, but cattle seemed to bear the brunt of it. When a cow died, the emigrants couldn't even use the meat because of the possibility of disease being passed on.

By the middle of August, the temperature had risen in the daytime to over one hundred degrees, and tempers were almost as high. One day, Terwilliger called for everyone to move out. As Will and America followed the Sanford wagon, they were suddenly called to a halt. After ten minutes of being stationary, Will became restless. America was worried. This had never happened before. The wagon train moved slowly, and there were sometimes slight delays, but never this long.

"Reverend Sanford, do you know why we've stopped?" Will called out to the preacher, who was seated in the back of the wagon. The preacher ignored him, his eyes glued to the pages of the Good Book, his lips stumbling over words in a passage. America looked for Lem, who had always been nice to her, but she spied him out on the prairie, chasing a couple of other boys. Mrs. Sanford was nowhere nearby.

"I need to stretch my legs," America said to Will as she climbed down from Betsy. "I'll walk up ahead and find out what's keeping us from moving."

As she passed wagon after wagon, others joined her—Gil and George, Catherine and Flavia, and Muriel Sanford. It was Isaac Moore's wagon that was the holdup. More to the point, it was Elva Moore who was delaying the trek.

"Elva, we must go," Moore was saying. His wife was sitting on a three-legged stool in the middle of the flat, scrubby ground, her hands clasped together, staring straight ahead.

"I'm not moving," was all she said. Mr. Moore got

down on his knees and placed his hands on her shoulders.

"Please, Elva. For me. For us. We have to go or Mr. Terwilliger will leave us here."

Elva Moore blinked and seemed to look at her husband, but America could have sworn that she was looking right through him. "Fine. Then you go, Isaac. You go on without me. I'm staying here. Maybe I'll finally have some peace and quiet."

Moore stood up and turned around to appeal to his fellow emigrants. "Can anyone talk sense to her?" He brushed dust off his knees, and held his hands out in appeal. Catherine was about to step forward, but Moore noticed her and glared, sending her back into the crowd.

America came up to her. "Why don't you try anyway, Catherine? She'd certainly listen to you before she'd listen to her own husband."

Catherine shook her head. "I think Elva has gone as far as she wants to go, and nothing I say will have any effect on her."

Mr. Terwilliger had overheard them and he nodded. "She's right. Some people just don't make it. They don't die from Indians or snake bites or cholera. Some just give up."

The wagon master turned back to confer with Moore. America overheard part of their conversation. "Mr. Moore," Terwilliger began, "I can't keep these good folks waiting much longer. Why don't you carry your wife to your wagon."

Together they looked over at her. She had crossed her arms and was scowling at both of them. It was clear that she had overheard him and didn't think much of the idea.

The captain scratched the back of his neck. "Maybe that ain't such a good idea. But we have to move, Mr. Moore. We can't stay here another night." He turned and pointed in the direction they were headed. "You can see the beginnings of those mountains up ahead, can't you?"

Moore nodded slowly. Terwilliger went on. "Well, we gotta find the pass through them mountains. And we got even bigger mountains beyond to get these wagons through. And it's gonna be a job hauling them up the sides when we get to the bigger mountains—the Sierras—we gotta use ropes and winches. We have to move full chisel now, and we can't set here waiting for your wife to decide when she wants to go."

Moore stood there with his hat in his hand. "Can anyone help me convince her?"

Gil stepped forward. "A group of us can load her and that stool in the wagon, if you want, Isaac."

"Oh, why didn't they do this in the first place?" America murmured to Catherine. Her friend gave her an enigmatic smile.

Moore nodded to Terwilliger and Gil, but when they started toward Mrs. Moore, she drew a pistol out of her skirts and aimed it at them. "I'm not going anywhere. I just don't want to move." Her voice cracked on her last words. "Go on."

"That's why," Catherine replied.

The men backed off, and Terwilliger shouted to Bowen to get the train moving.

Blinking rapidly, Isaac Moore jammed his hat back on his head. He turned back to Elva. America never heard Isaac Moore speak so tenderly to his wife before this moment. "Elva, I'm going to get back in the wagon and go because Mr. Terwilliger said I had to. Please come with me. I promise things will be different from now on."

Elva gave her husband a blank look. "You've said that before, Isaac. I'm tired. Nothing changes. I'm not going anywhere."

Isaac walked backward, watching his wife for any sign that she would change her mind, until he got to his wagon. Then he climbed up on the jump seat. The crowd dispersed, even Catherine, going back to their wagons to get ready to move on. America lingered a moment, stepping closer to the woman who had pulled a pistol on the wagon master.

"Mrs. Moore," she said.

Elva Moore's eyes were closed, as if she was too tired to keep them propped open. "Yes, child?"

"Why?"

Elva opened her eyes and stared at America, as if she herself hadn't fully explored why she was acting this way. "I don't know," she said, shaking her head and turning to stare out at the prairie. "It's so vast. I just can't go any farther. I'm tired and I don't think we're going anywhere better than the place we left."

"It does seem as if we haven't made any progress," America said.

Elva shook a finger at her. "Now don't you go thinking that, girl. You have that baby to think about."

"What about your husband?" America asked.

Elva seemed to think about that for a minute. "I think I've stopped loving him. And I reckon there's not a place for me out there."

"Do you want to go home?"

Elva Moore looked forlorn when she answered. "There's no home left to go back to. I just know I don't want to go any farther."

"America!" Will called her as the wagon creaked by on the trail, not yards from where Elva Moore sat.

"You don't have any food," America pointed out.

"I won't need any."

"What about Indians?"

"You'd better go. Your husband's calling you, child. Take care of him and that baby."

America hesitated.

"Good-bye," said Elva.

"Good-bye."

America sat in the back of the wagon, watching the sad woman grow smaller, waiting for a sign that she'd changed her mind. But she stayed seated on that stool in the middle of nowhere until the wagons came to a series of gradually bigger hills and Elva disappeared.

That night when they had come to a good water hole and had picketed the animals inside the circle of wagons,

America lay next to Will and thought about Elva and Isaac.

"Do you think she's all right?" America asked him when they were lying underneath the stars that night.

He was slow to answer. "I think she's in a better place than her life here."

"I could never leave my husband like that," she murmured, then realized what she had said and looked self-consciously at Will.

He grinned. "And I could never let you go like that."

America smiled. Jan finally was a memory, and her heart now belonged to Will.

He looked up and pointed a finger at the sky. "There's a falling star."

America followed his finger and saw the shimmering trail the star left behind. She felt a tear slide down her temple and into her hair. She wiped her face and Will turned over on his side to look at her. He reached out when the next tear came and stopped it with his finger, gently swabbing at it, then kissing her temple. She reached out for him and they took comfort in each other before falling asleep in each other's arms.

All night, America kept waking up, half-expecting Mrs. Moore to come staggering into the campsite. As she drifted off to sleep each time, she thought, *Maybe Elva will come back in the morning.*

But morning came and went, and Elva didn't come after them. Her husband was quieter than usual, and people had stopped kidding him about being "Injun" Moore.

After a week on the trail, Mr. Moore went off to hunt alone and never returned. The wagon train waited a few hours while Terwilliger, Pike, and several others formed a search party to track the man. When they returned with his flintlock, but without Moore, there were no explanations. His belongings were divided among the emigrants.

Will and America got a sack of flour and Mrs. Moore's dresses. The Hayeses got two of the horses. The Sanfords got some of the books and a bag of rice. The mail-order brides received the sugar and the coffee.

The next night in the campsite, America noticed that Pike was smoking Moore's peace pipe. It occurred to her that Moore had always kept that pipe on his person, even when he went hunting. It was then that she realized Mr. Moore was really gone, and wouldn't be coming back.

CHAPTER 9

Ever since she marked the passing of Emmaline Foley's gravesite two weeks ago, America had been counting the number of markers along the trail. In many cases, she couldn't tell who was buried or how many were in a gravesite because the names had been worn off the markers by the harsh winter. But one thing America was sure of—the markers numbered into the hundreds.

Even after seeing all those graves, she still was not prepared when cholera struck her own wagon train. The sickness began one morning when they were on the move. America saw Flavia walking slowly toward them, letting the Sanford wagon pass her by until their own wagon came abreast of her. Will reined in the horses.

"Flavia! What's the matter?" America scooted over so the mail-order bride could climb onto their jump seat.

Flavia was normally a good-looking woman—milk white skin, light golden hair, and green eyes. But today, her eyes were puffy and her complexion streaked with dried tears. "It's Catherine," she said. "She's awful sick with a fever."

America's heart fluttered in her breast. "Has anyone told Dr. Bauer?"

Flavia took her lace-edged handkerchief and dabbed daintily at her tear-stained cheeks. "Addie went to get him. They're up in our wagon right now. I thought I'd be in the way, so I came back here."

"You did right," America said, absently patting the woman's shoulder.

She didn't feel particularly close to Flavia. Over the past few months, she'd come to think of the young woman as vain, spoiled, and selfish. Flavia often talked about her privileged childhood, and it was Catherine who confided to America that she questioned Flavia's claim to wealth.

Coming from a privileged background herself, America had observed Flavia's social manners and wondered how a woman from a good background didn't even have a rudimentary knowledge of etiquette, French, embroidery, or ballroom dancing. In an odd sort of way, America felt sorry for Flavia, and therefore didn't challenge the young woman.

"It's the cholera, isn't it?" America said. Her hand protectively covered her belly.

Flavia nodded. "I just hope I don't get it." She reached up and touched her face, then looked at America and Will and quickly added, "But I'm certain I'm healthy." She smiled wanly, then crawled onto some sacks in the back of their wagon and immediately fell asleep.

America could feel Will's worried glance. She reached over and covered his hand with hers. No one really knew how cholera got started. The popular theory among doctors was that it was a mysterious virus that traveled on air currents, but America had heard that a doctor named John Evans had been studying the fatal disease and was trying to convince the medical community that it was passed by touch from one infected person to another. Dr. Evans had, so far, been unsuccessful.

"We're bringing up the rear," America reminded Will in a low voice.

"That won't stop us from getting whatever Catherine has," Will said. "If it's contagious, I'm worried about you and our baby."

"There's little that we can do now," she reminded him.

They traveled in silence, with just the comforting sway and creak of Betsy to interrupt their separate thoughts. She scanned the horizon north, west, and south as they rolled along. There was nothing to see but prairie grass and the Platte running about half a mile to the north. A hawk drifted up in the cloudless sky, searching for its dinner.

The sun seemed to reach into every pore of America's skin. She felt as if her temperature had risen to the point of bursting and she longed for a dip in the Platte or in some cool watering hole with weeping willows shading the banks.

Finally, Will spoke. "Maybe we should break off from the train, lag behind by a day or so."

"I don't think that's such a good idea. We're coming into hostile Indian country and a lone wagon would be an easy target," America replied. "Besides, how would it look to the rest of the emigrants if we avoided them?" She glanced back at Flavia. "And if this cholera is infectious, we've already been exposed. No quarantine can save us now."

The skin around Will's mouth tightened, but he didn't reply. Although the first few months of their married life had been strained, America had come to realize that she was falling in love with him. It wasn't an epiphany that came swiftly; it had been a more gradual realization.

The moment she accepted her love for Will was when she tried to picture life in the Territories without him—and couldn't. But she saw that her future happiness was now endangered by an invisible enemy—better that it had been a war party than something she couldn't see, couldn't understand, and, worse, couldn't fight back.

Her leg muscles cramped suddenly and she tried to shift her position, but her growing belly made every position uncomfortable. America looked back at the sleeping Flavia, and wished that the woman had stayed with her own wagon. She immediately regretted such a selfish thought.

"I need to walk," she said.

Will stopped the wagon and helped her down. She walked a couple of miles before the company stopped to rest. She heard a shuffling sound coming from inside her wagon. Fearing that Flavia had become ill, she walked to the back and lifted the cover. There sat Flavia, with her hand in America's jewelry box.

"What are you doing?" America asked coldly.

The young woman jumped and squeaked like a field mouse caught in a hawk's claws. Then she put one small, plump hand to her breast and let out a calming sigh. "Oh, America! Forgive me, but I recalled I'd lent you a mirror, and I thought I'd retrieve it while I was here."

America eyed her jewelry box, which was still sitting on Flavia's lap. "Then why are you searching my jewelry box? I wouldn't put it in there. And you didn't lend me a mirror. I have one," America said, pointing out her own silver-backed mirror that she had brought from Philadelphia.

Flavia blinked several times, blushed, and stammered. "Oh, well, I—I guess I must have lent it to Celeste." She returned the jewelry box to America, who eyed her treasures to make sure nothing was missing. "I suppose I should get back and see how Catherine is doing."

Flavia climbed out of the slow-moving wagon under America's stern silence, then caught America's hand and asked in a pleading tone, "You won't tell anyone about this visit, will you?"

America suddenly remembered that throughout the trip, emigrants had periodically complained that items were missing from their wagons. It was usually things such as a brooch or a ribbon or a small mirror—feminine articles that were pleasing to the eye. Harriet Tobias, a freed slave who lost a pair of rhinestone hairpins, had grumbled that the thief didn't seem interested in acquiring her three-legged skillet or her bar of lye soap.

Because the missing items were of a frivolous nature,

Terwilliger had expressed his reluctance to search the wagons, not wanting to incur hard feelings for the sake of a few pieces of jewelry.

"As long as those items are returned to their rightful owners, I won't say anything," America promised. "But if they are not returned by tomorrow morning, I will have to let the women know."

Flavia's face paled beneath her sunlit ringlets, and she nodded imperceptibly as she backed away from America. When she was gone, America let out a breath of relief and stared at her jewelry once more. Nothing appeared to be missing. Among other less important pieces of jewelry was a string of pearls that her father had given her for her first ball, and a pair of diamond earbobs that Will had presented to her during the first month of their marriage. And there was Jan's garnet ring. America fingered the soft leather bag around her neck. There was room, she decided. The medicine bundle would be a good place to hide the few precious possessions that meant the most to her.

America returned her jewelry box to the wagon, then reached for the water bucket. She felt as dry, withered, and brown as the grass that crackled beneath her feet. The dust had gotten into everything and she hadn't bathed for weeks. She had taken off her shoes to save on shoe leather and walking barefoot had toughened her feet over the last few weeks. She rarely felt the pebbles and sticks on the ground when she trampled them.

It was mid-August and there hadn't been a good rain since early June. The Platte was dirty and shrunken this time of year, and the water holes that Terwilliger and Pike sometimes led the wagons to weren't much better. In fact, the last water hole had been black and smelled nasty. No one let their cattle, horses, or mules drink it, and they had been forced to move on a few more miles until they found a hot spring.

A homemade sunbonnet shaded America's head from the unforgiving sun. She had made it herself out of scraps of material and reinforced it with potato starch. Her long-sleeved, high-necked calico dress had been let out to accommodate her rounded belly. The dress was an amalgamation of two dresses previously worn by Elva Moore. The plain red and the blue sprigged print went together well and America had received many compliments.

But she still felt as big as a buffalo, and about as ugly. No matter how often Will told her that she was beautiful, she saw a different America when she looked in her hand mirror. All she could see was her cracked lips and wind-burned cheeks. The fine, straight, shiny hair that she had been so proud of had turned to dry, tangled straw. Her hands, so white and fine once, were roughened and reddened by the chores she performed every day on the trail.

America should have been troubled by the changes in her physical appearance, but that wasn't what bothered her now. She had more immediate worries—the spread of cholera, the child she had to protect.

In a journal written by a former traveler of this trail, a woman told of an epidemic of cholera in her encampment. She had hated using the watering holes and instead had used the water from the Platte for drinking and cooking. She boiled the river water and strained it through a cheesecloth to rid it of impurities.

The writer had been convinced that this is what saved her family from the sickness. She had written: "The water in these holes, no matter how clean it looks, has been stagnant. Cows and horses drink from it and bathe in it, and I will not use it. On the other hand, the water from the Platte is forever moving, so if an animal bathes in the stream or if we do our washing in the river, I can still use the water if I go upriver."

Since their departure from Independence, America had been following this woman's example, using the Platte River water for cooking and drinking. She had noticed that several other families had followed her example as well. If this writer's theory had been correct, this practice just might save America and the others from cholera.

By the time Terwilliger called a halt to the company to noon that day, Catherine was in worse shape than Flavia had led America to believe. When America approached the wagon, she heard moans coming from within. She peeked inside and found Addie bathing Catherine's forehead with a damp rag while two men held down the thrashing woman.

"It hurts," she cried. America started forward, but Addie caught sight of her.

"Don't come in here, America," she said sharply. In a softer voice, she added, "Please go. Catherine would never forgive herself, or me, if you got the cholera."

"But what about you—?"

Addie shook her head. "I've been traveling with her and I've put myself in danger already."

"But I have to do something," America said, hovering on the outside of the wagon. Desperation pressed heavy on her chest, laboring each breath she took.

Catherine was panting; her hair was damp with sweat. She managed to croak out one sentence. "Get her out of here."

One of the men who had been holding her down looked up at America. "Go away. You can't do her any good." He pulled the canvas cover closed and America stepped back.

When she went back to their wagon, Will was there, upset that she hadn't told him where she was going.

"How could you blithely go wandering off without telling me? I was worried," he shouted as he paced in front of their wagon.

"So I should just stay in our wagon?" she asked. She knew she shouldn't be angry with him for his concern, but she wasn't happy about the way he showed it.

Will's brow darkened, his eyes sparked with fury. "Yes," he said. "The other women would do the same thing if they were carrying a child."

She crossed her arms and felt her cheeks burn with anger.

Will took her by the shoulders. "There are dangers out here, America—not just cholera and hostile Indians, but wild animals and snakes. I don't want to lose you."

It was their first serious disagreement, but she reluctantly nodded, seeing his reasoning. And although she would never admit it to him, she knew he was right.

The day passed by slowly. Flavia came by with news of others in the wagon train who were stricken. America cooked supper for herself and Will, and did all the domestic chores that needed to be done while they were stationary. Still, she could smell the fever and sickness and hear her friend's screams of agony while she tended the stew, darned stockings, and mended a pair of Will's pants.

Later in the afternoon, America looked up from writing in her journal to see Dr. Bauer leaving Catherine's wagon. He was a short and wiry man, balding on top, but with a full beard to compensate for it, and he wore a stethoscope around his neck. America had only seen him wear suits the entire time they were on the trail, but he seemed comfortable dressed in such formal attire.

He caught sight of America and came over, studying her over his wire-rim bifocals.

"I heard from Miss Addie that you were very foolish earlier today," he said in a severe manner.

"But Catherine's my friend, Doctor."

Dr. Bauer shook his head. "You can't help. And you have another to think about right now."

"Will Catherine be all right?"

"I did my best for her. Gave her calomel and opium stringents." America knew that both calomel and opium stringents were medicines that helped the sick cope with pain. Dr. Bauer avoided her gaze. "I have to go see the Hayeses."

She caught his sleeve. "What's wrong with them?"

"George and Gil Hayes are sick," he replied.

America thought about delicate Mary Elizabeth. "What about Celeste and Mary?"

"They seem to have escaped the symptoms thus far," the doctor assured her.

America went back to the wagon to lie down with Will, who had fallen asleep after their midday meal, but she couldn't get any rest. She finally got up an hour later to write a letter to her parents and noticed the doctor entering the Sanford wagon. He came out just a few minutes later.

"Doctor," she called out, "how are the Sanfords?"

Dr. Bauer came over. "They have dysentery, not cholera, and I think they'll recover."

America had crossed her arms protectively over her belly. "Can you tell me how Addie and Flavia are feeling?"

The doctor raised his eyebrows. "Addie Schreck is healthy, and has been nursing her two companions. Flavia has been vomiting, but I've given her some calomel. She's resting now outside the wagon. Like the Sanfords, I don't think she has cholera."

"Will George and Gil Hayes be all right?"

The doctor gave her a tired smile. "We caught the symptoms early and the calomel and opium stringents seem to have done some good. I think they will be back on their feet soon." He looked around the encampment and shook his head. "But there are others here, like Miss Welborne, who are too far along. And once cholera takes hold of a person, there's no hope."

He told her he had to check on some other patients and took his leave.

Later in the day, America went down to the river to do some washing and to get away from the sounds of the dying. As she scrubbed one of Will's shirts with her bar of lye soap, she heard someone approaching.

She looked up and recognized the young man as a member of her wagon train. His name was Peter Miller and she had talked to his wife, Caroline, several times. They were traveling with her parents. Peter looked desperate and wild-eyed. He carried a flintlock with him and was breathing hard, as if he'd been running.

"Is everything all right back at the camp?" she called out, alarmed by his appearance.

He looked at her as if he hadn't seen her until she'd spoken. He slowed down and backed away from her. "If you're not sick yet, you should get away now," he said. America could hear the panic in his voice. "Don't go back there; you'll only die. There are others who've run away already."

She stood up, but didn't approach Miller. "What are you talking about?"

"The sickness. Cholera, they call it," he replied, sobbing. "My wife, Caroline, she's dead. Her parents are both down with it. I couldn't stay and watch. I have to leave. I have to find a safe place."

America took a step toward him, talking softly. "They probably need you now. Why don't we go back."

He shook his head. "No. I can't go back. I can't face them. I'd rather die in the wilderness alone than die in agony like that." He paused. "You have your child to consider. Come with me." He took a couple of steps toward her and grabbed her elbow. "I'll protect you."

America resisted his insistent tugging. "My husband is back there, and my friends, too."

The man let go of her and backed away. "They're all dead, madam. They may walk and talk, but they're all dead." He turned and started walking away from her, then paused in mid-step and said over his shoulder, "And you are, too, if you go back there."

She watched him walk, then break into a run. She stood watching his retreat until Peter Miller was a speck on the horizon.

When America got back to camp, she went immediately to Mr. Terwilliger and told him about Peter Miller.

The wagon master looked grim and shook his head. "I can't spare anyone to go after him."

"Maybe my husband could go after Mr. Miller," America said.

Terwilliger shook his head. "I think young Peter is beyond anyone's help. He'll either come back on his own, or we'll never see him again."

America didn't think she could ever get used to the harsh way the emigrants were treated out here on the trail. She regretted what happened to Peter Miller, and thought about going after him herself, but realized that Mr. Terwilliger, as hard as he sounded, was right.

What she could do was find out how her friend was progressing. As she started to head toward the doctor's wagon, she encountered her husband. Will was looking pasty in the face, and there were new lines around his nose and mouth that she hadn't noticed before.

"Where are you going?" he demanded.

America started to take offense to his tone of voice, but checked herself when she realized what a strain he must be under. "To ask about Catherine," she replied.

He gently took her elbow and tried to steer her away. "I don't think that's a good idea. Let's get away from here. Now."

America gave him a strange look. Will was perspiring. He had the sort of expression that Peter Miller had when she talked to him. "Are you all right?" She reached up and felt his forehead. He was cool to the touch.

He shook off her hand. "I'm fine," he replied shortly. "I just think we should leave here now."

She stepped back from him and indicated her washing. "I've just come from the Platte." She told him about her encounter with Peter Miller.

He dropped his head. "I believe it would be a good idea if we left, too. There are several families who are still healthy. They are packing up their wagons and getting ready to break off from the wagon train. I talked to one of the men, Sam Hawbaker, who told me that they will leave tonight. And if we're smart, we will leave with them."

A moan of agony, then the sound of dry retching, came from a wagon nearby. "Let me die. Please kill me," a feeble voice cried out.

America swallowed the fear that was building up inside of her. It would be so easy to go. Just pack up their wagon and leave with the healthy ones, leave the sick and the dying.

"How will we know that we won't be taking the sickness with us? Or that some of the other healthy people with us won't contract cholera? And if we do come down with it, would they stay to nurse us back to health or until we die? I think not. At least there's a doctor in the camp right now."

Will looked at her steadily. "He's sick, too."

She closed her eyes momentarily. "Will, we can't leave these people. It's—inhumane."

He grabbed her by the elbows. "But what can we do, America? How can we help them? What about the risk to ourselves and the baby?"

She yanked herself free. When she looked in his eyes, she saw panic and dread. "Will," she replied gently, "if we did go now, how could you live with yourself? I know I couldn't live with myself."

She started to lay a comforting hand on his shoulder, but he turned and walked away.

A few hours later she saw the two men who had been tending to Catherine. They eased a body wrapped in a blanket out of Catherine's wagon and carried it out of the camp. She felt bile rising in her throat and her legs melted from underneath her. She had to grab the side of the wagon to keep from sliding onto the ground. Wishing Will were there to hold her, she allowed the hot tears to flow freely down her face as sobs wracked her body.

In the morning, America paid the doctor a visit. She passed three wagons that were already empty, or in the process of being emptied of the dead. America was appalled at how quickly a person could die if cholera was discovered too late.

She passed the Hayes wagon. Mary Elizabeth and Celeste were outside, stirring a pot of cornmeal mush. Celeste looked up and America saw the dark circles under her eyes.

"How are you doing?" she asked.

Celeste managed a shadowed smile. "Gil is resting, but George had the worst of it. I think if I got an hour's sleep last night, it was a miracle."

America turned her attention to Mary Elizabeth. "You look healthy, Mary."

"I'm fine, Mrs. Hollis. But I do worry about poor George." She turned to the coffeepot. "In fact, I'm going to take him a cup of coffee and see if he holds it down."

"Broth would do him better," America suggested. "Coffee can be awful strong on a delicate stomach."

Celeste gave her a grateful smile. "We'll boil some water and mix a little pocket soup in it."

Pocket soup was one of the many things America had never heard of until she started this trip. The stock, made from pig's trotters, was the consistency of solid glue and created a suitable broth when mixed with heated water. Although it had never found its way onto a dining table in high society in Philadelphia, America had used it as a base for many stews over the last few months.

She moved on to the doctor's wagon. Dr. Bauer was resting on a blanket under a tree, looking pale and worn. Eliza, his wife, came out of their wagon with a wet rag. She was quite a few years younger than he, and had dark, expressive eyes and slender wrists. "Why, hello, America," she said, cocking her head slightly. "I hope you're feeling well."

She smiled. "Yes, but I'm worried about the others. What can I do to help?"

Eliza placed the damp rag over her husband's eyes. He spoke. "Just continue to avoid the sick people, Mrs. Hollis. There is nothing you can do except put yourself at risk."

"I can't ignore what's happening in our encampment."

Someone in a nearby wagon screamed.

The doctor sighed and took off the compress. "That was Mr. Hanley. His daughter died this morning and his wife died an hour ago."

America recalled Peter Miller. The Hanleys were his in-laws.

The doctor pulled himself into a sitting position. "I suppose you can help Eliza with cooking broth. We could use an extra hand here, and it will keep you away from the cholera."

"I was told that you had contracted the sickness as well, Doctor," America said.

Dr. Bauer and his wife exchanged glances. "I've been up for almost twenty-four hours straight, Mrs. Hollis. I'm not sick with cholera or dysentery. It's a sickness of the spirit."

"I hope you are feeling better now," she replied.

The doctor smiled. Before he could reply, Terwilliger appeared. He looked older than when they had started. She wondered if it was just layers of trail dust emphasizing the lines in his face, or if the wagon master truly was aging.

He nodded to Eliza Bauer and America. "Ma'ams." Then he turned to the doctor. "What do you think, Doc? Can we continue tonight? We should try to make at least twelve miles today."

The doctor had put his glasses back on. "Mr. Terwilliger, I don't think we should move these sick people at all today. Let's see how people are feeling in the morning."

Terwilliger took off his hat and slapped it against his thigh, creating puffy brown clouds of trail dust. "We might as well settle in for the night," he said. "Looks like we may be here awhile."

CHAPTER 10

The next morning, four wagons were gone. Late into the night, America had awakened to the creak of wagons moving out under the cover of dark. She heard the angry voices of the wagon master and Tal Bowen as they confronted the deserters, but the crack of a whip and the sound of horses and oxen pulling those wagons continued. Then there was silence.

During a breakfast of cold leftover biscuits and coffee warmed over the embers of yesterday's fire, Tal Bowen came over to give them the news. America poured him a cup of coffee.

"Most folks are ready to leave. There's fourteen dead and we'll have to abandon three wagons, including the wagon for the mail-order brides."

"How are Miss Addie and Miss Flavia feeling this morning?" America asked.

Bowen ducked his head and suppressed a smile. "Miss Addie must have the constitution of an ox, and that's meant as no offense, ma'am. She's as healthy as you are right now. And Miss Flavia, well, she's feeling a mite better. Her digestive troubles weren't too bad in the first place. I kind of thought it was a case of feeling the way other folks is feeling in order for attention."

America thought a little guilt at being caught might have contributed to Flavia's illness, as well.

Will broke in. "We heard the commotion last night."

Bowen showed his disapproval. "Several wagons pulled out."

Will nodded. "Mr. Hawbaker approached me yesterday and asked if I wanted to leave with them." He glanced at America. "But I decided against it."

Bowen frowned. "I wish you'd told me yesterday. I might have prevented them from making a very foolish mistake."

"What do you mean?" America asked.

"Well, ma'am, four wagons ain't got much protection out there. And the Indians in this part of the country are very unfriendly. I've heard they attacked several wagon trains just before they reached the South Pass." He stood up and threw the dregs of his coffee on the embers. "I don't like being divided like this, but at least we still have the bulk of wagons."

The company moved out. Three days later, they came within a mile of Fort Laramie and camped for the day. Mr. Terwilliger made it clear that if the company wanted to make it through the mountain passes before the first snowfall, they were behind schedule and would have to make it up. Dr. Bauer announced that his wife wasn't feeling well, and that they had decided to stay in Fort Laramie until next spring.

America could almost hear the sigh of disappointment from her fellow emigrants. Even Reverend Sanford had been especially subdued during those past few days. America attributed his change of behavior to recovering from the sickness, but she hoped it would continue. The women bid farewell to Eliza Bauer, all of them, especially America, disappointed to see the doctor and his wife leave. The rest of the trek would be more of a hardship if there was a sickness or accident among the emigrants.

Several men were chosen to go to the fort to renew the company's supplies and were provided with money and a list from each wagon. While Will and the others were visiting Fort Laramie, the rest of the company was visited by Indians that Bowen called the Dakota. They wanted to trade buffalo meat and fresh melons and vegetables for tobacco and other items from the East.

America admired the beautiful clothing and beading that the men, women, and children wore, and the colorful banners that they carried, waving in the summer breeze. She rooted around in her personal things, anxious to find something she could exchange for a little fresh produce and meat. She had acquired a taste for buffalo meat and could already smell the stew that would be cooking over her fire before the sun set. She found two brightly colored kerchiefs that she wouldn't need, and a beaded bracelet. While Pike sat with the Dakota men, passing Mr. Moore's peace pipe, America and the other women approached the Dakota women.

America showed her items to a woman with high

cheekbones and long black hair wrapped in red cloth at the ends. Feather and beads adorned her hair and clothes. America showed the woman how to drape one of the scarves around her neck. The Dakota woman smiled and handed America a chunk of meat. Without a word being spoken, the transaction was completed.

America then wandered over to a young girl who displayed fruits and vegetables. She showed the girl her bracelet, and exchanged it for two melons and several turnips, which would go well with the meat. If Will brought back some paprika, she would have a nice-tasting stew.

One of the Dakota women noticed the bulge under America's shirtwaist, where her medicine bundle hung around her neck. She began to speak excitedly to her companions in their language. America pulled the fetish out for display and the women gathered around America and took turns handling the bag, then touching America's belly, nodding to themselves and smiling at her. The young girl came up to America and shyly handed her a feather. America was touched when the Indian women indicated that it should be included in her bundle.

"Get away from me, you heathens!" Mrs. Sanford walked briskly by, shooing the Dakota women and their offerings away with hand gestures and her acid-tongued words.

The reverend was back from his bout with dysentery, standing by the wayside, glaring at the Indians, his Bible tucked firmly under his arm. As America passed by him, he reached out a hand to stop her. "How can you stand to let them touch you, Mrs. Hollis? And only the devil could possess you to carry that barbaric leather pouch around your pretty neck."

America had plenty she wanted to say to him, but she bit back her bitter reply and said instead, "We are in their country now, Reverend. Some folks might even say that we are the intruders here. If you cannot abide them, I suggest you retire to your wagon." With that, America continued on her way without another word.

When Will and the others returned from the fort, they had news of the four wagons that had broken off from the company. "They stayed here for two days, then headed toward the South Pass," Terwilliger told the emigrants. "We may catch up to them."

There was some grumbling among the company, some people voicing the opinion that those who abandoned the camp so heartlessly didn't deserve to travel with them the rest of the way, but Terwilliger made it clear that they were welcome back. "The more wagons in our company, the better chance we will have if we encounter hostile Indians."

Two days later they came across what was left of the small rebel train. Three of the wagons had been burnt to a cinder by a war party. Bodies were scattered around on the ground—most of them scalped and with looks of terror on their faces. There were no pistols or flintlocks in sight—the war party had taken the weapons.

Pike and Bowen had tracked the fourth wagon and

found it a few miles off the trail in a ravine. Mr. and Mrs. Hughes were barely alive. Their two small girls, Emily and Rose, were nowhere to be found.

"They were carried off by those savages," America heard Mr. Hughes say while his wounds were being dressed. His wife was resting in one of the other families' wagon. She had been given laudanum to ease the pain from the wound on her head. "We need to go after them."

"Comanche," said Pike, examining the arrows that had been pulled out of Mr. Hughes's thigh.

Terwilliger nodded in agreement. Gil Hayes stepped up. "Well, let's go after them."

"They'll be long gone," Bowen replied.

"They have my children," Hughes said, trying to get up, but wincing with the effort.

Bowen, Terwilliger, and Pike exchanged silent looks. When they walked away from Mr. Hughes, America approached them. "Why don't you go after them?"

Tal Bowen wore a troubled expression. Pike looked away and scratched the back of his neck. The uncomfortable silence grew, but America could stay silent no longer.

"Mr. Terwilliger, will you form a posse? They have taken this couple's children."

Will stepped to her side and put his arm lightly on her shoulders. "America, Mr. Terwilliger has been through this situation before. He knows what can and can't be done."

America didn't have a response. She placed a protective hand on her belly and thought about what it would be like to have a child ripped away from her in that way. Were Indians the godless savages that Reverend Sanford would like her to believe? Maybe some were. Maybe she just didn't understand them, and they didn't understand her ways.

Mr. Terwilliger flushed, bested by a woman. "We can try, ma'am. But don't expect much," he said to the Hugheses, who were huddled together, bandages covering their wounds. "Comanches are good at covering their tracks."

Bowen took over. "Mr. Terwilliger hasn't told you everything." He glanced at the wagon master, who shrugged and nodded as if it didn't matter—telling the emigrants everything now wouldn't make any difference. Bowen continued. "At the fort, I was told that there had been a murder two months ago. A nearby rancher and his family were killed and everyone thought that a Comanche war party did it. So a group of vigilantes found some Comanche and strung 'em up—" He paused in deference to Mrs. Hughes and added, "that means they hanged 'em, ma'am—and the Comanche have been on the warpath ever since."

"So why doesn't the army do anything about it?" America asked. She couldn't understand why the men in charge of Fort Laramie hadn't met with the Indians to come to some agreement. But if there was one thing America had learned on this journey, it was that men had a different way of handling a tragic situation like this.

Terwilliger answered wearily. "It's not for us to do

anything about it. We have to let the commander at the fort know what happened and let him handle it."

"Why would they take the two girls?"

Pike spoke up. "It was a way of replacing their lost warriors. They probably would have preferred boys, but they took what they could get."

"Don't forget the other wagon trains—there are probably several other children who were taken by the Comanche," Bowen added.

That night, Terwilliger sent Bowen and Pike to the fort to relay the message. The emigrants were on edge, every man, woman, and child carrying a flintlock or a pistol. No one was allowed to go outside the encampment unless accompanied by several men.

When Bowen and Pike got back late that night, the men set up a schedule to guard the wagons. Three men stayed awake in three-hour shifts all night long. The next morning, the wagon train continued on its way.

They didn't encounter the Comanche or any other Indians as they made their way toward the Continental Divide. The muggy summer days turned cold by the time they reached the South Pass, a wide valley about thirty miles across and one hundred miles long, which allowed a gradual ascent through the Rocky Mountains. Although it was only early September, America felt as if winter had already come to visit.

Their ascent through the Rockies slowed to ten miles a day as the emigrants adjusted to seeing their breath come out in wet clouds. It seemed to delight the children who were too young to understand the hardships they were enduring, but most of the adults, America and Will included, left them to their fantasies.

Waking up had become as unpleasant as a slap in the face every morning. America soon learned to loathe getting out from underneath the warm Indian blankets to start a fire by stirring the previous day's still-warm embers and adding tinder. Her woolen cloak was the only thing that kept the mornings from becoming too hard to bear. While Will checked on the horses, which were picketed nearby, America had to break the ice on the water buckets so she could start the coffee boiling.

At eight months along, she had grown too big to do much more than lumber around the campfire and make breakfast or mend torn clothes. For most of the trip, America had helped Will hook up the team of horses to the wagon, and when Terwilliger announced to the emigrants that there were hardnuts or wild mushrooms for the picking, she had gone along to forage her share. But no more. She couldn't see her feet, and she often felt the baby kicking inside.

As if the cold wasn't enough to contend with, the rains began—and didn't end. They went on and on, hard driving rains that slowed the wagon train down. Terwilliger became a taskmaster, forcing the emigrants to keep up a grueling pace.

Accidents became commonplace—wheels would stick

in the muddy, slippery ground; children fell off the backs of wagons and were nearly trampled by the horses pulling the wagon behind.

One clear night, America hung her damp woolen cloak out on the back of the wagon. It was a surprisingly warm night and she decided to take advantage of the turn in the weather. The cottage cloak had kept her warm in more then the physical sense—it was a reminder of where she came from, of Philadelphia, of her mother.

In the morning, while Will led the horses to the watering hole, she discovered that her cottage cloak was gone. One of the Sanfords' oxen walked by and with dismay America noticed a dark blue wool patch hanging from the corner of its mouth. She approached the animal and gently removed the piece of wool.

One of the complaints she and other emigrants had about the Sanfords was that they didn't picket their oxen like everyone else. They insisted on hobbling the animals, which gave them enough room to roam about inside the encampment. Those emigrants who slept outside under the stars instead of under their wagon were in constant danger of being trampled.

She approached Mrs. Sanford, who was busy taking the hobbles off the oxen. "Mrs. Sanford, your oxen ate my woolen cloak."

The dour woman finished and straightened up, a hobble in her hand. She turned to peer at America. "How do you know it was my ox?"

America held out the piece of fabric. "I took this from its mouth."

"What do you expect me to do about it?"

For the last few months, America had noticed that her emotions ruled her actions. She cried more easily; she was giddy at the drop of a hat. Now, frustration ripped through her the moment Mrs. Sanford opened her mouth. She didn't think as she started to speak.

"You might start by apologizing for your oxen." As her voice became louder, the other nearby emigrants stopped what they were doing to watch the drama unfold. "Then you might consider picketing them to keep this from happening to others whose clothes are hanging out to dry."

She moved closer to Mrs. Sanford, her hands on her hips, bending slightly to come nose to nose with the shorter woman. "And if you practiced the Christian charity that your husband insists on preaching to the rest of us, you might consider finding some sort of replacement garment for me to wear so I don't freeze and become sick."

America stepped back, realizing that she had attracted a crowd. She quietly turned away, went back to her wagon, and burst into tears.

Celeste came into her wagon a few minutes later. America quickly wiped the angry tears away with the back of a sleeve.

"That woman is enough to make anyone as mad as a March hare," Celeste said with a bitter laugh.

"You heard our quarrel?"

Her friend smiled kindly. "How could I not hear it? The whole camp heard it." America looked away. Celeste chuckled again. "And those who weren't there to hear it have probably heard the story already."

America hugged herself. "I shouldn't have said the things I did."

"Why? You just told the old biddy off, something she deserved. The only thing I regret was that the reverend wasn't there to hear it along with his wife."

America sighed. "I shouldn't have left the cloak out."

Celeste took her friend's hand and squeezed it. "I don't think you have anything to apologize for, America. We all leave clothes out to dry. Even the captain has requested that the Sanfords picket their oxen. Those people just don't like to be told anything. They're the kind of people who have to be right about everything."

America allowed herself a slight smile. "But I do think I overreacted."

Celeste gave her a hug. "When I was with child both times, I do recall feeling everything much more than I do now. You have nothing to be ashamed of."

The next day, America woke up to find Lem Sanford holding a folded up plain white Indian blanket coat. "I know it's not much to look at, but it's kept me warm," he said, offering the coat to her. "And I think it'll fit you. I'm sorry about the ox."

America smiled and tried the coat on. It fit and was even

warmer than her cottage cloak. "But what about you? Will you be all right?" she asked.

Lem grinned. "I got my father's old coat, since he can't wear it anymore. I'm getting too big for this coat anyway."

"Thank you, Lem," America said softly.

The gangling boy stopped smiling. "I told my parents that hobbling the oxen would get them in trouble. I'm sure sorry about your cloak. It looked good on you," he added with a blush.

America sighed. "It was nice, wasn't it? But it wasn't very practical for being on the trail," she admitted. "It flared out and if I got near a flame, there was a chance it could catch fire. This is much better."

Later that day, although the reverend and his wife saw America wearing the coat, they never made any mention of it, and she wondered if they even knew that Lem had done this favor for her.

CHAPTER 11

As the wagon train moved through the South Pass, the rain stopped, but only long enough to give America and the other emigrants false hope. Travelers had used the Pass since its discovery in 1812, but not so much as in the last three or four years when people decided to migrate out to the western territories in search of adventure and a better life.

As the wagons made their way toward the timber-lined summit, America hoped the sun would break out. She was sure that the rain had soaked into her skin and she would never feel dry again. For the next eleven days it rained, and when it wasn't raining, it was damp and cold. America's new coat kept her warm, but she missed her cottage cloak. Whenever she saw the ox that had lunched on it, she glared at it.

The first night on the Pass, America and Will were bundled up in their wagon, lying on sacks of sugar and flour that had gotten wet. An animal howled in the distance.

"What's that?" she whispered, snuggling closer to him. Even though they had never completely made up from their fight during the cholera epidemic, America still felt close to Will.

He wrapped an arm around her. "That's the sound of wolves. Terwilliger once told me that he wasn't sure whether it was better to keep a fire going all night to keep the wolves away, or continue the policy of not building a fire after dark in order to keep the Indians away."

She knew that she should be frightened by the sound, but it only made her heart ache with loneliness. America had seen drawings and paintings of wolves, and they reminded her of an undomesticated dog. She hoped to catch a glimpse of a wolf before they reached Oregon.

The day the wagon train came out of the wide Pass through the Rockies, it was with dismay that America saw the other side of the mountain. The ground was rocky and fell away at a steep angle. "How will we ever get down there?" she murmured.

Fortunately, Terwilliger had made this trip several times and was well prepared. Over the next few days, the men cut down several trees and tied them to the backs of the wagons to slow their descent. When the men weren't working on outfitting the wagons, they were hunting for elk or moose. The emigrants ate very well during these days.

The rain held back, allowing the women to build their cooking fires in the cold, clean air. America and the other women took advantage of the break in routine to bake breads and cook roasts from the game brought back by the men. Sometimes they went out foraging for wild asparagus, onions, and the last of the summer service berries.

Then came the night when everything was done. Terwilliger announced that the entire wagon train would have a community meal to celebrate the halfway point of their journey. America had found some nice, black service berries and made a pudding, using some of the sugar that had gotten wet. Celeste brought a couple of pies made with elk meat and rice.

The captain allowed George to play the fiddle and he accompanied on his flute. There was dancing and singing and a blazing campfire. But everyone, America included, was aware that there were men staked out on watch for Indians. It was unlikely this high up in the mountains at this time of year that the Indians would be here, since they migrated to warmer climates at the first sign of cold weather. Still, their wagon master was taking no chances.

"We met a party of Shoshone one fall day up here in the South Pass," Terwilliger recalled between bites of stew and bread. "They gave us a wide berth, but with hostilities rising, I'm a mite suspicious of any Indian around these parts at this time of year."

They danced and sang and played music until late into the night; then the emigrants fell into an exhausted sleep.

America awoke in the middle of the night, feeling the urgent need to relieve herself. She looked over at Will, but decided not to wake him from his deep sleep. She crept out from under the Indian blankets that kept them warm in their wagon, and slipped into her blanket coat. The chill night air seemed to slip down her neck and run down her spine. She shivered as she slipped behind a bush.

When she was finished, she came back around the bush and stopped. A yellow-eyed wolf stood outside in the clearing, puffs of cold breath escaping from its black snout. America huddled where she was and watched the wolf with fascination. She knew she should feel fear, but something told her she would be safe if she stayed still.

A moment later, three pups romped up to the adult wolf, playfully nipping at her legs. The mother wolf snapped at them once, then turned around and trotted back into the timber area, her pups following behind.

America stayed there for another few minutes before slipping back into her wagon.

The next day, it rained again. Hard, cold, large raindrops pelted down from the sky as if God himself was hurling them to the ground. It made for tough going with the wagons, but soon everyone but the Hollises was heading down the mountain. America felt as if the hard part of the journey was over with—they were now descending, not ascending, the mountain.

America and Will began their descent about an hour after the last wagon had gone, waiting plenty of time so that if they lost control, they wouldn't run into the wagon ahead of them. The mud was everywhere, sticking to their wheels, splattering from the horses' hooves, getting on the underworkings of the wagon.

Halfway down the mountain, they heard a creak and crack; then the front of the wagon dropped suddenly.

America let out a yelp and Will jumped down from the seat to see what was the matter.

America had to shout to be heard by Will over the rain. "What's wrong?"

His answer came out muffled.

"What?" she asked.

He crawled out from under the wagon. "I said, the axle's broken."

America peered down the mountain, hoping to see one of the other wagons. There was nothing but an unbroken curtain of rain and mist. She groaned. Will helped her down before he unhooked the team of horses. They seemed content to stay nearby, grazing for any bit of grass that clung to the mountainside.

"I don't think it's much of a problem," Will said. "I've seen several others in our company fix their axles. We've got a spare in the back of the wagon, and it's just a matter of pulling the old one out and slipping the new one in its place."

America followed Will to the back, where he rummaged around until he pulled out their jack. A few more minutes, and he produced the spare axle.

America brought the jack to the front while Will dragged the axle into position. He jacked up the wagon and took off the wheels. Then he searched for a large rock to prop the new axle on. After he found one, he rubbed bear grease on the large piece of lumber to make it easier to slip into place.

America recalled the days and weeks on the plains when all they saw was dust. The Platte River, although close at hand, had had no cover for privacy, and that made it impossible for use in bathing. Now it seemed as if being dry was just a memory.

"America!" She started when Will called her name. "Can you get on the other side and push on the broken axle to loosen it? The rain has made it too slippery for me to get a good grip on it."

She trudged over to the other side of the wagon and inspected the axle. "Will, maybe we should wait for Mr. Pike and Mr. Terwilliger to come look for us."

"No," he shouted. "We can do it. Just give it a push."

The axle looked dry and she wondered if she should grease it before trying, but Will was being impatient.

"America, just push it a bit. It will come loose."

She gave it a timid push. Nothing happened.

Will's voice floated through the rain. "America, it won't give if you don't push harder."

She used a little more leverage, planting her feet farther apart on the muddy ground and bending her knees slightly. She pushed again. With a groan of protest, the wagon tipped slightly away from her and the axle shot free.

"We did it, Will!" America felt a momentary satisfaction in doing her part. There was no response. "Will?"

She heard a groan. By now, she should have heard him dragging the broken axle out of the way, but there was no

movement from the other side of the wagon. America walked around to see what was wrong. Will lay on the ground, the shaft of the broken axle stuck through his chest.

America rushed to his side. His eyelids drooped and he was having trouble breathing. She leaned over and kissed his lips, not able to think clearly. "Oh, God, help me!" She rocked back and forth, wondering what to do. What would Dr. Bauer do now? How would Mr. Terwilliger or Mr. Pike handle this situation?

The only doctoring America had done was to fix herbal teas for a bad cold. Without thinking, she ran to the edge of the mountain and screamed for help. There was no answer. She had to help her wounded husband, but she didn't know how.

When she got back, Will's lips were blue. America reached out and lightly touched his chest near where the axle was stuck.

Will muttered something and she had to lean forward to hear him. "For God's sake, America, pull it out of me. I'm pinned to the ground."

He was losing consciousness fast. The nerves on the ends of her fingers seemed to be attached to her stomach—both were tingling as she firmly grasped the axle. Ignoring the splinters that dug into the palms of her hands, America tugged until it came free. Blood spurted wildly from the gaping hole in his chest.

"Will!" she screamed. She ran to the back of the wagon

and grabbed anything she could find to stop the blood. Stumbling back to her husband, America knelt beside him and tried to staunch the gushing blood.

The notion of getting on a horse and riding after the wagon train entered her mind, but she pushed it aside. Will couldn't stay alive without anyone to watch him. But without getting help, he didn't have a chance to live, either. She packed the clothes and rags around the wound as best she could and struggled to get up in the slippery mud.

The day had become as dark as night and she could hear thunder rolling toward the mountain. The team of horses had stopped eating and were nervously looking around. Thunder rolled and lightning cracked, striking a Ponderosa pine nearby and sending the team of horses into a wild, whinnying, prancing dance.

America ran toward them. "No! Please, stop!" The horses skittered away from her, then bolted down the mountain. She stood there, watching them disappear into the rain before turning back to Will.

Kneeling beside him, she felt raindrops stinging her cheeks. Will searched for her hand. His breath came out in labored, wheezing gasps, but his chest wasn't moving. He whispered something to her that she couldn't understand and she bent closer. "I love you, America."

Hot tears mingled with the cold rain on her face. "Oh, my darling, I love you, too."

She kissed his gray lips once before he let go of his last breath. After a time, she closed his eyelids.

It was still raining when she pulled the shovel and the blankets out of the wagon. Numb with grief, America dug a shallow grave, wrapped Will's body into a blanket, and buried him. Then she gathered several items from the wagon, covered herself up, and sat vigil for her mourning.

She was still sitting there when Mr. Pike and Tal Bowen found her several hours later. The wagon had begun to slide down the mountain on an avalanche of mud, and America remembered hearing it smash somewhere beyond the wall of rain. The only items she had unwittingly saved were her blankets, some of the money she carried with her at all times, and a few cooking utensils. The medicine bundle was safely dangling from the leather thong and nestled between her breasts, and she wore her Indian blanket coat and an India rubber poncho for shelter from the rain.

America told the men what had happened to Will.

"Are you all right, Mrs. Hollis?" Mr. Pike asked as they stood over Will's grave.

"I am fine, Mr. Pike," she replied in a dead tone of voice, "for a woman who has just lost her husband. But I seem to be without a wagon or team of horses. Everything has been lost."

America had already gone through a range of emotions from hysteria to horror to grief, and now, a calm was settling on her. She knew that she shouldn't feel this way, that she should be crying and grief-stricken, but so much had happened, so much tragedy and misery. She couldn't dredge up the energy to mourn the loss of Will in the proper way. Not now. Maybe she would feel differently when she got into the encampment.

Pike glanced at Bowen and nodded slightly. "I'm sorry about your husband, Mrs. Hollis. Let's get you back to camp. Mr. Bowen will take you back. I'll go in search of the horses. I'm sure they're not far away."

"Thank you, Mr. Pike." She walked stiffly over to Tal Bowen's horse and allowed him to help her into the saddle. Before they started down the mountain, she took one last look at Will's grave and said good-bye to her future.

$\mathcal{P}$ART . 2

CHAPTER 12

For the first week after Will's death, the emigrants passed America from wagon to wagon, much like the mail-order brides who had been forced to abandon their wagon after Catherine died in it. America and her few possessions took up little room, and she kept to herself, grieving privately for the loss of her husband and her friend.

The families on the wagon train had been kind to her, giving her their sympathies over the death of her husband and letting her know that they would help her in any way they could. During the third week of September, she took up the Hayes' offer to take her under their wing, even though she knew what a hardship it would be for them. Gil and George had recovered from the dysentery, but the sickness had weakened them.

Mr. Pike had found her team of horses a mile off the trail, and brought them back. Gil had offered to look after her horses for her. When she protested, he insisted.

"You can't take care of them in your condition, and a few more horses won't be any more work for George."

The young man had agreed, and it was settled.

When the train reached the bottom of the Rockies, they

were faced with a river to ford. The morning they arrived at the riverbanks, the settlers realized it wouldn't be easy to ford this river. The men began to take apart the wagons and fit the boxes and covers together with rods. One box was used to row in, the other to ferry supplies. With each river crossing the emigrants had become so used to taking their wagons apart and putting them back together that it took them but little time. By sunset, it was clear they wouldn't get all the wagons and people across before dark.

Half the families were already on the other side of the Green River with Mr. Terwilliger. Since the remaining people would have to wait until the following day, Tal Bowen and Pike stayed with them for protection. The Hayeses, along with America, had stayed behind, as had the Sanfords. The Tobiases and the Sorensons were also still there.

She pitched her bed, spreading her India rubber poncho on the damp, sandy soil. She had chosen a place behind a rock for protection against a cold wind that had come up ever since the rain had stopped, and she hoped that she wouldn't need to find shelter halfway through the night.

"I don't see how she can continue," she overheard one woman say while they waited for the makeshift boat to come back across for more supplies. America couldn't make out the woman's facial features in the gathering darkness, but she guessed the voice belonged to Harriet Tobias. She and her husband, Bundy, were ex-slaves who had bought their freedom down in Georgia.

"Maybe Mr. Terwilliger will leave her at the next available fort." She recognized Mrs. Sanford's clipped voice. "With a baby on the way, the journey would just be too hard on her now that she's a widow. I always thought she would be the first to turn back, coming from Philadelphia." Her mean-spirited comments didn't surprise America at all.

A familiar voice spoke sharply—she recognized Celeste Hayes. "I don't know what you ladies are so worried about. America has gone through a lot since Independence. She's lost her dear friend, Catherine Welborne, and her husband. And from what Gil tells me, America buried Will up there on that mountainside all by herself."

"By herself?" Harriet Tobias echoed in a sympathetic tone. "The poor thing. That takes spirit and determination. She must be feeling mighty lonely about now."

America closed her eyes and held her breath to keep the tears from running down her face. Losing Will was still fresh and hard for her to accept. Since the beginning of the journey, she had come to rely on him in so many ways, and had only recently begun to feel as if they would soon be a real family when the baby was delivered.

Now she would have to start thinking of how to raise her child alone, and how she would make a living when she got to Oregon. She briefly entertained the idea of going back to Philadelphia, but there wasn't a way to get back there alone, not with winter setting in. And she didn't anticipate a warm reception from her parents. She would be better off staying with the wagon train until she reached the Oregon or California Territories.

Maybe she could get married again. It wouldn't be difficult. She could easily take Catherine's place and marry the widower with children. But she didn't think marrying again so soon would be right, and she certainly wasn't ready to take on another man's children.

America pulled the blankets up around her chin, her coat still wrapped around her, the hood a makeshift pillow. She slipped into a sleep filled with dreams that kept her feeling warm and safe. It was the only time she felt that way anymore.

The river crossing passed without incident. They were just starting to put the last wagon together when, in the middle of the afternoon of the following day, company arrived. It was a small train, five wagons, that had left from Council Bluffs a few days after America's train had left Independence.

The men forded the river to help the small wagon train, and it appeared that everyone was glad of the company.

"We've been fortunate so far," said Captain Conway, the wagon master of the expedition from Iowa Territory. "We haven't met any Indians yet, but we've heard the stories."

Terwilliger nodded, and Pike took out his pipe and tamped it with dried weeds. He had run out of tobacco and there had been none at Fort Laramie, so he was forced to dry pungent weeds and smoke them in the place of tobacco. America was within earshot when the men put their heads together and began talking in low tones.

She was aware that they were talking about her because every once in a while, a head would pop up and gaze at her as if assessing her worth. At one point, a man from the Iowa train looked at her for so long that she turned and met his gaze until, embarrassed, he dropped his eyes.

"How are you feeling?" America turned around to encounter Tal Bowen.

"I am doing quite well, thank you," she replied shortly, then thought better of her response. "It's hard sometimes, but I know things will be better for me when we get to California."

Bowen raised his eyebrows. "California! I thought you were heading north." Until that moment, she had assumed she would take the path that led to Oregon. But once she said it, she knew that California was where she was bound.

America laughed for the first time in days. She caught herself, realizing that it didn't befit a newly widowed woman. "I guess I didn't realize it until now, either. But I think I want to go to California."

There were stories about the southern Territory being a land of sunshine, flowing with milk and honey. She wasn't so sure she believed the milk and honey part. She had discovered on this trip that writers tended to exaggerate about the good things and downplay the bad, but she was intrigued. Oregon had been Will's destination. Maybe going to California appealed to her simply because it was her idea.

"Are you free to take a walk?" Bowen asked.

America was surprised at his invitation, but saw no wrong in it. They walked down by the river.

"It's beautiful here," she said. "But it's so lonely."

"I always thought that this would be a good place to settle down," Bowen said.

He had always just been second-in-command as far as America was concerned. But talking to him now made her give him another look. He wasn't terribly attractive, more plain and honest-looking. His eyes were his best feature, and he had a charming crooked grin that probably made the ladies sit up and take notice.

"So this is where you plan on settling down?"

He nodded. "I have a stake not far from here. I go check on it whenever we come this way."

"When do you plan to settle on your property?"

"This is my last journey west. On the way back, I'll stay here and build."

They stopped, hearing a cry from across the river. A woman stood on the other bank, shouting at them to get their attention.

"It seems someone needs help over there," America said.

"Excuse me, Mrs. Hollis," he said, touching his hat, "it looks like one of the Council Bluffs party was forgotten."

America laughed at the thought, then turned to wave at the woman to assure her that she would soon be rescued.

Two men, one on horseback and one on a mule, crossed the river to help the woman over. On the way back, the mule stopped dead in the middle and refused to go any farther. When its rider cussed it out, it threw him into the water and almost trampled him getting across riderless. The rescued woman and the man on horseback arrived safely—and dry—on the other side. They stood on the bank with America and a gathering crowd, watching as the other man finally got to his feet to wade the rest of the way.

"I lost my damn hat," said the short, stocky man, trudging out of the river. He was dripping from head to toe and his rough cotton flannel shirt and black wool vest clung to him. His wife, a dumpling of a woman, wrapped a blanket around his shivering body.

"You knew you shouldn't have taken Sara out there. She's ornery as can be," his wife clucked. "Dotty would have gotten you across and back just fine."

"I can't tell the difference between the blamed mules," he muttered. "One mule looks the same as the other."

America's heart lurched at the loving exchange between the couple. She and Will had barely gotten to that stage when they had their big fight. And he had died before they could make up.

Terwilliger seemed pleased to have another captain and more wagons join them at this point in the journey. Before they could get on with the trip, however, Reverend Sanford was called upon to perform a wedding. A young couple, whose parents had both started the trip with America and Will, had been courting ever since Independence.

The wagons formed a circle by the river, with a tent set

up in the center for the ceremony, decorated with whatever pretty wildflowers the women could find. The ceremony took only a few minutes, and afterward, the company celebrated by eating and playing music and dancing. Terwilliger wouldn't allow a campfire, but the food that was set out tasted good even if it was cold. Tal Bowen asked America to dance, but she couldn't bring herself to accept.

The next day, she walked with Celeste beside the Hayes wagon as the train continued on its way. "I've had the same dream the last few nights," she said, breaking a long, comfortable silence. She fingered the medicine bundle around her neck.

"What kind of dream?" Celeste asked. "Was it about Will?"

America smiled. "No. At least, I don't think so. I dreamed that a wolf came and laid down beside me. I was warm and I felt as if the wolf was looking after me." She then told Celeste about her one encounter with the mother wolf and her cubs.

"Could it be related?" America wondered aloud.

Celeste shrugged. "I don't know. I don't believe in spirits other than our Lord, but Mr. Pike tells me that the Indians have beliefs that involve animal spirits. You should talk to him about it."

America fell into a pensive silence.

She had grown to rely on Gil and Celeste Hayes as her friends and traveling companions. They were helpful and didn't seem to mind the fact that she spent so much time with them. She had also grown fond of George and Mary Elizabeth, and hoped that she could raise a child as pleasant and well mannered. Often, she would help Mary Elizabeth with one of her embroidery projects, and they had even begun another quilt, this time for the newlyweds. All of the women in the company were helping with it, even Mrs. Sanford.

Tal Bowen became a regular visitor. Wherever America was staying, he would come to see how she was doing. At first, she was puzzled by his interest, but Celeste cleared that up for her one afternoon.

"Don't you know?" her friend laughed. "He's smitten with you." Suddenly she clamped her mouth shut, as if she thought she'd said something wrong.

America waved away her friend's apprehension. "Will was a part of my life, and always will be. I loved him, but I have to move on now."

Celeste gave her friend a sly look. "Well, I think Tal Bowen wants you to move on with him."

Her cryptic response proved to be right a few days later when he showed up one afternoon. The wagon train had gone through a beautiful forest full of fir trees and evergreens, and settled in a lovely, sunny valley for their nooning. Tal asked her to take a walk and, since she enjoyed his company, she agreed.

As they walked, America stopped to smell the air along the way.

"Mrs. Hollis, America, I got to ask you a question." Bowen had taken his hat off and was worrying the brim.

America thought he'd wear a path right through the material if he wasn't careful. "But I'm not sure it's proper at this time."

"Why don't you ask me the question, and I will tell you if it's appropriate, Mr. Bowen." America hid the smile she felt coming to her lips.

He stopped and faced her. "It's just, I've been thinking, ever since Sally Tronsgaard married that Sorenson fella, that you're stuck with no husband. And I know in proper society, you should mourn for a year. But I don't hold to that out here." He reached out and gently took one of her hands in both of his. "A woman in your condition needs a husband to help raise that child, and, well, I'm suggesting that you consider marrying me."

America raised her eyebrows and managed a smile. Tal Bowen stood there, sincere, earnest, and a mite arrogant. She wasn't sure she agreed with his assumption that she needed a husband, but it was sweet of him to ask her and she didn't want to hurt his feelings. And she saw absolutely no reason to inform him that Will had not been the father of her child.

"Mr. Bowen, I do thank you for your offer." She smiled and detached her hand from his. "But please let me consider your proposal for a few days. As you said before, it is a little early for me to consider marriage." She started to walk away.

"Mrs. Hollis," Bowen called out, making her stop and turn around. He was looking down at the ground. "If it means anything to you, I am enamoured."

She smiled again and nodded her thank you, then went in search of Celeste. She found Addie and Flavia first, and explained her dilemma. She was more interested in Addie's reaction than Flavia's and was a bit irritated when Addie remained silent.

Flavia, however, spoke right up. "He proposed?" she giggled. "And you didn't accept?"

"That is correct," America replied tersely. Flavia didn't seem to understand. She seemed to think that if a man proposed, a woman should immediately say yes.

Addie was viciously stabbing the quilt with her needle. "Well, I think America did the sensible thing. You don't just up and marry a man right after losing your husband." She jabbed her finger, bringing tears and a look of surprise to her face. "Ow!"

A drop of bright red blood appeared and she stuck her finger in her mouth. She stood up and excused herself, running off toward the wagon she had been sharing with one of the new families.

America thought it was an extreme reaction to pricking her finger. "Is something the matter?"

Flavia laughed gaily. "Why, don't you know, America? Addie has been in love with Tal Bowen for many a mile."

America was appalled. "Why didn't somebody say something to me? I indiscreetly mention Tal's proposal, and she's sick with love for him."

Flavia shrugged. "Nothing can be done about it. She's going off to marry some old man in Oregon, and there isn't any way for her to get out of it."

Anger flared up at Flavia's insensitivity. She stood up. "I'm ashamed of you, Flavia Townsend."

Flavia stopped laughing and blinked. "What?"

"How could you be so cruel? How could you let me be so cruel? Addie nursed you back to health during the cholera epidemic. Now she is sick, lovesick, and this is how you repay her." Before Flavia could reply, America turned and left.

Later that day, she caught sight of Flavia, who looked sheepishly at America, then turned her head. America knew she should feel guilty for being so hard on Flavia; then she remembered catching the woman ransacking her wagon.

America couldn't help feeling bad about Addie. The quiet woman continued to avoid her, and America tried to figure out a way to help her. She wasn't in love with Tal Bowen herself, and if there was some way to get them together, America wanted to help. She wondered if Flavia's careless comment about there not being a way to get out of marrying the man she'd never met was correct.

She enlisted Celeste's help. "How can we get them together?"

Celeste frowned. "I'm not sure it would work, America. He's smitten with you. He's told you that already. And Addie is promised to a man in Oregon."

America caught Celeste's hand in hers. "I want to help her. She's desperately unhappy, and tonight, I'm telling Tal Bowen that I must refuse his offer."

Celeste studied her friend for a moment, then sighed. "What can I do?"

"Arrange for Addie to meet me at the bend in the river tonight after I refuse Tal Bowen's offer of marriage." America knew that she couldn't force Tal to love Addie, but she hoped that events might take a natural course if she stepped out of the way.

CHAPTER 13

Later that night, America wandered down to the river and dipped her hand into the sweet-tasting water. She sensed another presence nearby and turned around. Tal was there, watching her as she smoothed her skirt and tried to smile.

"I apologize for bothering you, America," he said. She noted how easily he said her Christian name, as if he'd practiced saying it to himself several hundred times. "Celeste told me that you wanted to meet me. I know it's only been a few hours since I proposed, but have you thought it over?"

"Oh, Tal," she began, and she saw his face fall as if he already knew her answer. "I am so honored that you would want me to be your wife, but I must decline. I am still in love with Will, and it wouldn't be right."

Tal didn't do anything immediately; he just stood there, head bowed. Then he took her by the shoulders and pressed a fierce kiss on her lips. America was too startled to respond, but when he stepped back, she could feel the heat radiating from her cheeks.

Tal averted his eyes. "Whether you love Will or not

makes no difference to me. Life out here is different from the fairy tales you grew up with back east."

America could no longer abide his arrogance. He had kissed her without her permission. She was newly widowed and his presumption that she lived on fairy tales when he knew nothing about her life angered her. Resisting the impulse to wipe her mouth on her sleeve in front of him, America nodded her thanks.

As she turned to leave, she couldn't help saying, "If you're so set on finding a wife, there are others in this wagon train who would welcome your advances, Mr. Bowen."

"The only other unmarried women on this journey are mail-order brides."

"My status as a new widow didn't stop you from kissing me without my permission," America replied, hoping her voice didn't tremble and give her anger away. She walked away without looking back.

She saw Addie coming and hid before the woman spotted her. America hoped that if Tal and Addie fell in love, Tal would treat Addie better than he had treated her. She thought back to the Moores and Catherine, and hoped she hadn't made a mistake in getting these two together.

The emigrants continued on their way the next day. The trail continued to follow the Bear River Mountains, which were not quite as rough as the Rockies, but offered challenges for the wagons along the way. After the first mile, the road became hilly. The wagon wheels dug into the sandy soil and the going was slow. Finally, the wagon train came to a small creek with clear running water. Some of the emigrants were grumbling that there was no grass nearby, but they stopped there anyway.

There had been no wood since they came over the mountains. All around them was sagebrush. They nooned near it, and slept with it, and even cooked with it. Many of the women didn't like it because they said it caught fast and burned hot, but America liked the musky scent. It was much better than picking up buffalo chips and using them for fuel as they had done back on the prairie.

As America helped Celeste and Mary Elizabeth prepare a stew and bake bread, she noticed that the men, Terwilliger, Pike, and Bowen in particular, were carrying their flintlocks and looking vigilant.

While they ate their midday meal, everyone in the encampment seemed tense to America. Several men kept looking over their shoulders after every few bites, and they kept their families close by. But then, America knew that ever since they had come across the victims of the Indian attack, the company was unnerved.

The weather for mid-September had turned unseasonably cold for the entire day. America had just become used to the frost on the water bucket in the mornings, and breaking the thin layer of ice that formed over the water. In late August, it had usually warmed up nicely by midmorning. But for the last two days, it had stayed cold through the entire day, and the temperature dropped to almost freezing after the sun set.

The company was nooning on the Sweetwater River,

cooking their midday meals, when a strong gust of wind buffeted the wagon where America was measuring flour for flapjacks. As she was scooping up the precious flour from the wagon floor, America heard screams. As quickly as she could, she scrambled out of the wagon and discovered Celeste using a wooden spoon to beat at flames that were climbing up her skirt.

America had no water bucket of her own and, after a quick search, couldn't find the Hayeses' bucket. Scanning the area, she found a full bucket hanging on a hook from the Sanfords' empty wagon. She grabbed it, hauled it over to Celeste, and splashed some on the fast disappearing skirt.

Other members of the encircled wagon train soon emerged from behind their wagons, but America was still closest to Celeste. As she stood there, not sure what else to do, Celeste continued to dance, her cries becoming high-pitched. "Ow! Oh! Help me!"

"It's all right," she assured her friend. "The fire is out." Celeste's skirt hung in soggy blackened tatters, but she continued to yell.

"Are you hurt? Have you burned your legs?" America asked as she approached. Just as she reached Celeste, she watched in horror as black smoke and red flames licked at the back of her friend's head. Even though the front of her skirt had been put out, the fire had climbed around her back and was engulfing her.

Celeste whirled around, running and screaming, until America could get close enough to push the woman down onto the ground. She beat at the flames with her Indian blanket coat as Celeste continued to scream.

Pike grabbed the coat from her and took over beating out the blaze. Someone splashed more water on Celeste, and finally the fire was out.

But the damage was done. Other members of the wagon train had gathered to help, but some didn't have strong enough stomachs for what they found. America looked around for any member of Celeste's family, until she remembered that some of the men had gone after an antelope they'd seen from a distance, and she had seen Mary Elizabeth heading toward the river with the empty water bucket earlier.

America took charge. "Someone get a blanket and cover her." She scanned the crowd and picked out Flavia's pale face. "Flavia, get a rag so we can wash her wounds."

Mrs. Sanford stepped forward, her face bright pink. "Whose water bucket is that?" she snapped.

"Yours, if it makes any difference," America returned quickly, handing the empty bucket over. "I have none and yours was closest at hand."

Mrs. Sanford's face flushed a deep red and she stepped back. America peered at Celeste, who lay prone on the ground, moaning. Her face was black and smoking. Her hands, almost unrecognizable, were blackened shriveled masses. America felt faint from the smell and sight of burned flesh, but she swallowed hard and took a deep breath.

She started to ask if anyone had gone after the doctor,

but remembered that Dr. Bauer and Eliza were back in Fort Laramie. Dr. Bauer had been apologetic, and had instructed several people in the wagon train on treating common sicknesses. He'd also left them several bottles of laudanum and ointments for ailments.

Celeste began calling the names of her children and her husband. Tal Bowen pushed through the crowd and rushed to her side. When he reached her, his eyes glazed and a sheen of perspiration popped out on his forehead.

When another woman came up with a blanket, America left Celeste's side. "Sit down, Tal," she said. He continued to stare, not reacting to her order. She grasped his shoulder and pushed him down on the ground. He looked up at her, but couldn't speak.

America spotted Addie nearby and motioned her over. Even though she had avoided America for the last few days, she nodded and came over to take America's place.

"It will be all right," Addie said softly as she stroked Tal's hair and dipped her handkerchief in a nearby bucket of water. She wrung it out and pressed it to his forehead. "When you feel better, someone needs to find Gil and George," America told him before returning to Celeste. Tal nodded his understanding, still too overwhelmed to speak coherently.

The reverend pushed his way past America and through the gathering crowd. He gasped and took a step backward, then took a deep breath to steel himself. "The best thing we can do," he intoned, "is to pray for this unfortunate woman."

"You pray while I try to make her comfortable," America said in a sharp tone. "Then at least one of us will be doing something useful."

Mary Elizabeth ran through the gathering.

"Mama!" she cried, stumbling toward the shivering, almost unrecognizable figure. America got to her before she could touch her mother.

"Careful, child," she chided. "Touching her may hurt her. Mary Elizabeth, you go make a place in the wagon for your mother to lie on."

As long as the girl was kept busy, she wouldn't have time to think about the terrible condition her mother was in. America knew the same was true of herself. Taking charge was the best way she knew to keep from going into shock.

She looked over to Addie. "Is Tal better now?"

Addie nodded.

"Good, then get him out to find Gil and George."

A short while later, the men charged into camp. America could see tears well in George's eyes.

"George," America said gently, "could you help Tal and your father carry your mother to the wagon?"

The boy sniffled once, then straightened himself tall. "Yes, ma'am."

America directed them as they picked her up. "Try not to touch her bare skin, and don't go too fast." She continued to intone instructions as they moved to the wagon, more to keep their minds off of Celeste's charred body than because they needed to be told what to do. "Keep her steady. That's it. Watch that rock to your left. Slowly now."

As they settled Celeste onto her makeshift bed, one of the emigrants brought a bottle of laudanum. "It'll help with the pain," she said, taking a quick look at Celeste and then hurrying away.

America poured a portion of the drug into a spoon and held it to Celeste's lips. She seemed to be beyond pain, but sipped the drug greedily. America wanted to pat her friend in reassurance, but knew that the touch would cause pain instead of its intended comfort.

The wagon train didn't move for three days, while the women took turns at Celeste's side. The rains started shortly after she was moved into the wagon and didn't let up for days. The first day, America was grateful for the cool, damp air, hoping it would soothe Celeste's ravaged body and spur healing. She had been so badly burned that many, including Reverend Sanford, thought it was a miracle she was still alive.

Celeste didn't recover consciousness until a week later. America was sitting with her, bathing her face in cool water. She opened her eyes in the late afternoon, just as the sun was setting.

"How do I look?" she croaked.

America looked at her friend's ruined face and tried to smile. She, along with everyone else in the camp, had been surprised that Celeste had survived the flames. Her patient shifted, then let out a gasp of pain. America opened the bottle of laudanum at her side and gave her friend a sip.

"I can't feel my hands." Celeste brought them up to look at them.

Celeste's hands were no longer black, but the flesh had melted together like candlewax. America and Mary Elizabeth had taken turns washing the flesh as gently as possible during the first few days. Now after a week, the skin was shiny and pink, and probably no longer useful.

A strangled cry came from deep inside her throat. "God, why have you allowed me to live?" Celeste sobbed and tears rolled from the corners of her eyes. She looked at America and asked again in a low whisper, "Why have you allowed me to live?"

Breath caught in America's chest and she had to force herself to breathe again. In, out, in, out. "Celeste, you're alive, and that's all that counts. Your daughter, son, and husband are so grateful."

The woman's eyes closed. "But not like this, America, not like this." She turned her head away. "Please go."

"Celeste—" America reached out, then hesitated. What part of Celeste could she touch without causing pain? Her hand dropped back into her lap.

The request came sharply this time. "Please go, America. Thank you for all you've done."

America stood up, instinctively reaching for the bottle of laudanum.

"Leave it there," Celeste ordered.

America's hand hovered over the bottle, but left it

where it lay and took her leave. Mary Elizabeth would be staying with her mother for the night, but America bedded down nearby in case she could be of help.

Later that night, Mary Elizabeth's thin, plaintive voice woke America from a deep slumber. "Mother? Mother? Wake up. Please wake up."

America pulled herself out of her blankets and stumbled over to the wagon in the dark. "Mary Elizabeth? What's wrong?" she asked as she stuck her head into the back cover.

"Mother won't wake up," the girl said. "She's been asleep ever since I got here. A few minutes ago I heard her moan, so I was going to give her some laudanum." Her voice was quavering so, America could hardly understand her.

"Then I noticed that the bottle wasn't where it usually is. I found it in Mother's hand, and it's empty. And she won't wake up," she said again.

America climbed into the wagon with some difficulty and checked Celeste. She wasn't breathing, and the bottle was indeed empty. After clambering back out, she woke Gil. America thought he looked twenty years older than when they started the journey. She told him what happened, then left to find the captain.

"When did this happen?" Terwilliger asked as they walked back to the Hayes wagon.

"She must have died some time after I left the wagon. I left Celeste alone for a few minutes, and then Mary Elizabeth took over." Realization came over her with horror and her knees buckled.

"Mrs. Hollis, are you all right?" the captain asked, grabbing her elbow in support.

"I left the laudanum with her. What could I have been thinking?" America buried her face in her hands. "She told me she wanted to die rather than live life like that. I— I didn't think she would really do it."

"You couldn't have known what she was going to do," Terwilliger said brusquely. After America had taken a deep breath to calm herself, he added gently, "It's probably for the best."

The captain checked in with Gil, then roused some men to help with the body. They buried Celeste Hayes that night, not wanting to wait until daybreak. The short service was attended by most of the camp, as word spread fast, even in the middle of the night. Reverend Sanford had started into a long, wrathful sermon at the gravesite, but was stopped by Gil Hayes's quiet command.

"Just a short prayer, if you would, Reverend."

That night, as America climbed back into her bedroll, she began to shiver violently. No matter how many blankets she wrapped around herself, she couldn't get warm. She lay awake for the rest of the night, her body freezing, her mind filled with the images of Catherine, Will, and Celeste.

CHAPTER 14

While the Hayes family grieved their loss, America ended up traveling with the Sanfords in their wagon. She spent as much time away from them as she possibly could, wishing often that someone else had been able to take her.

It would have been unseemly for America to take up residence in Mr. Tronsgaard's wagon. His wife had died in the cholera epidemic and his daughter, Sally, and new son-in-law, Justin, were sharing the wagon. Even though Justin no longer lived in his parents' wagon, they still had nine children to contend with.

Harriet Tobias had come by to apologetically explain that while they would love to share their wagon with her, it wouldn't look right for her to reside with ex-slaves. There were still so many prejudices, even after everything the emigrants had gone through together.

America was tempted to tell Harriet that it mattered not a whit to her what others thought, but she just smiled and thanked the quiet woman. She knew it would matter to the Tobiases—some of the other emigrants might make life difficult for them.

Addie and Flavia had each found a family to ride with,

too. But no one seemed to be able to take America in except the Sanfords, and that only under duress from Terwilliger, she was sure. She recalled seeing him go to their wagon one night and stay for a long time. There had been raised voices and some grumbling, but the next day, the Reverend and Mrs. Sanford grudgingly offered her a place in their wagon.

She could easily have continued rotating wagons until the trail divided, and even beyond to California. But the reverend and his wife finally invited her to stay with them until the end of the journey. They made it clear that they were none too happy to take her in but, burden that she was, because they were Christians, they would take it upon themselves to give her shelter.

America felt that she had no choice in the matter, and she agreed to travel with them all the way to California. Or until Terwilliger put her off at the first convenient place. But she paid a high price.

Mrs. Sanford squeezed as much work out of America as she could, even though it was only two weeks to a month until her delivery time. One afternoon, America hauled water up from the river, started the fire, and cooked the afternoon meal. When she was done, Mrs. Sanford handed her the washing.

"These need to be done while we're still stopped. Maybe they'll dry a bit over the fire."

Together the women brought the laundry down to the river and scrubbed the clothing with a bar of lye until

America's hands were raw and chapped and stinging from the cold weather.

They worked without talking, because Mrs. Sanford didn't believe in idle conversation while their hands were busy. She liked to quote the Bible, but didn't seem to know more than a few verses. Her favorite passages were from Psalms. When they finally stumbled into the Sanfords' camp, weighed down with wet clothes and bedding, Mrs. Sanford began to make bread.

"Well, don't just stand there; you'll drop the clean clothes on the ground," she snapped. "I had Lem set up a rack for you to hang the clothes on." The rickety rack was set near the fire, and America prayed that it wouldn't give under the weight of the wet clothes. When she was finished with that chore, she stoked up the fire, shuddering with the sudden onset of a vision of Celeste engulfed in flames.

As if being made to work from morning until night wasn't enough, Reverend Sanford bullied America into giving up most of her money as payment for giving her shelter. Lem was the only consolation. He was polite and enjoyed talking to her whenever they had a free moment, which didn't happen often. In the presence of his parents, he often didn't talk to her, but would catch her eye occasionally and wink. She always returned the wink with one of her own.

America knew that many of the emigrants thought that with her husband gone, maybe it would be for the best if America stayed for the winter at the next fort they came to. She thought back to the conversation she had over-heard on the other side of Green River. Would she be conveniently left at the next fort? She cornered the captain one day while they were nooning.

"Mr. Terwilliger, there is something I must ask you. It has been preying on my mind ever since I buried my husband back on the mountain."

Terwilliger was squatting beside one of his mules, inspecting its hooves. He straightened up and faced her. "Well, I'm awfully busy at the moment, Mrs. Hollis, but go ahead. Ask your question."

America couldn't help but wonder if he would be so busy if Will were still alive and they still had their wagon. As it stood now, she was a destitute widow who had been reduced to indentured servitude for the Sanfords. She pushed the self-pitying thought out of her mind.

"I was curious about your plans for me. I know my condition, a new widow with child, is a bit unusual, but I was wondering if it was your intention to let me continue to travel with you until California."

Terwilliger let out a frosty breath and looked down. "I kind of thought it would be your decision, Mrs. Hollis, not mine. As far as I'm concerned, you paid to be on this journey, and you should expect to go as far as you decide to go."

America blinked in surprise. She had come to take the rumors she had heard earlier as gospel.

"Why do you ask such a question?"

"Oh, I was under the impression that due to my reduced circumstances, I would be left behind at the next fort."

Terwilliger smiled kindly and shook his head. "I don't know who told you that, but it just ain't so. At least as long as one of the emigrants shares their shelter with you. And I've been told that Mrs. Sanford has some midwiving experience, so you'll have someone there to help when it's time."

America suppressed a shudder at the thought of Mrs. Sanford by her side and forced a smile for Captain Terwilliger's sake. No doubt he knew how reptilian Mrs. Sanford was, but they wouldn't speak of it. She would bear up under the strain until she got to California Territory.

As she walked back to the Sanfords' wagon, America suddenly felt the pressure and the loneliness of her situation—no parents, no husband, no friends left. She pressed her eyelids tightly shut and bit her lip to keep the tears at bay. There was Tal Bowen's proposal, and at the moment, she was sorely tempted to go back to him and ask if he would marry her after all.

When she opened her eyes, she caught sight of Tal and Addie together, her hand on his arm as they talked and laughed. No, Tal wasn't the answer to her predicament.

Voices raised in anger distracted her from dark thoughts. She looked around and realized they were coming from the Tobias wagon. Bundy Tobias was standing between his wife, Harriet, and Captain Conway.

America hadn't taken to the new captain ever since his

wagons joined theirs. He was a brash older man who ridiculed men when they showed softness in a decision, and who had nothing good to say about women. He often told tales of the Indian women he bought from their tribes, how he would take one as his wife at the beginning of winter and leave her as soon as the wagon train season began in the spring.

"I don't need a woman around to take care of while I'm out on the trail," he'd said, "but it's sure nice to have one to take care of me on those cold winter nights." Here, he winked at the men, then tipped his hat to the women, America included, who had overheard. "Uh, no offense to you ladies."

Conway intimated that once he left for his journey west in the spring, he never returned to the same woman again.

Conway was trying to grab Harriet's arm and Bundy was protecting her. America hurried over. Terwilliger was there by the time she got there.

"She's no free woman, nigger, and I mean to have her as my cook in Oregon," Conway was saying. "You can come along if you like, but she hasn't proof she bought her freedom, so she's there for the taking."

America realized with horror that he was talking about Harriet's status as a former slave.

"Now hold on, Captain," Terwilliger said, stepping in front of Bundy. "These are members of my wagon train you're talking about so freely."

"Thank you, suh," Bundy replied. Harriet cowered behind him, and she was shaking.

Conway hitched up his pants, which had a tendency to slide down his corpulent waistline. "I aim to have a slave cook for me and do my wash," he said, pointing a finger at the Tobiases, "and these two ain't proved the woman's standing as a freed slave. He says they lost the paperwork."

America thought back to Flavia's raiding of wagons and wondered if she'd taken more than a pair of rhinestone hairpins from the Tobias wagon. But Harriet hadn't mentioned it. Then again, it was the sort of thing you might not want to mention if you were a recently freed slave.

Terwilliger turned around to address Harriet. "Is what he says true?"

Harriet blinked back tears. "Yes, suh. The papers are lost and I don't know how to prove I'm free."

Terwilliger scratched his head. "I don't know what I can do about it."

Bundy stepped forward. "But, Captain, she's married to me. Don't that count for somethin'?"

Terwilliger shook his head.

America tried to remember some of the things Will used to talk about when he discussed slavery and the law. She stepped up. "What about where we are now? Aren't the Territories free?"

Terwilliger looked up, startled to see her there. He shook his head. "All the Territories are different about how they treat slavery. California Territory is free. Oregon is more likely to let a man bring his slaves in."

America looked at the couple. "Which Territory are you going to?"

Bundy exchanged looks with Harriet. "California." She nodded imperceptibly.

"Well, tarnation! Of course they're gonna say that now. You just told 'em which Territory to choose." Conway neatly stepped around Terwilliger and Bundy and claimed Harriet as his own. "You got no rights to this nigger, mister," he said to Bundy. "She's my property now and I aim to make it official at the next fort."

"How much would you take for her?" Four pairs of eyes turned to America, who stood there with her hands on her hips. "Well? You're so eager to put a price on a human being."

Conway sneered. "You want to buy her from me, little lady?"

"Since you insist on it, yes. I'll buy her."

Terwilliger put a hand out. "Now, Mrs. Hollis, maybe you should lie down for a while. You have enough problems of your own. Don't be taking on these people's problems as well." He put a hand on her shoulder and she shook it off.

Bundy shook his head and looked at America with sad eyes. "Ma'am, you don't have to do this—"

"Be quiet," she cut in, her eyes still locked with Conway's. She could see him calculating what would be best in this situation. His eyes flicked away from hers for a moment, a sign from Terwilliger, no doubt, to refuse the offer.

"Now, ma'am," he said in a soothing tone, "I just been told by your wagon master here that I should turn you down flat. A little woman like yourself with no husband, about to have a baby, it would be a crime—"

America turned around and surreptitiously dug the string of pearls from her medicine bundle. She turned back to the arguing group and held it up. "Is this enough? Will this buy Harriet's freedom?" Tears stung her eyes from the humiliation of bargaining for a life, for someone's happiness.

Conway narrowed his eyes and licked his lips. "Well, now, Mrs. Hollis, I do believe you bought yourself a slave."

Conjuring up every ounce of contempt she felt, she threw the pearls at him. They fell past him and Conway let go of Harriet to scramble after them. Harriet looked at America uncertainly.

She nodded. "You have your freedom, Harriet. Captain Terwilliger is our witness. I'll make out the paperwork, if the captain has a piece of paper and a pen."

The next day she delivered the signed paper to the Tobiases. Bundy took it and put it with his own papers.

"We don't know how to repay you, Mrs. Hollis," Bundy said, averting his eyes.

"There is nothing to repay," she said. "Maybe when the time comes for the baby, Harriet will be there for me."

Harriet grasped America's hand and squeezed it. "I will be there, Mrs. Hollis; you can count on that."

CHAPTER 15

The wagon train was well into Idaho Territory. It was a crisp, sunny late September day, something America hadn't seen in at least three weeks, when the emigrants came to Soda Springs, a wondrous place where a dozen pools of water bubbled up from the earth. America marveled, along with Addie and Flavia, at the mineral formations around the constantly boiling springs. They dipped their fingers, then their hands, in one of the pools and laughed at the cold sensation as small bubbles raced across their skin.

America made a cup with her hands and sipped the water. "Ugh!" she said, making a face.

"Does it taste that bad?" Addie asked.

"Too much alkaline."

"You ladies could use a little refreshment, I think." The women turned to see that Tal Bowen had come up behind them. He carried a battered pot in his hand. "Is this a cold spring?"

America nodded and looked from the pot to the spring. "It's cold, but it tastes terrible."

Bowen smiled and squatted to fill his pot. "I've been

here before, and there's a little trick to it." He left with the water and came back a few minutes later with a dipper. "Try it now."

America obliged by taking the first sip. It was sweet and effervescent. It tasted a little like lemon. "This is good. Is it the same water?"

Addie took a sip, then Flavia. Bowen tipped his hat and nodded shortly. "The same. You just have to balance the alkaline with a little cream of tartar. Then I added sugar and the juice of a lemon for taste."

He looked so pleased with himself that the women praised him again. Tal Bowen beamed under the lavish acclaim, and America started to wonder what kind of man she had turned down. He was certainly self-sufficient, and had knowledge of some wonderful exotic practices out here in the Territories. Still, whenever she saw the way Addie looked at Tal, it reminded America of the way she had once looked at Jan, and how, after she had fallen in love with Will, she had admired him. America had to concede that she might never look at another man that way again. She'd loved two men, and it was against all odds that she should love again.

Over the next four days, the company passed over the divide between the Bear and the Snake Rivers, then crossed a sandy plain about ten miles long. They were nearly through the Rocky Mountains when the company reached Fort Hall, a large building made of unburnt brick.

Captain Grant was the man in charge, and was welcoming and interested in how the emigrants had done on the trail. He invited them to a lavish supper in his dining hall. The spacious hall was decorated with wall sconces and a large painting of the captain in military uniform.

As America sat near Captain Grant during supper, Mr. Terwilliger formally introduced them.

After exchanging pleasantries, the captain was sober for a moment. "Mr. Terwilliger has told me of your misfortune. And at such a time." He made it clear he was talking about her pregnancy while not looking pointedly at her figure. "Let me extend my condolences."

"I appreciate that, Captain."

Before she was able to resume eating the excellent stewed venison with wild carrots and potatoes, the captain spoke again, more gently this time. "Mrs. Hollis, I know this journey has been sorrowful for you, and I commend you for coming this far. But now that your reason for going on this trek is no more, let me extend the hospitality of Fort Hall to you for the duration of the autumn and impending winter."

America was touched, and slightly surprised, by the offer. She saw the captain glance at Terwilliger, and got the impression that the wagon master had nodded his appreciation to Captain Grant. But she didn't want to stay in Fort Hall, as attractive as the offer was.

"We don't have a physician," Captain Grant said, "but we do have several experienced midwives at your disposal."

"Oh, that is kind of you, Captain," America replied cautiously. "Please let me think over your offer."

He bowed his head and smiled again. "As you wish. Now let me leave you to your meal."

America finished her supper without tasting it. She thought about what would be best for the baby, what would be best for her, and knew that the easy answer was to stay in Fort Hall. But she needed to complete this journey for Will. It had been his dream, and it had become hers.

As they finished up the acorn squash pie, America turned to the captain. "I must decline your offer," she said. "But thank you for giving me the choice."

The captain touched his napkin to his lips. There was a gleam in his eye. "You have to finish it, don't you?"

America was startled by the captain's remark. "Pardon?"

He leaned forward. "You have to go on, finish what you started. This trail has become more than a means to an end for you, hasn't it?"

America felt breathless. She answered slowly. "You understand, don't you?"

"Indeed I do," he replied. "I remember the first time I journeyed out to California Territory." His eyes had a faraway look in them for a moment, then became shrouded with reality. "But you do know that we're at war with Mexico in California. Are you sure you have to go?"

"Yes. And I will stay in the northern part of the Territory."

He shook his head. "Doesn't matter. The Mexicans are ambushing small groups of wagons as they pass through the Sierras. Be careful. Reconsider going to Oregon Territory. It's a safer place to be."

Much to America's sorrow, the wagon train had to leave the next day, and she bid good-bye to Captain Grant, regretting that she wasn't able to get to know him better. Terwilliger made sure everyone was well stocked with supplies before they continued on their way. By then the rest of the company had learned about the war being waged between Mexico and the United States over the California Territory. Even though she did not question her decision to continue, America began to have second thoughts about going south. She still had a few days before the train would split up, some going southwest and the others heading northwest.

Before they had reached Fort Hall, America had noticed the sound of rushing water, but was so excited about seeing a group of new people that she hadn't inquired into its source. As they journeyed on past the fort, the sound seemed to be getting nearer, but she still couldn't see anything that could make such a noise.

When they nooned, America stood and listened to the rushing sound, trying to puzzle it out. She caught sight of Mr. Pike with the peace pipe in his mouth. He was seated on a rock, whittling the figure of an otter.

"What is that?" America asked him.

He looked up and squinted at her, never taking the pipe out of his mouth. "What?"

She cocked her head. "That sound."

His face cleared and he grinned, his teeth clenched

around the pipe stem. "Oh, that. Amurrcn Fahhs."

"Pardon me?"

He blinked, then put his whittling knife down and removed the pipe before repeating, "American Falls."

"It sounds so close by. Why didn't we wait to noon there?"

Mr. Pike frowned. "Well, it sounds close, but it's still quite a few miles away. We'll be there tomorrow." He looked thoughtful. "It's quite a sight."

The next day, they crossed the Snake River once more, about nine miles past Fort Hall, and finally came to American Falls. America was thrilled at the sight of the wide, rushing water. It wasn't that she hadn't seen a waterfall before—she'd been to Niagara Falls with her family when she was a child, and that was far more majestic. But Niagara had been surrounded with people—it seemed tame compared with American Falls. The water fell from above like an avalanche of snow.

They camped nearby for the night, and by mid-morning of the next day, the company came to the fork in the road that was called the "Parting of the Ways." Some wagons would head northwest to Oregon, and the others would head southwest to California. America had decided to continue on to California Territory, despite the war.

All the women had tears in their voices when they said good-bye.

"Oh, America," Addie said breathlessly, "I must tell you before we part. Tal has asked me to marry him."

America kissed Addie's cheek and squeezed her hand. "That's wonderful news. Tell me, what will happen to the man you were coming out here to marry?"

Addie blushed. "Tal has offered to pay my intended for my passage out west. He told me last night, after he proposed, that this had been done before, and assured me that it was proper."

"I am so happy for you, Addie," America said. And a little envious, she admitted privately.

Flavia hugged America and cried a little before she was helped by Captain Conway into the back of one of the wagons. It was rumored that back at Fort Hall, Conway had traded the pearl necklace for a case of whiskey and several flintlocks, powder, and lead.

Gil Hayes and his children were also going to Oregon Territory, and America was sad to see them go. Mary Elizabeth came up to her before they went on. "I'm sure if you asked my father, he'd take you to Oregon Territory," she said shyly. "But he said it would have to be your choice."

"Thank you, Mary," America said, hugging the young girl. "But I have my mind set. Look after your father and brother, won't you?"

Mary Elizabeth returned the hug and was gone. Gil came up to her and took her hand. "Come with us, America. I said I wouldn't ask you, but it's so hard to see a friend of Celeste's leave us."

"Oh, Gil, thank you. It seems that everyone is conspiring to stop me from going to California."

He smiled, but she could see that smiling was still painful to him. "I'm just worried about seeing a lovely widow going into a strange Territory without a friend. Come with us and you'll have friends to help you."

She touched his hand briefly. "Thank you, Gil, but no. I intend to arrive in California with my baby."

Gil squeezed her hand and nodded. "I understand. I'll unhook the horses and—"

"Keep the horses, Gil. No one will take better care of them than you will."

He looked startled. "I—I couldn't. You have so little left—"

"Then pay me for them."

"I can't offer as much as they're likely to be worth."

"Whatever you can spare. I can't take care of them, and you can keep or sell them when you get to Oregon."

"All right." He nodded and offered her a fair price. She accepted and tucked the money in her medicine bag. George and Mary Elizabeth waved from the wagon as Gil pulled out behind Captain Conway's wagon. America could still see the wounded look in Gil's face.

"We've both lost so much, Gil," she murmured to herself, then shook her head.

America had never seen anything like the forty-mile desert they crossed over the next week. Barren, dry, and hot in the day and brittle cold at night, she wasn't sure she would make it through each day. They lacked water for several days, with no sign of a spring or a creek, or even a trickle of water nearby. All she could see for miles was sagebrush, which seemed to survive under the cruelest of temperatures, and greasewood.

To make it worse, the treatment she received from the Sanfords had gotten much worse. She figured now that her only friends had departed, the Sanfords didn't feel that they had to put up any pretense of being kind to her.

Often during the day, they insisted she walk, even though she was almost ready to deliver her child. Reverend Sanford had tried earlier to procure her horses under the guise that she hadn't paid them enough for her keep. He was angry that she had sold the horses to Gil Hayes, and made her life a misery for several days. America was beginning to wish that she had stayed back at Fort Hall. Or that she had gone to the Oregon Territory.

To avoid the Sanfords, America began to spend more time with Harriet and Bundy Tobias. Harriet was teaching her how to darn socks properly. Will had never complained about America's lack of domestic skills, even though she had been brought up in an aristocratic household where fluency in French, the art of embroidery, and the ability to play the piano had been more useful talents for the future wife of a lawyer or politician.

The Tobiases made some of the hard times easier to bear. Many of the emigrants looked down on America's befriending the Negro couple, but America was past caring what people thought. The Tobiases didn't seem to mind her presence.

"We owe you a debt, Mizz Hollis," Bundy would often say, "and if all it takes to repay it is to give you a place to escape to, it's a small price."

No matter how many times America told the Tobiases that they didn't owe her anything, they continued to remind her of the debt owed. It took a few days for America to reason it out—since they had both been slaves, and had bought their freedom, it meant more to them. The fact that America had bought Harriet's freedom a second time meant that they felt beholden to her.

It was about a week later that Harriet made a confession to America. After hearing Harriet remind America once again of the debt she owed, America burst out, "For goodness sake, Harriet, I only did what was right under the circumstances. You were already free, and I only reinforced it for you."

There was an uncomfortable silence. Harriet kept her eyes down. America sensed that there was more to the story than she had been told. "That's right, isn't it? You *were* already a free woman."

Harriet sighed and bit her lip. "I wasn't truthful with you and Captain Conway. I ran away to be with Bundy. I had no papers."

America paused to think about it, but didn't find the news upsetting, only a relief. She hadn't given the pearls away for nothing; she had honestly bought Harriet's freedom. With a little laugh, she said lightly, "Well, then, it's a good thing I was there with those pearls, isn't it?" She bent over as far as she could in her condition, in order to meet Harriet's eyes. "And there won't be any more talk about owing anyone a debt, will there?"

A slow smile came to Harriet's face. "No, ma'am. No more talk about debts."

Often when America returned to the Sanfords' wagon at night, the reverend accosted her with biblical quotes and stern lectures. She would let him rant until he had nothing left to say; then she would retire to her bedding under the wagon. Muriel Sanford just stayed out of America's way, studying her from across the encampment as if America was evil incarnate.

Aside from her growing attachment to the Tobiases, the only other thing that kept America going on was the horizon. Every day as they made their way across the seemingly endless desert, America could see the mountains in the distance. She had read about them in previous emigrants' accounts of their journey. The Sierra Mountains were the last wall to breach before the wagon train reached the land that she had read about and heard about—a land so beautiful and bountiful that it was a wonder more people didn't migrate to California.

The problem that kept most emigrants from going south was that Mexico hadn't completely abandoned the land. Those emigrants who went to California Territory might be living under Spanish rule in a few years. The reason that so many people ignored that threat and migrated south anyway was the rumor that there was gold to be had in the hills and rivers of California. In fact, there was talk of gold to be found in the streets of the small towns that dotted the countryside.

The Sierras loomed in the distance, and for a while, America thought they would forever be shadowy purple rises on the horizon. But with each passing day, the mountains took on more definition. By the first week of October, she could see the Ponderosa pines on the mountainside, and the snow-capped top wreathed in mist.

And with each day closer to the Sierras, America was that much closer to delivering her baby. One night, she dreamed she had her baby and it was a girl. The next morning, America recounted her dream to Muriel Sanford. Even though she still did not like the woman, there were so few people to talk to out here.

"That's ridiculous," Mrs. Sanford said in a matter-of-fact manner. "No woman can predict what she is going to have. And to be quite frank, my dear, you should be praying that it is a boy. Boys are hardier than girls, and when they grow up, they can support their mothers."

"But you once told me that you wanted a daughter," America recalled.

Muriel looked away, the wattle under her chin trembling. "That is true. But I've had a healthy boy, and my husband is grateful for that. A girl would be a frivolous thing to want. And I became too old to bear another child. I've put my fancies aside and made do with what I have now."

She turned back to America and gave her a stern look.

"And that's what you should do as well, Mrs. Hollis. Put your dreams aside and make do." She got up and started bustling around. "I understand that the assistant wagon master, Talmadge Bowen, proposed to you and you turned him down."

"How—how did you know?" America felt a cramp in her stomach and she took a slow, deep breath to make it go away.

Mrs. Sanford wouldn't look at America. "He asked me if he had a chance. I told him that you being a young widow ready to have a child, I thought you would be smart enough to agree to marriage." She paused for effect, then looked at America. "I see that I was wrong. You are a silly, vain thing, and foolish besides."

Although America was highly insulted, she managed to squeak, "Foolish?"

Mrs. Sanford had gotten started and couldn't seem to stop herself. With hands on her hips, she added, "Befriending that nigger couple. What is the matter with you? It was a very stupid thing to do, giving up your pearl necklace for a Negro. Those people are born to serve us."

"Excuse me," America replied coldly. "I have to attend to the meal." She began to walk over to the fire that Lem had started, but had to stop when she felt another cramp. They hadn't found a good water supply, and making a meal with little water would prove to be a challenge.

Ever since she had awoken that morning, America had been having these cramps, and she was worried about her baby. Suddenly, she felt a pressure between her legs, then the release of water. She gasped and put a hand to her belly, looking for a place to sit down. She looked around for someone who would notice her predicament. Mrs. Sanford had disappeared, but Harriet Tobias spied America from across the encampment.

"Bundy, fetch us some water and be quick about it," Harriet cried out. "And while you're at it, see to the fire." Bundy moved quickly and Harriet was by America's side in an instant.

America smiled through gritted teeth. "I do believe I'm about to have my baby, Harriet."

Harriet's rough hand came up and smoothed America's brow. "Looks that way, child."

She started to respond to Harriet's kindly smile, but a sudden contraction made her gasp with pain and double over.

$\mathscr{C}$HAPTER 16

"There's so much blood." America could hear Harriet's voice as if she were speaking through a dense fog.

"Here, let me take a look." Another voice floated past her, but she couldn't grasp who it belonged to.

She closed her eyes for a minute, and when she opened them again, Harriet had disappeared and in her place was Muriel Sanford. America struggled to talk. She wanted to tell Muriel that she wanted Harriet back. After several failed attempts to speak through the pain, she finally gave up.

Focusing all her attention on her body, she tried to relax, but another contraction came and her body tensed up again.

"America, can you hear me? The baby's almost here. It's time to push." America thought Harriet had said that. She tried to comply with her friend's request, but as she pushed, she experienced a sharp pain. A whimper ended her attempt.

"Is the baby all right?" America recognized Mrs. Sanford's voice.

"There's so much blood."

America spoke in gasps. "Harriet. Can—you see—the—baby?"

"I see it," her friend answered in a low voice. "It's a breech birth." There was a pause, then, "Wait; here it comes."

Through the pain, America could feel the baby sliding out. She panted. "Boy or girl?"

"It's a girl," Harriet answered. Her voice was a mixture of awe and another emotion America couldn't place. After a pause, she could hear Harriet whisper, "We have to do something about the blood, Mrs. Sanford. She's bleeding too much."

America felt a surge of joy. She had a girl! Her dream had come true.

"Somebody get me some rags." There was a tinge of desperation in Harriet's voice. "Is there anyone here who knows what to do?"

America thought that she should be feeling better since her baby had been born, but she continued to struggle to breathe. The air in front of her was hazy and she felt as if her life was draining away.

"I'll take the baby," she heard Mrs. Sanford say in a brisk tone. "Here, give it to me."

"Sierra," America murmured. "I want Sierra." She could hear her baby crying. America teetered on the brink of unconsciousness. She felt as if she were holding onto the edge of a black crevice with her fingertips. She jerked as cold, stiff fingers pressed hard on her wrist.

Through the thickening fog, she heard Muriel Sanford say, "I think she's gone."

"America! America! Wake up, please." America felt Harriet shaking her shoulder, but she couldn't find the energy to open her eyes. She was having trouble breathing and had to focus all her concentration on that one action.

"We have room in our wagon for the baby," Mrs. Sanford said. "The men can take care of the body."

"I'm not sure we're doing the right thing," came Harriet's uncertain voice. "How can you be so cold?"

There was the sound of a hand hitting a face. Then Mrs. Sanford spoke. "How dare you talk to me like that! You should know your place. I may not show my emotions as easily as your people do, but I know Mrs. Hollis has gone to God to be with her husband. And I'm the proper one to take this baby."

"You weren't even her friend," Harriet argued.

America desperately wanted to open her eyes, or move a hand, but she felt as if in a dream, or tied down. She had no control over her body, and was unable to will it to do the things needed to show that she was indeed alive.

"That may be so," Muriel Sanford said bitterly, "but it wouldn't look proper if a black couple took care of this baby—"

She's my baby! America thought. *You can't take her away from me!* Still unable to say the words, she slipped further down the thin thread of life, then plunged deep into the blackness of unconsciousness.

CHAPTER 17

America slowly opened her eyes. Even though she felt too groggy and weak to move, she moved her head from side to side, searching for Harriet and her baby.

Her vision cleared enough for her to make out the Indian woman bent over her. America gasped. The dark-skinned woman wore a grass skirt around her waist, but her breasts were bared. Several necklaces that looked as if they were made of colorful seeds dangled around her neck. Her hair was worn loose and brushed the tips of her breasts like feathers.

America's own breasts ached as she tried to sit up. "Where is my baby?" she asked the woman.

The woman smiled and said something in her own language.

America cradled an invisible form in her arms and repeated, "Ba-by?"

The young woman frowned, then looked sadly at America. She made a similar gesture and shook her head. "Baa-bee."

Panic welled up inside America. She had lost her home and her husband. Had she now lost Sierra as well?

Barely able to sit up, America took in her surroundings. She was sitting on a grass mat in some kind of small grass shelter, being tended by an Indian woman who spoke no English. Had her encampment been attacked? Had she been captured? If so, maybe her baby was nearby. But what about the others in the wagon train?

America desperately wished she could communicate with this gentle woman. Just as she opened her mouth to speak again, an older woman entered the shelter carrying a crude bowl. She handed the bowl to the other woman, then quickly left.

The younger woman held the bowl up to America's lips and she sipped it tentatively. It smelled like an herbal concoction, but was not unpleasant to the taste. She drank it greedily.

When she was done, the young Indian pointed to herself and said, "Pan-tak-i."

"Pan-tak-i," America repeated. "That is a nice name," she said, knowing the woman couldn't understand a word, "but I think I shall call you Dancing Feather."

At the woman's puzzled look, America pointed to the long, straight black hair. "Your hair dances like feathers around your shoulders."

She then pointed to herself and said her name. "America."

"A-mer-i-ca." Dancing Feather rolled the syllables around in her mouth a couple of times. "America." She smiled, then held the empty bowl in front of America.

She wondered if it was part of their introduction ritual,

but wasn't sure what to do next. Dancing Feather said something in her own language and pointed to her own breasts. America was still puzzled. The woman then held the empty bowl to America's right breast.

It dawned on America that Dancing Feather was trying to tell her that she should force out the milk. "But my baby may need—" She stopped trying to explain. If her baby had been captured by this tribe, this woman would surely have brought the baby to her to be fed.

America's shoulders slumped and her heart felt as heavy as lead. It must be true—Sierra was gone. Vague snippets of memory convinced her that her daughter was alive, although she couldn't figure out what made her hold onto that belief so strongly.

Even though America's arms ached for her baby, she knew she needed to get rid of the milk that engorged her breasts. She removed her medicine bundle from around her neck and tucked it into the pocket of her now tattered skirt. Hesitantly at first, she touched her left breast. Both were heavy with milk, and she wondered how on earth she was supposed to perform this act.

It was a much different action than milking cows at her uncle's farm. Dancing Feather remained by her side, smiling encouragement, and, when America was empty, the woman took the full bowl out of the grass hut.

Dancing Feather took care of America for the first week, bringing her food and water and herbal remedies that America took without question. She gradually recovered physically, but was still ailing emotionally.

She spent most of her time thinking about her baby, and was constantly being reminded of the loss through little things. Often, just before waking, the smell of a newborn baby would fill her senses. She would open her eyes in anticipation, only to find herself alone once again.

The days ran into one another until America wasn't sure how long she had been with the tribe.

One day, Dancing Feather brought her a small smooth leather pillow stuffed with aromatic herbs. America stroked the butter-soft leather, thinking it felt just like a newborn's skin. At night, America would sometimes hear the cry of an animal that reminded her of the cry of a baby. She would turn over and lie awake just to listen to the sound, vowing that when she was better, she would search for her daughter.

Many of the villagers came by to keep her company, even though none of them spoke English and she didn't understand their language. Slowly, she learned the names of things that were brought to her. The Indians were patient and gentle teachers, and didn't pressure her to learn unless she asked.

America's strength gradually returned, and she continued to build her vocabulary of Indian words. She also taught some English words to Dancing Feather, who seemed eager to communicate.

It gradually occurred to America that she must be in the camp of the dreaded "Diggers," Paiute Indians who lived in the barren basin near the foot of the Sierra Mountains. She had once read about them—the Paiute were the poorest of Indians, having been driven out of the mountains by more ferocious tribes. The written account had described ambushes of lone wagons that the "Diggers" sometimes resorted to in order to stay alive.

As she moved about the village, America discovered that the Indians who had saved her did not seem to exist as a whole tribe, but rather, were a nomadic band of several combined families. After she had explored the camp, she noted that the "Diggers" weren't as bad off as she'd read about. They had a few flintlocks and pistols, and horses as well.

Of course, she reasoned, if they were raiding emigrants who passed by, they would have these possessions. America began to wonder if she was a prisoner of their camp. What would happen if she decided to walk out of the village one day and didn't return? Would they go after her?

She had only read about the dangers that existed in the desert, but would she know danger if she saw it? And without the knowledge of foods to be foraged, America knew that she was dependent on the people who had nursed her back to health.

In the end, she decided that leaving would be useless. She had no horse, no weapons, and no survival skills for the desert. On the other hand, Dancing Feather proved to be a faithful friend and helpful to America in her introduction to Paiute existence. The leader of their group, Chief Truckee, was a fatherly presence who paid polite attention to America, often stopping to see how she was feeling.

The older woman who had brought the herbal tea that first day turned out to be Chief Truckee's wife, whom America called "Mrs. Truckee." Mrs. Truckee was the medicine woman and came often to the wickiup where America was staying, bringing different herbal brews and ointments. She always seemed to know how America was feeling and what would make her feel better.

The only thing the medicine woman could not cure was America's broken heart. Some days, she couldn't even get up in the morning. The melancholy would cover her like a thick woolen blanket and she would begin to cry.

Gradually, America learned more about the families who lived in the small community. Dancing Feather had a sister who had two young daughters, Sarah and Mary. America was surprised, but could not understand enough Paiute to discover how they had come to have English names.

She did, however, begin to realize that the "Diggers" were not the band of thieving Indians that the written accounts had portrayed. In fact, many of the Paiute had initially been afraid of her, and they seemed to loathe the Emigrant Trail. After spending some time observing them while they gathered food, she thought she understood why—the trail cut right through the best area for foraging.

America's strength returned enough for her to help with many of the chores. It felt good to help them as an accepted part of the community, and not to be treated like a servant as she had been by the Sanfords.

One of her first duties was to help the group gather piñon nuts for the fast approaching winter. While the men and boys shook the branches of the trees with long sticks, the women used large baskets to gather the nuts that fell on the ground. America listened to the families chatter conversationally as they worked, and she wished she were better acquainted with the language.

The weather alternated between warm and sunny, and bitter cold, as if it couldn't make up its mind. Autumn was firmly entrenched in this high desert area, but the concept of time as America knew it was not as the Paiutes knew it. America had counted the days since she had awakened here. Even though she didn't know how long she'd been unconscious, she figured her baby must be close to a month old by now.

Soon she noticed a growing excitement among the families, especially the men. America would frequently see the Indians gathered together, facing the mountains, talking and gesturing as if they were shooting bows and arrows. She finally asked Dancing Feather, in halting Paiute, what everyone was so excited about.

"Running antlers," was the only part of the response she understood.

The following morning was when she learned what "running antlers" meant. Dancing Feather came into the wickiup and gestured that America should pack up for a short journey.

The group started out early in the morning, some walking and the rest on horseback, heading toward the mountains. America's good health was back, but after a few hours of walking, Dancing Feather convinced her to ride a horse.

By late afternoon, she was glad to see that they had reached their goal—the foot of the Sierras. There was already a large gathering of Paiutes waiting for them. America presumed that they were all there for the "running antlers."

The other Paiute women came over and surrounded America and Dancing Feather, reaching out to touch the white woman. They chattered to Dancing Feather, who responded in kind, touching America's shoulder and smiling at her to reassure her that she was accepted by these women.

In the distance, America could see graceful deerlike creatures grazing near the foot of the mountains. Dancing Feather motioned for her to follow. The other women had gone ahead and America walked beside her friend and the two little girls, Sarah and Mary.

"What are we doing?" America asked.

"Shut antlers," was the elusive reply.

A few minutes later, she understood. They came to a place where someone, perhaps the Paiutes whom they had met there, had cleared a large area and built up sagebrush all around into a corral-type enclosure. After greeting each other, the men mounted their horses and left the women to forage the area for roots and lizards, to socialize and cook.

America did the best she could, working beside Dancing Feather. But when her friend came to her with a smile on her face and a basket full of dried grasshoppers, America didn't know what to make of it. And when Dancing Feather began to grind the insects into powder, America thought she would faint.

Dancing Feather, noting the expression on America's face, frowned in concern and turned to get something. Then she offered a piece of bread to America, who took it and began to chew on it. It had a nutty, grainy flavor. Dancing Feather touched America's shoulder and said one word in Paiute, a word that America had only recently learned—"Life." Then she indicated the basket of dried grasshoppers and the bread.

America understood immediately. The bread she ate was made from grasshopper flour. Taking a deep breath to keep from getting sick to her stomach, America gave her friend a decisive nod, picked up a pestle, and started grinding the insects into flour. She conjured up an image of her family dining room, remembering the lavish dinner parties her parents had given. Exotic foods often graced their table, always waited on by servants, and America laughed at the thought of grasshopper bread next to the unusual meats, tropical fruits, and gourmet soups.

Late in the afternoon, America had just finished with her chore when she heard a sound like thunder. She looked up in time to see a herd of antelope stampeding toward the brush corral. The other women got up from their work and hurried to the enclosure. Each woman picked out a stick from a large pile nearby. Leaving a wide enough berth for the antelope to be driven into, they formed an ever-narrowing human fence to the opening of corral.

The men on horses came on the heels of the animals and soon the antelope were cornered in the corral, panicking as they tried to find a way out. After the last antelope was inside, the women closed rank. The men got off their horses and entered the corral with their weapons—spears, knives, bows and arrows—and began to kill the animals.

America shut her eyes and clamped her hands over her ears when she heard the first dying scream of a doe.

CHAPTER 18

Together, the men and women of the tribe dressed the antelope and prepared the hides for tanning. America worked alongside Dancing Feather, mimicking whatever her friend did and feeling clumsy for her efforts. This was the sort of thing Dancing Feather had probably grown up with, so it was second nature to her. But America found the act of skinning antelope to be hard, messy, smelly work.

Eventually, Dancing Feather seemed to notice that America was having a difficult time, and she led her friend over to the cookfire that blazed cheerily as the sun began to set. An antelope was roasting over the fire, and a woman turned a crank to keep the meat roasting evenly. The woman grinned and stepped aside, indicating that America should take over roasting the antelope. Hours later, when America thought her arm would fall off from slowly turning the crank, she handed the job to someone else and helped fashion the grasshopper bread and shell the nuts.

Later that night there was a feast of crisp, roasted antelope meat, warm grasshopper bread, nuts, and berries. America stayed in the background to watch the dancing and socializing. She observed the Paiutes, Dancing Feather included, and was envious of their life. She wasn't sure if it was the closeness and the caring that was displayed by everyone or the fact that they all seemed to accept each other and belong together.

America thought back to her own life, her own family, and realized that even now, after all she had been through, if she were to go home tomorrow, her family might not accept her or welcome her in the same way that these people had done. In private, her mother might express relief that her daughter was home, but the fact that America had been pregnant by another man before her marriage to Will would continue to isolate her from the rest of Philadelphia society.

With a start, America realized that she hadn't written a letter to her family since Nebraska, and she wondered if her parents worried about not hearing from her, or if they were relieved that she was gone. They didn't know that Will was dead or that her baby had been taken from her. There was nothing she could do about it now but wait until the spring. She knew she had to find her daughter before making any further decisions.

After the feast, a group of drummers began beating out a strange tattoo. Two or three flutes joined in, and several of the men who had been sitting around the fire after their meal stood up to dance. First slowly, then with more vigor, they shuffled around the fire in an intricate series of steps and turns. A ghostly voice started a steady droning series of notes, an alien form of singing to America, but she soon found herself caught up in it.

One man caught her eye several times. He didn't have the same look as the rest of the Paiutes. He was taller and, in America's eyes, had a handsome profile quite unlike the squat, round faces of the Paiutes. He didn't dress as they did, either. Most of the Paiute men were simply dressed in unadorned tanned hide breeches and shirts. He wore a fringed buckskin shirt and breeches, and a breastplate made of bone with an elaborate design. On the back of his head there was a sunburst of feathers that America thought might be from a hawk. She wondered where he came from.

Dancing Feather plucked America's sleeve and gestured to the dancing. America shook her head shyly and watched as her friend got up and joined the group. Seated near the fire, watching the slow, rhythmic movements of the dancers lulled her into a semi-conscious state. She forced herself to move slightly away from the fire and breathe in the cold night air. She turned her head toward the mountains, and tried to imagine the distance that was left to traverse before she actually got to the foothills.

A light touch startled her and she turned around to face the man she had been admiring. He was smiling at her.

"Oh!" she said. "Thank you, but I'd rather not dance."

"I didn't ask for you to dance," he replied pleasantly.

She blinked. "You speak English?" was all she could think of to say.

"I was educated by a Christian missionary," he replied.

"I see." Thoughts whirled around her head; questions fought to be asked first. After spending so long with people who didn't speak her language, America had to keep herself from clinging to him as if he were a bastion of civilization. The people she had stayed with had been so kind to her—had, in fact, saved her life. She was grateful to them. But now she wanted to go back to her own world. She had to stop herself from begging.

He spoke first. "My name is Black Wolf. I have heard your story from Chief Truckee."

America looked away, the sharp memory of the loss of her baby washing over her like a tidal wave.

"My people have asked me to question you, if you are willing," Black Wolf said. "They admire your spirit and are pleased that you have tried to learn their language."

"I don't mind relating what has happened to me," America replied. She took a deep breath to collect her thoughts, then told Black Wolf of her journey west, Will's death, Sierra's birth.

He listened without interruption and when she was finished, he nodded shortly. "So you are a widow, and some of the people you were traveling with took your baby with them."

"From the best I can figure out, it seems that is what happened to my daughter." America replied, although she still couldn't believe it herself. "Perhaps you can answer a question for me," she continued. "How did I come to be here?"

A look of disgust mingled with disbelief crossed over his handsome face before he answered. "Chief Truckee related the story to me this way: His family had decided to move to a new area for foraging the piñon nuts, and they had to cross the wagon trail. I believe many whites call it the Emigrant Trail."

America nodded.

"It was your friend, Pan-tak-i, who saw the grave."

"The grave?"

Black Wolf nodded. "Pan-tak-i had just passed a mound of stones when she thought she heard a moan. When she went over to satisfy her curiosity, your hand reached up from between the rocks. She called to the others and they moved the stones, digging you out of a shallow hole."

America could feel the blood draining from her face. "I see." So the Sanfords had stolen her baby and then left her to die. America was dumbstruck.

Black Wolf watched her silence.

"I owe these people my life," she finally said.

He frowned. "They would not see it that way. You are free to leave at any time."

"I have felt for some time that I could leave," she admitted, "but I have nowhere to go." She tried not to let the bleakness of her own words overwhelm her.

"You are welcome to stay with them as long as you would like. The chief has told me that you are a woman of brave heart. He could see that during your recovery, and afterward, when you have helped them with tasks that are obviously beyond your experience."

America suppressed a smile. "Like grinding grasshoppers into flour?"

Black Wolf allowed a small smile to cross his face. "Insects are a part of our existence here in the desert. A locust invasion is a boon for my people. It means the difference between life and death."

"I understand." America broached the subject she had been wondering about ever since she set eyes on him. "Please forgive me if I sound rude, but you don't look like the rest of this tribe."

He nodded. "That is true. I do look more like my father, a Shoshone. My mother was Paiute, and I spent most of my childhood growing up in the mountains. But my mother would come back to visit our Paiute kin often and bring me with her. Since her death three years ago, I have come back to visit and help with the annual antelope hunt. Sometimes I stay with them for the winter."

"Where do you go when you're not with your tribe?" America asked.

"I help wagon trains cross the mountains and occasionally the army uses me as a scout," Black Wolf replied.

"So that explains the luxuries I have seen," America said in a thoughtful manner.

"Luxuries?" Black Wolf seemed puzzled.

"You are able to get these people the guns and horses because of your work."

His eyes hardened. "I do not consider these to be luxuries. These items have made the difference between living and dying for my people."

"I'm sorry, I spoke out of turn—"

Black Wolf stood up. "I must go see that the antelope is prepared and divided up among the people." He left her alone.

America blinked back tears of frustration. Here was the one person she could talk to without struggling to be understood, and she had insulted him. She looked around at the rest of the tribe. The music and dancing had stopped and Chief Truckee had everyone under his spell as he wove a story.

America tried to focus on his tale, but couldn't understand very much of it. She recognized a word here and there—the words for coyote and wolf were used frequently, and she recognized the word for sun. But the more she tried to understand, the harder it became for her. Her head began to hurt from the concentration and she finally gave up.

Curling up next to the fire, she let Chief Truckee's words wash over her as she entered the state between reality and the dream world. With the heat on her face and the flames flickering over her closed eyelids, she found herself watching his story unfold.

Wolf, the strongest man in the universe, was lonely paddling his canoe around in the water by himself, so created Coyote and called him brother. But Brother Coyote soon tired of paddling the canoe, so they created the earth by taking a handful of dirt and placing it in the water to make an island. The island was shaky, and Coyote ran around on it and declared it too small. So Wolf added more and more dirt until Coyote was satisfied. That is how earth was created.

America opened her eyes and sat up. She had understood the meaning of Chief Truckee's story. And she felt she had comprehended it on a deeper level—it was about the Indians, Wolf, and white men, Coyote.

She got up and searched for Black Wolf. She didn't have to look far—he was sitting by himself on a rock overlooking the rest of the tribe's activities. When he saw her approach, his expression dismissed her and he looked away.

"Please accept my apologies, Black Wolf," she began. "My assumption was inexcusable."

He looked back at her with renewed interest. She sat beside him and told him about her experience understanding Chief Truckee's story. He nodded. "That is a good interpretation. But you have missed some of the other stories by seeking me out. The chief is now telling the story of what you call the Milky Way."

They looked up at the clear sky together and America found the starry white path that cut a swath across the dark sky. "What do the Paiute call it?"

"It is the road of the dead to the spirit world," he explained.

"How do you mourn your dead loved ones?" she asked. "By telling stories of where they go after they leave their physical existence?"

"That is part of it," Black Wolf conceded, "but there is also the emotional loss that is demonstrated in physical ways. The loss of a partner is usually displayed by cutting off the hair." He held his long braid up to show with a cutting gesture. "Sometimes the mourner will cut herself to display the pain of her loss." He used his finger to slash a mark on his forearm.

"What do you do with the hair?" she asked.

"A wife will braid it and lay it across her dead husband's breast."

America fingered her own hair. "And what if her husband's body was lost in a war, or in the mountains?"

Black Wolf thought for a moment. "It is a symbolic gesture. The body need only be symbolic."

Ever since Will had died, living on the trail made it impossible for America to grieve properly. And now she had so many people to grieve—Jan, Catherine, Will, Celeste, and Sierra.

As if in a trance, America began to plait her fine, blond hair. When she had completed the braid, she asked, "May I use your knife?"

Tears ran down her face, but she barely took notice of them. Black Wolf handed her his knife without a word. She cut her braid, gave him back his knife, and laid her hair on the rock between them. He didn't say a word during or after her ritual, but sat silently with her on the rock late into the night, both of them listening to Chief Truckee tell his stories.

CHAPTER 19

The next day, after the feasting, the men held council while America helped the women pack up the tribe's possessions and make ready to leave the area. When the council broke up, America got the impression that her group would be seeking a new place to set up their domed grass huts for the winter. She wondered how they would stay warm. It came as a pleasant surprise to America that Black Wolf traveled with her group.

They spent the next few days moving south across the desert. The location they finally stopped at was similar to the place they had left, but it seemed slightly warmer, and it was nearer to the Sierras, something she was grateful for. America gained comfort from the belief that she was nearer to her daughter, assuming the Sanfords had gone over the mountains and settled someplace on the other side.

America helped to reconstruct the wickiups, which were bundles of cattails tied to a framework of poles. To keep the chilly winter wind at bay, they were reinforced with antelope and buffalo skins secured around the outside of the huts. Each shelter had an opening at the top for smoke and a small entry which was covered with another skin to keep the cold wind from blowing through.

During those long winter days that turned into weeks and months, America and Black Wolf spent much time together. It was more comfortable conversing in her own language without worrying whether any of her words were being misinterpreted. While Black Wolf would speak in English once in a while to accommodate her, he spoke more often to her in his native language.

At first she thought that he was scornful of her language, but after a time, she realized he was teaching her to adapt to her surroundings.

"Why do you do that?" she asked one day in frustration. She had been struggling to understand the difference between sun and moon in Paiute. "It would have been easier if you had told me that in English."

Black Wolf grinned. "But then you wouldn't know what Chief Truckee is talking about when he tells his stories of Coyote and Wolf."

America realized he was right. She was becoming lazy and dependent on him to interpret whatever she wanted to say to anyone in the camp. She resolved to learn the Paiute language before the snow melted on the foothills of the Sierras.

It only took her a couple more months to start having halting conversations with Dancing Feather. Her friend had stuck by her throughout her recovery and her grief. Now the two women could finally talk without using Black Wolf as a go-between.

Winter was a dreary, dull prospect for the Paiute tribe. There was very little to do—most of the foraging was gone and the families sat in their wickiups on the coldest days, feeding sagebrush to the fires. On warmer days, the men might go hunting for jackrabbits or the occasional stray deer, but most animals in the wintertime were hardly worth the trouble of hunting. They, too, were having trouble finding food to forage, and many came near to starving to death. Still, the Paiutes had plenty of flour for bread, and piñon nuts as well. And they had smoked a good portion of the antelope meat for storage.

Even though America had led a pampered life in Philadelphia, her months on the trail had built in her an eagerness to keep busy. One of the first items on her agenda this winter was to make herself a new set of clothes, with Dancing Feather's help, of course.

America only had one dress, the thin, cotton shift which she had been wearing when she was discovered. The warm coat Lem had given her was not found in the grave. Even after washing the dress several times, it was still stained from the birth of her daughter, and America decided to adopt the Paiute style of dress. Dancing Feather was delighted to help her sew a buckskin dress and leggings from the antelope hides they had brought back. America's cloth dress was carefully folded and put away.

After they completed her new clothing, basketweaving became a source of fascination for America during those long winter months. She found herself mesmerized by Dancing Feather's nimble fingers weaving and sewing baskets together. Some of these containers, used to hold bread or other loose items, had beautiful designs woven into them. Other baskets were covered with pine gum and made watertight so they could be used as drinking vessels.

One cold night, America finally asked Dancing Feather if she could learn to make baskets, too.

"Yes, I was hoping you would ask," her friend replied, making a place for America on the mat next to her mound of supplies.

At first, America's attempts were clumsy and by the end of a day, her fingers would be raw and sore from weaving the tule rushes into shapes. By the end of winter, even if she wasn't an artisan, America's calloused fingers flew over the reeds and she was able to weave a simple small basket in half a day.

The act of weaving became enjoyable to her and she was proud of the finished product. Dancing Feather and the other women praised her efforts, but in the end, America had to admit that she would never be able to attain the artistry that made Dancing Feather's baskets works of art.

Still, weaving baskets became a way of escaping the problems that loomed in her future. Come spring, she would have to make a decision—should she stay with these people who had accepted her so easily, or should she go look for her child?

She brought up the question to Dancing Feather one day as they worked on large water baskets. "I sometimes think that it would be the best thing for my baby if I didn't try to find her. She probably already has people who love her." But even as she said this, America couldn't convince herself that her words were true. She was certain that the Sanfords had her baby, and she had never seen any indication that they were loving people.

Dancing Feather frowned. "I have not had a child yet, but I cannot imagine not ever seeing my baby. It must be difficult to know that she is out there."

"Yes, it is," America admitted. "The question is, can I live with the idea of never knowing my daughter, never seeing her?"

It was a difficult question to answer, so she brought her dilemma to Chief Truckee. Up close in the firelight, America was aware of every sun-wizened wrinkle on his face, and felt comforted by the good humor twinkling in his dark eyes.

"You are asking me for advice. I do not consider myself a wise man, but I do have a belief that mothers and their children are never separated in spirit."

"Father," America said, addressing him in the polite Paiute manner, "if that is the case, then I must go away in the spring to find Sierra. But I don't know where to begin."

Chief Truckee frowned. "Pay attention to your dreams, child. They have allowed you to interpret my stories, and your dreams will show you the way." He fell silent for a moment, then added, "And I will talk to Black Wolf. I will see that he goes with you for protection."

America thanked the old chief and left the wickiup. Later that night, she told Dancing Feather about her conversation with the chief.

"It is true," Dancing Feather replied as she sorted medicinal herbs. "Many times, I have had dreams that came true or that have helped to guide me in a decision."

"Tell me one," America urged. Even if Dancing Feather's story couldn't help her own decision, she was still fascinated.

Dancing Feather thought a moment. "When I was nine years old, I dreamed that white-faced skeletons were running toward me. I hid in the sagebrush and they passed me by. Two days after my dream, my tribe saw the first white men from afar. The children were terrified."

"Were you scared?" America asked.

Dancing Feather nodded. "I told my father about my dream and he took it seriously, hiding me and my sister in holes under the sagebrush. Other families heard about my dream and followed my father's example. Some of the women were also hidden in case everyone else was killed."

"Why?"

"Someone needed to take care of the children."

America nodded. She could understand that.

Dancing Feather finished her story. "The rest of the tribe met with the white men and it turned out to be a friendly meeting."

America breathed a sigh of relief. "So not all dreams are about bad things."

Dancing Feather paused. "I think dreams give you a glimpse into what could happen. How you react is within your own command."

Besides Dancing Feather, Black Wolf had become increasingly important in America's life. He was there to help her understand complicated communications from the others in their encampment and to discuss the differences in their cultures. With his assistance, America found it easier to adapt to the Paiute life than she had originally thought possible.

As they grew to be closer friends, she became aware that it had been many months since she had experienced the love of a man. By the white man's standards, she should still be mourning. But the day that she braided and cut off her hair was the day that America showed her grief openly to the people of this tribe. She had since learned that her mourning period was as long or as short as she wanted it to be. In the Paiute culture, the widow could begin living again as soon as her parents and in-laws gave her permission. One day, the chief summoned her to his wickiup. Upon her entering, the chief greeted her. "My child, please sit down."

Wordlessly, America had obliged. Mrs. Truckee sat beside her husband.

"America," the chief said, "we know that for many months, you have grieved the loss of your husband, but he is gone now, and you must go on living."

America didn't understand. "But, Chief Truckee, I am living. I am going on."

Mrs. Truckee smiled and held out a hand. America took it. "No, America, I don't think you understand. When Black Wolf told you about our custom of mourning, he did not tell you everything."

America remained silent, waiting for them to finish.

The chief picked up where his wife left off. "America, the parents of the widow and the parents of her dead husband usually go through ritual mourning with her. But you have no one to tell you when it is acceptable to join society again."

America was still puzzled. She had been taking part in the Paiutes' everyday existence. Her bewilderment must have shown. Mrs. Truckee clicked her tongue and leaned forward. "No one is here to tell you when to start loving again, America," she said gently. "But we willingly take up that role. You are free to start loving again. If you love another man, and agree to be his wife, you have our permission."

America felt tears stinging her eyes and she blinked rapidly. "Thank you for your kindness. But I don't think I will ever marry again."

"You are free to do whatever you want to do, America." The chief smiled and bobbed his head. America left, musing over what they had said.

Black Wolf approached her later that afternoon as she sat weaving baskets and staring at the mountains.

"You are still thinking of your daughter."

America turned and nodded. "How can I forget her?"

"The tribe cannot understand how this could happen," he said as he crouched near her.

America sighed and shrugged. "The child needed to be taken care of. The people who came west with me thought I was dead and they buried me."

"Have you decided what you will do, come spring?"

She shook her head. "I'm waiting to make a decision. I'm happy here, and I'm afraid to leave. What if I never find my daughter? What if I can never come back here? I'm hoping for a sign that will help me decide what to do."

Black Wolf took her hand. They hadn't touched often, and she found his hand strong and cool.

"Dreams do not always come when you need them as much as you do. Perhaps you should stop wanting a vision and make a decision on the way that you feel." He stroked the back of her hand. America felt her heart pounding at his touch. "I hope I do not speak out of turn when I tell you that I would like you to consider staying with the tribe, America. I would like you to be my wife."

"You haven't spoken out of turn, Black Wolf," America replied hesitantly.

She had established a deep friendship with this man, but had not experienced any feelings of love for him. She wasn't sure how to answer, since she felt burdened by the other decisions she had to make.

She smiled at him. "I can't give you an answer right now. I need to know that Sierra is alive before I make any decisions about my future. I just don't feel complete without my daughter."

America put aside the unfinished basket and stood up. "I think that the Sanfords are basically good people. We don't see things in the same way, but I think Muriel Sanford will love my little girl like the daughter she never had.

But I am still bothered by the fact that they left me to die. I need to know why they did."

Black Wolf stood beside her. "Then I will go with you, if that is what you decide."

It was toward the end of winter that America had her dream: She was standing in a vast field and from afar, she could see her daughter at the age of one, the Sanfords standing behind her. When she tried to get to Sierra, her feet seemed to be rooted to the ground. But when Black Wolf appeared at her right side, he took her hand and she was able to move. They walked toward Sierra together. When America looked to her left, Dancing Feather was at her side as well.

The next morning, a warm, sunny day on the desert, America told Dancing Feather of her dream. Her friend nodded solemnly. "Then I must go with you across the mountains."

"But that would mean giving up your life here," America replied, stunned that her friend would take her dream so literally.

Dancing Feather smiled. "I can always come back here, if it is what I am meant to do."

Black Wolf had gone away to scout for the cavalry and it was expected that he would not be back for several weeks. It was a pleasant surprise when he turned up suddenly a few days later. Tribe members greeted him warmly, but he hardly acknowledged them, as though something weighed heavily on his mind. He spent a long time in council in the chief's wickiup. When he came out, he still looked lost in thought.

America was elated that she had had a vision that spoke so clearly to her and she saw Black Wolf's return as a sign. She sought him out in his wickiup.

"May I enter?" she asked from outside.

There was a long silence, then a short, "Enter."

America greeted him and told him of her dream. When she was finished, she had expected Black Wolf to offer his scouting abilities without her having to ask him. Instead, he sat without speaking.

"Will you help me?" she finally asked, hating to plead. She wondered if she had done something to offend him, to cause him to turn away from their friendship and his offers.

Black Wolf looked at her, his expression unfathomable. "I stand by my word. I will go with you." He turned away abruptly.

"Black Wolf," she hesitated, not wanting to bring up her recent fears, "have your feelings for me changed?"

He turned back, a startled expression on his face. "No, no." He caught her hand in his. "It's just—I cannot tell you now. But I will help you. We will find Sierra together."

America was relieved to find out that he still wished to be with her, and that he would help her find Sierra. When the time came for her to give him an answer, she already knew what that answer would be. She left the wickiup without another thought about his strange behavior.

PART 3

$\mathcal{C}$ H A P T E R   2 0

Black Wolf suggested that they start out across the Sierras after the piñon nut gathering. America's best guess was that the gathering took place in May. "A party of white men and women tried to cross the mountains in early winter and were caught there," he explained when America asked why they couldn't leave any sooner.

"I was scouting with the army during their search for these people," Black Wolf told her. "We finally found what was left of the wagon train, but there were few survivors and they were in bad condition."

When spring came and they prepared for the journey, the tribe members brought her gifts that would help her on her way. Chief Truckee presented her with a fantailed dapple gray horse for her trip, which America immediately named Fanny. The chief made sure she had plenty of food and supplies, and his wife presented America with a new pair of moccasins she had made herself. On the morning that the trio set out, there were emotional farewells made by all.

The Sierras were nothing like the South Pass that America had crossed with Will and the wagon train. Through the Rockies, the pass had been ten miles wide and thirty miles long. The Sierras rose up like a sheer wall against the backdrop of the basin area.

As they approached, America couldn't help but feel intimidated by the majestic mountains. Even Dancing Feather, who had been chatty most of the first day, fell silent in the shadow of the giant peaks. When America glanced over at Black Wolf, he wore a grim expression.

Day after day, they continued on their way, climbing higher and higher. When they weren't making camp by blue lakes and cool, green pine forests laced with melting white snow, they were traveling through mists so thick America could hardly see her hand in front of her face. The weather turned cooler the higher they went, but she could feel the change as soon as they started to come down the other side. Suddenly the weather became warm, almost like summer.

Throughout the trip, Black Wolf remained as impassive as he had been since his council with Chief Truckee. America was puzzled by his silence, but even more so by his behavior. At first, she thought that his careful actions, such as doubling back and brushing out their tracks in areas where their prints were clearly seen, were just the way of a scout. As time went on, she realized that Black Wolf was concerned about someone following them.

She tried to broach the subject with him several times, but was always met with a rebuff. When she tried to talk to Dancing Feather about it, her friend would change the subject. It was a source of great concern for America and she began to wonder what was being kept from her.

Then the day came when the mists parted and America found herself standing on a ridge, overlooking a valley in which a small town was nestled.

"Sutter's Fort," Black Wolf responded to America's unasked question. He reined back his horse. "This is as far as I can go with you." She started to ask why, but the look on his face did not invite a question.

"I will come to you when you need me," were his only words before he wheeled his horse around and left America and Dancing Feather to make their way down the mountainside.

Sutter's Fort was a dusty little town that had been built up from an old fortress. The bleached wooden storefronts displayed signs with fading paint announcing the dry goods store, the saloons, the hotel, the jail, and the assayer's office. The main street was a well-traveled dirt road—there were rutted wagon tracks and uneven spots where numerous horses had ridden through.

Traveling west affected people in different ways. America could see the look of hope gone from the eyes of some of the people who had made their way west for a better life, only to be bitterly disappointed. In others, she saw the gleam of freedom in their faces and their manners.

America and Dancing Feather got several suspicious looks from the townspeople as they rode into town. The distrustful looks only increased in the days to follow as they conversed in the company of others in Paiute.

America's first act was to find out that it was May 27th. The second thing she did was to find a room and figure out how to make enough money to continue their journey in search of her daughter. It wasn't easy to find a place, as America soon discovered, when accompanied by an Indian woman.

Digging into her medicine bundle once again, this time to save herself, she was able to parlay Jan's garnet ring and Will's diamond earbobs into enough money to rent a small room attached to the back of a blacksmith shop. America thought about Gil Hayes and his children as she parted with the last keepsakes of her former life.

As soon as she was settled, America wrote a letter to her parents, telling them that Will was dead.

"Please convey my deepest sympathies to his dear parents," she wrote to her mother. "I miss him every day, and would give anything to have him by my side again."

She wrote nothing of her missing daughter. That could be saved for another letter, one that would be written after she knew what had become of Sierra. She posted the letter at the general store, where the letter would most likely languish until someone passed through town who was heading east. America wondered how long it would take to reach her parents. Once it reached Independence, it would not be a long journey, but getting from California to Missouri would be a haphazard situation.

America and Dancing Feather had brought rushes along with them, and began making baskets. After they had completed a dozen of them, America carried the baskets through the streets, selling them to the townswomen. At first, it was difficult for her to go from door to door, begging housewives to buy her wares, but after a few days, she discovered she had a knack for talking to the women and getting them interested in buying a basket or two.

As she chatted with these women, she slipped in questions about her daughter and the wagon train that would have arrived in late October. One of her great fears was that her wagon train was the party that had been trapped in the Sierras over the winter.

She soon discovered that the company was called the Donner party, and she hadn't known anyone in her wagon train named Donner. It was a small comfort that several women remembered a wagon train traveling through town around late fall, but they couldn't tell America any more about it.

The two women earned enough money from selling baskets to keep them fed and to pay the rent for the second month. Through word of mouth, housewives sought them out to buy their baskets. One day, one of the women who came to their room to buy a basket brought a child with her. The child had a dry, hacking cough.

"I have something for that," Dancing Feather told America, who translated for the woman.

The woman hesitated, but at last said, "We've tried everything, including remedies given to her by the town doctor. She's had the cough for over four weeks."

Dancing Feather gave her a bag of licorice root, wild cherry, and ginger root. "Mix this with lemon and boil one part to three parts water. Boil it down to a syrup with some sugar or honey and give it to your daughter whenever she needs it."

"I don't remember any lemons back in the village," America said after the woman left. "Where did you learn about those?"

"From Black Wolf."

A few days later the woman with the ill daughter returned. America was afraid that the child had taken a turn for the worse and the woman was going to try to place the blame on Dancing Feather.

"My daughter is better," she said, handing America some coins. "Your friend has cured her. And I've brought my neighbor with me." She indicated the woman by her side.

"You would like to buy a basket?" America asked, getting ready to display their wares.

"No," the neighbor woman replied, shaking her head. "Imogene told me about your cure. If I hadn't seen it with my own eyes . . ." She trailed off, then explained, "My husband had an accident several months ago and his wound won't heal." Her eyes strayed to the Indian woman. "The town doctor has done everything he can. Is there something she can do?"

Although Dancing Feather wasn't familiar enough with English to speak it, she could understand most of the language now. She nodded, gathered herbs and roots together, and began to make a poultice.

Soon word spread that if the doctor couldn't fix up a

person, Dancing Feather had a remedy. Between the baskets and the herbal remedies, the two women did a brisk, profitable business among the townspeople of Sutter's Fort over the next month.

Dancing Feather made friends with several of the town Indians and asked questions about the wagon train as well. She was more successful than America, finding out that it did indeed come through Sutter's Fort in late October, but no one had stayed on in the town.

Since the war with Mexico had still been going on, all of the wagons had taken a northern turn, heading through the Sacramento Valley. The families could have settled anywhere, Dancing Feather told America. They could even have homesteaded nearby and not come to town yet. People who lived in Sutter's Fort wouldn't necessarily notice new settlers who lived outside the area and only came in for supplies.

America had been worried about Black Wolf's disappearance, and questioned Dancing Feather about it. It was clear to her that her friend knew more than she was willing to tell, but the woman wouldn't reveal what she knew.

One night in early June, America went to the town well to fill their basin. When she returned, she heard a rustling from the bushes on the edge of the ravine fifty yards from the entrance to their room. She dropped her basin and let out a small yelp. A strong hand closed around her mouth and dragged her around the corner of the building. When she recognized Black Wolf's voice, she relaxed.

"Do not call attention to yourself," he whispered.

She turned around and reached out to touch his face. "I have been worried about you," she said. In the darkness, she thought she saw him smile. "And I've missed you, too. I wish you could stay with us," she said.

Black Wolf took America by the shoulders and held her away from him. "It is something I wish I could do as well. But I cannot live among white people now."

"Why not?" America asked. "You were educated in a mission."

Black Wolf grimaced and nodded. "It has nothing to do with that."

"Then tell me," America persisted. "Why can't you stay here with us? And why are you sneaking around in the dark like this?"

He fell silent, as if thinking about his options. "America," he finally said, "I have found Sierra."

Her earlier thoughts of Black Wolf's stubbornness were forgotten.

"Where? Is she all right? Do the Sanfords have her? How far away is she?" She stopped herself, knowing how desperate she must sound.

Black Wolf touched her cheek tenderly. "She is with the Sanfords. They are homesteading about twenty-five miles west of here."

America stood as if transfixed. Images of Sierra raced through her mind, her first smile, her first tooth. She must be crawling now, scooting about in a cabin just a short ways from here.

"What do you plan to do?" he asked quietly.

She thought for a minute. It hadn't occurred to her that it would take such a short time to find her daughter. She had spent all her energy preparing for the search, instead of thinking about what she would do once she located her.

Now that America knew where Sierra was, all the anger that had built up the last eight months exploded inside her. She was enraged at Mrs. Sanford's eagerness to bury her and raise her child. She resented the Sanfords for the way they had treated her after Will died, the way the reverend bullied her into giving him money to cover her expenses, not leaving her enough to get settled. The only Sanford she had no ill will toward was their son, Lem.

America had a simple plan, one that would require swallowing her anger when she faced them for the first time since giving birth—she would tell them that she bore no hard feelings about leaving her for dead. And she would get Sierra back.

When she told Black Wolf about her idea, he nodded. "What will you do after you reclaim her?"

"I will go wherever you go," she answered quietly.

His dark brown eyes bore deeply into hers. "Are you telling me you will be my wife?"

"Yes." America blinked. "You accompanied me here even though I hadn't given you an answer to your proposal, and now you've found my daughter. I would be honored to be your wife."

"Then I should tell you why I can't show myself—"

Black Wolf stopped and started again. "Last autumn, after I finished tracking the Donner party for the army, I came by the fort to get my pay. When I got to the captain's office, I found him dead, shot through the heart. The pistol lay on the floor next to his chair."

"Did this happen just before we left the village?"

He nodded.

She was beginning to understand now. "And that's why you were reluctant to go with me."

"Yes."

"So there's a reward for your capture," America said.

"Yes," he repeated. "And the law here in town knows that I've been seen. There were a few young soldiers who spotted me, but they were too drunk to chase me."

America felt Black Wolf tense up as several voices drifted toward them from the street. He let go of her and stepped back into a shadow. When the voices floated away, America whispered, "There has to be a way of proving that you're not guilty. Do they know who the pistol belonged to?"

Her question was met with silence and she looked around to find that Black Wolf had melted back into the darkness. She sat waiting for a half hour, but he did not return.

When she got back to her room, Dancing Feather looked up from dying some rushes red, using goose grass root. "What took you so long?"

"I was visited by Black Wolf," America replied absently.

Dancing Feather looked up from sorting her rushes. "Is something wrong, America?"

"He found my daughter."

"Why, that's wonderful!" Dancing Feather had dropped her handful of rushes and clapped her hands together in delight.

"I also agreed to marry him after we have rescued Sierra." America bit her lip and looked down.

Dancing Feather picked up several reeds and slowly began to weave them together. She cocked her head. "I am happy for you both. I have wanted this ever since you and Black Wolf met at the antelope hunt." She paused, then added, "But you are worried about getting your daughter back, am I right?"

America hesitated, then asked the question that had been bothering her since she had come into the room. "Did you know about the murder in the fort, Dancing Feather?"

Her friend nodded. "Yes, and I'm glad Black Wolf finally told you."

America began pacing the small open space in their room. "I've suffered so many hardships these past two years. I don't know if I can face living with a man who has a reward on his head."

Dancing Feather stood up from her chair with such force that it fell over backward. "I cannot believe this. Your own people left you for dead and my people took you in. Now Black Wolf has found your daughter and wants to provide for both of you, but you would abandon him." She shook her head and mumbled, "I do not understand white ways," before picking up her chair and sitting back down.

America stood silently, watching Dancing Feather put more tule rushes into the red dye. Her long black hair fell forward and with one red-stained hand she pushed the hair back over her shoulder. America could see anger and frustration in each movement.

She sat next to her friend and picked up a rush. "Maybe I was just hurt that you and Black Wolf didn't trust me enough to tell me that he was a wanted man."

Dancing Feather smiled solemnly and put a hand on her friend's shoulder. "I know Black Wolf well. We grew up together and I consider him my brother. If he didn't tell you immediately, it was because he was afraid of losing you. I know that he respects you and wants to make a life with you and your daughter." She hesitated.

"Is there more?" America asked.

"He hasn't said this aloud, but he may think you will stay here in this town, or move to some other town, once you find your daughter."

America thought back to her conversation with Black Wolf. He had seemed surprised that she still wanted to be his wife. It had never occurred to her he might wonder whether she would change her mind once she was back in civilization.

Frankly, since she had been here, she hadn't felt comfortable. As a widow, civilized society had no use for her. She was an outcast, made further so by her close associa-

tion with Dancing Feather and the town Indians. Back in
the desert with the Paiute, she had originally felt out of
place, but the people had accepted her and her situation.

Was there any place on this earth that she belonged?

CHAPTER 21

The next day, America rented a horse and buggy from the stables down the street. She could have used the dapple gray that Chief Truckee had given her for the journey here, but would need a buggy to carry her daughter home.

"Do you want me to go with you?" Dancing Feather looked disquieted as America climbed in.

She shook her head.

"You've heard me speak of my friend, Roaring Bear?" Dancing Feather asked, her cheeks beginning to show a slight flush.

America nodded as she took the reins.

"We've become . . . friendly recently. I hope you don't mind that I told him about Sierra. If you need someone to accompany you—"

"Thank you, dear friend," America said with a smile. "But it would be best if I go unescorted. Knowing the reverend, if he saw me with an Indian, he would probably open fire on us." She sighed. "I'll probably be lucky if he doesn't point his gun in my direction anyway."

"When will you be back?" Dancing Feather asked, her voice thick with concern.

"If I am not back by sunset, you and Roaring Bear should come looking for me." America gave her friend's hand a squeeze, then set the horses into a slow trot.

The trip out to the Sanfords' cabin was hilly and bumpy. If America hadn't become so used to handling rough situations on the journey out west, she might have lost a wheel or worse, a horse.

Wanting to know more about where the Sanfords were living, America had approached some of the women in town earlier this morning. She described the Sanfords and the homestead Black Wolf had told her about. One woman finally recollected the blustery preacher, although she didn't recall him ever having a baby with him. She did have an interesting story to share, however.

The cabin the Sanfords now lived in had stood abandoned since its first owner, a gold prospector, took sick and died. The body had lain there for over six months before anyone came by to find out why the prospector hadn't been into town for supplies over the summer. The stench had kept people from moving in, and before long people had forgotten that the cabin existed.

According to town gossip, when the Sanfords found the place, the reverend believed that God had spoken to him. This was the place that his family was destined to live, so they bid farewell to the wagon train and claimed the cabin and its land as their own.

America felt anxious for most of the trip out to the cabin. She was eager to see her daughter, the baby that had been taken away from her at birth, but she was dreading the first encounter she would have with the Reverend and Mrs. Sanford. She hoped to use the shock the Sanfords would undoubtedly feel upon seeing her alive to convince them to give up her daughter. Deep inside, she had a suspicion that they would fight to keep the baby anyway.

America found the place with no problem. She passed the orchard first, recognizing the peach, pear, and plum trees from back east. The cabin was set back by a stream that ran through the homestead. It was clear that originally it had been a bachelor's one-room, but had been expanded to two rooms by the current owners. The door to the cabin was open when America pulled up, and the moment she stepped from her buggy, Mrs. Sanford came to the door.

Muriel Sanford's hand went to her heart and her mouth dropped open. She seemed to be trying to speak, but nothing came out except a squeak.

America called out, "Mrs. Sanford, I know this is a shock, but—"

As she came toward the cabin, Mrs. Sanford stepped back inside and shut the door. America paused, considering what to do. A moment later, the cabin door opened slightly, and Muriel stuck her nose out the door.

"Mrs. Sanford, I'm sorry to upset you, but I wanted you to know I'm alive and well."

The woman slipped out the door, closing it carefully behind her. "I—I don't know what to say."

America found herself twisting her hands and tried to calm them. "I wanted to know if Sierra is all right."

"Sierra?"

"My daughter."

Mrs. Sanford's eyes shifted toward the cabin door; then, crossing her arms, she turned back to America. "I'm afraid I don't know what you're talking about, Mrs. Hollis."

America became impatient. "I know very well that I bore a little girl, and I am also well aware of the fact that you took her away and left me for dead."

"I'm afraid we don't have her," Mrs. Sanford replied shortly.

"Then where is she?" America couldn't understand Mrs. Sanford's elusive replies.

"She's dead."

America felt as if her heart had stopped. "Dead?"

"Dead." The words came out in a rush. "She died on our way across the Sierras. We buried her up in the snow. The wolves probably got to her body by now."

America thought that she would faint. After all these months, she had finally made the decision to look for her daughter. She had invested all of her emotions in finding the baby, but never for a moment considered that Sierra might not be alive.

She dropped her head and turned back to the buggy when suddenly she heard the sound of a baby crying.

America turned back and looked at Mrs. Sanford. "My daughter is in that cabin, isn't she?" The words came out harshly, in anger.

Mrs. Sanford blocked the cabin door with her body. "You can't have her, Mrs. Hollis." There was a pleading tone in her voice. "I've taken such good care of her and she's mine now."

"You've taken such good care of her, yes," America agreed, before she let the truth spill out, "after you left her mother to die out in the desert. You weren't even sure I was dead, were you? But you convinced everyone in the wagon train that I was gone." A tremble ran through her body and she couldn't control it.

"You wouldn't be a good mother. You're a widow, and you couldn't make a life for Rebecca."

"Rebecca?"

Mrs. Sanford demurred. "We gave her a good Christian name, not some heathen name like Sierra or America. We are bringing her up in a good Christian home."

"She's my daughter," America said in a hard tone. "I've come for her. Please don't do this."

"Rebecca will go nowhere with this godless creature," boomed a voice from behind America. She turned around to face a wrathful Reverend Sanford. "You have no claim to this child."

"I almost *died* for her," America replied, wondering how this man could call himself a Christian. She looked around, but Lem was nowhere in sight. "I'm grateful to you for taking care of her, but as a Christian, you know that you have no right to her."

The reverend strode over to the door to stand beside his wife. "I cannot, in good conscience, let Rebecca leave here with the likes of you."

America blinked. "The likes of me? What do you know of me?"

The reverend shook his finger at her. "Come now, Mrs. Hollis. I have gone into town and seen you in the company of that savage. You are an outcast, poor as Job's turkey. Would you allow your daughter to be raised as such?"

"Better than being raised by a self-righteous devil such as yourself," she retorted before she could get control of her rage.

Mrs. Sanford's hand went to her mouth and the reverend's face turned purple. He pointed down the road, his finger trembling. "Now you git, you whore. Don't come back here."

America ran toward them, determined to see her daughter. The Sanfords were so startled that she got past them and through the open cabin door. When she stepped inside, she saw her daughter playing on the dirt floor with a wooden spoon. Lem sat beside her, holding out a metal pot for Sierra to hit. For a split second, she stopped and marveled at how much Sierra looked like her father.

Lem turned around and his mouth gaped open. Then he broke into a grin. "Mrs. Hollis! You're alive."

"Lem," she said, taking a few slow steps toward the two children, "it's good to see you."

Lem turned to Sierra, then back to America, a knowing look in his eye.

America got down on her knees and spread her arms. "Sierra!" she called out softly.

The child looked up at her with inquisitive eyes just as the reverend's strong hands grabbed America. She could see Lem's pale face and astonished expression as she was dragged backward outside.

"Get away from my daughter, you strumpet!" the reverend shouted.

"No! She's mine; why won't you let me have her?"

Muriel Sanford stood in front of her with a horsewhip in her hand. She snapped it a few inches from America, who instinctively brought her hands up to protect her face. The sting of the lash swept across her wrist, leaving a red welt that started to bleed. Muriel dropped the whip and put her hand to her mouth, obviously startled to see the damage she had done to America.

"Get in your buggy and leave us alone. Leave us alone," the reverend said grimly.

Summoning all her remaining strength, America climbed back into the buggy and took up the reins. She would not let them see her cry. Instead, she turned to them and said calmly, "Why are you doing this?" Her eyes met Muriel Sanford's; then the other woman looked away. She knew the answer. Mrs. Sanford had told her that she wanted a daughter. "I will be back. With the marshal next time."

Muriel and Reverend Sanford looked at each other, then looked back at America. "Fine," the reverend said. "Bring him. We'll see who he decides is fit to raise this child."

As soon as America reached town, she ran into her

room. Sobbing between each word, she was finally able to tell Dancing Feather what had happened. Her friend's expression became more distressed with each detail of cruelty.

"This cannot happen, America. This would not happen in our world."

America nodded sadly. "I think I was expecting everything to turn out happily, but I forgot how much Mrs. Sanford wanted a daughter. They believe it was the hand of God that gave them this baby, and the fact that I have presented myself and asked for my baby back is just another test of their faith in God."

"But you believe in this God as well," Dancing Feather pointed out.

America smiled weakly, wondering how much of that was true these days. Faith had been a difficult ideal to maintain during her journey west. Her faith had remained strong when Jan died and when she discovered she was pregnant. She lost a little of it the day she consented to marry Will Hollis, but found her faith again when she discovered she loved him. It had diminished when Will died, then faded almost completely when she woke up without her baby.

But now, America had faith that she would get her child back. She couldn't help remembering that her husband had been a lawyer, and would have known what to do. Her father had been one of the finest lawyers in Philadelphia and was one of the most respected judges in the city. What would he do under such circumstances? She wished he were here to advise her, but there was no time to waste. She could only hope that the Sutter's Fort marshal would be able to help her.

The following day, after she had gotten what little sleep she could manage, America dressed carefully in her new store-bought dress. As soon as she and Dancing Feather had earned enough money for rent and food, America had gone to the general store and bought a plain blue-sprigged calico and the undergarments that she hadn't missed during her time in the desert. With reluctance, she took off the medicine bag from around her neck.

She also donned the new boots that she had bought for appearing in public. When she was making baskets, America went barefoot, as did Dancing Feather, but she didn't want the townspeople to think of her as primitive, especially since she wanted to make a good impression on the marshal. Dancing Feather didn't offer to go with her this time. In fact, her friend had gone off to meet Roaring Bear.

There wasn't a mirror in their room—mirrors were expensive—and this was one time that America wished she still had her silver-back hand mirror to see what she looked like. Her hair had grown to shoulder-length and was coming in wavy. It was long enough for her to catch it up in a snood that she had made with a bit of lace and a length of red ribbon.

As she walked to the marshal's office, she caught sight of herself briefly in the big front window of the dry goods store and was amazed that she looked like most of the women here in town. It was reassuring to know that on the exterior, America seemed to fit in.

When America entered Marshal Nick Gates's office, she was encouraged to see that the lawman was there. He was in his mid-forties, with slicked back hair and a clipped beard with no mustache. He was a handsome man, and America had heard from some of the women who bought her baskets and Dancing Feather's herbal remedies that Marshal Gates was an eligible bachelor. The marshal stood up behind his desk and looked her over.

"How can I help you, Miss—" he asked eagerly.

"Mrs. Hollis," America replied. "America Hollis."

He came out from behind the desk and offered his hand. Summoning all of her Philadelphia charm, America took his hand and smiled. "I'm afraid I've come with a sad story."

He looked around and found a chair for her to sit in. "Please. Tell me your story, Mrs. Hollis," he said in a solicitous manner that told America that he found her attractive. The twinkle in his eye told America that she had to be careful—he might not take her seriously if she flirted too much to gain his attention.

She launched into her tale of losing her daughter and finding her again, leaving out some of the details.

"And these people ran you off their property?" He was stroking his beard now as if he was in deep thought.

"Yes. And they won't give me back my daughter," America said, finding it hard to keep the tremor out of her voice.

"And what have you come to me for?" He had stopped flirting. It was clear that her story disturbed him. But his reaction wasn't what she had expected.

America put her hand on her breast and fluttered her eyelashes. "Why, I thought you might go out to the Sanfords' place with me and talk to them."

"Mrs. Hollis." He hesitated, then went on, avoiding her eyes. "The Sanfords have already been in this morning, and their tale is quite different from yours."

America stood up, startled by the extent of the Sanfords' duplicity.

The marshal gestured for her to sit down. "They say that you lost your baby on the trip here."

"But that's not true! I saw my child in their cabin."

Marshal Gates's expression was troubled. "But you can't positively identify this little girl as your own, can you?"

America sat in stunned silence for a moment. "Marshal Gates, a mother knows her own child. Besides, Reverend and Mrs. Sanford admitted to me that she was my child, but they wouldn't let me have her."

She could see from his expression that he would need more convincing. "You don't believe me, do you? Reverend Sanford and his wife are lying so they can keep my daughter and raise her as their own. On the wagon train, Muriel Sanford told me several times that she wished she had been able to bear a daughter. And when my daughter was born, they left me by the side of the road in a shallow grave." The marshal winced. "If it weren't for the Paiute—"

He leaned forward, folded his hands, and studied them as he talked to her. "Look, Mrs. Hollis, there is very little I can do without evidence. I have no reason to believe the reverend is lying, other than your word. Is there someone else who can confirm your version, someone who was on the wagon train?"

America slumped in her chair. So it was still up to her. Nothing came easy out here in the West—including her daughter. She took a minute to collect herself, then stood up and smoothed her skirt. "I can see that you are not willing to help me with my plight," she replied with as much dignity as she could muster. "Thank you for your time, Marshal."

"Mrs. Hollis," he called out as she reached for the door. She turned. There was compassion in his eyes. "Maybe your daughter would best be left with the Sanfords. She knows them as her parents now, and," he hesitated before going on, "they say that you live with an Indian woman here in town. Now, there's nothing wrong with an Indian as a servant, but they say you act as if you're friends, not mistress and servant. Is that how you want to bring up your daughter?"

"Dancing Feather *is* my friend, Marshal Gates. She saved my life, which is more than I can say for the Sanfords."

CHAPTER 22

Dancing Feather was back in the room when America returned. It appeared that her friend had gone on a gathering trip without her to replenish their tule rush supply. Herbs and roots for the dyes were scattered all around her in individual piles on the floor. There was also a large Indian with her. The frown he wore probably made a lot of townsfolk nervous. If he wasn't obviously a friend of Dancing Feather's America would have been a bit nervous herself.

"Roaring Bear, this is my friend, America," Dancing Feather formally introduced them in halting English. She tucked her arm into his. "America, this is Roaring Bear, of the Klamath tribe."

America smiled, but Roaring Bear didn't. She glanced at her friend, who smiled sadly and continued comfortably in Paiute. "We know about the Sanfords coming into town to meet with the marshal this morning. I'm so sorry."

Roaring Bear came forward, his hands reaching out toward America. She had to force herself not to take a step back. "I, too, am sorry. I discovered the information too late to stop you from going to the marshal."

America smiled and touched his shoulder. "Thank you, Roaring Bear. But I probably would have gone anyway."

Dancing Feather stood up with a bunch of rosemary and hung it from the rafter that crossed the middle of the room. America inhaled the smell, the phrase, "Rosemary for remembrance," coming to her mind. "What will you do now?"

America sat down on the bed. Would she be able to find someone from the wagon train who would remember? "I suppose I must look for other members of the wagon train to confirm my story. Someone else must have settled nearby."

America knew that if anyone she knew from the wagon train was living nearby, it wasn't here in Sutter's Fort. She had been here over a month and had not run across anyone familiar. No, she decided, the emigrants would probably be living in similar circumstances to the way the Sanfords lived—near a town, but not in a town. That meant that she would have to outfit herself so that she could travel by horse.

With some of the money they had amassed from their business, America bought a saddle for Fanny. As an afterthought, she purchased a gun as well. As she well knew, there were many dangers out on the trail—some she could not plan for, but other dangers would be easily dealt with if she had a loaded pistol by her side.

The night before she left, someone knocked on the

door. When she opened it, a package of dressed venison sat on the ground outside.

Dancing Feather stood just behind her. "Black Wolf wants you to meet him by the ravine."

America turned around, startled. "You can tell all that from the deer meat?"

Dancing Feather laughed. "No. He told Roaring Bear this morning, and the message was relayed to me. The meat is just the signal."

It was a clear, starry night with no moon in the sky—dark by most white people's standards, but out in the desert, America had become comfortable with the blackness that surrounded her.

"Did you see your daughter?" Black Wolf asked immediately upon meeting.

"Yes, I did," she answered, grasping his outstretched hands in hers.

"You do not sound happy. What is the matter?"

"Sierra is with the Sanfords, but they lied to the marshal and told him that she's not my daughter." She told him of her visit, and the disrespect with which they treated her. "The marshal thinks I am one of those grief-stricken women who sees her dead daughter in every babe she encounters."

Black Wolf inspected the lash mark on her wrist and his expression grew dark. "You cannot allow them to keep Sierra."

She nodded wearily. "I'm afraid for her."

Black Wolf's hand touched her cheek. "We will go after her together. Tonight."

America pulled away. "No. I can't allow you to get in more trouble."

He looked amused. "I have nothing to lose. If I am caught for killing that soldier, I will be hanged."

"I couldn't bear to lose you if you were caught trying to get Sierra for me. And what if the army finds the real killer?"

He shook his head. "They will not try. It is convenient for an Indian to be blamed. The army wants to believe that I am the killer."

"Tell me the whole story," she urged, clutching his hand tightly.

"I was scouting for the army, searching for the party that was lost in the Sierras last winter. I came back to the fort to report my findings, and found the colonel at his desk, shot. The pistol was laying on the floor beside him." Black Wolf walked to the edge of the ravine, his back to America. She came up behind him and laid her hand on his shoulder. "I made the mistake of picking up the gun to examine it, thinking I might recognize it. Lieutenant Markham walked in then."

"Did you tell him what you had found?"

Black Wolf turned around to face her. She could see that it was hard for him to talk about it. "The lieutenant and I are not friendly. I knew immediately that I would be blamed. I pointed the pistol at him and used him as a hostage to make my escape. Then I left him a few miles out in the desert. Later, I doubled back and made my way to your village."

"Do you have any idea who killed the colonel?"

Black Wolf squatted and picked up a stick. He drew random figures in the moist dirt by the ravine. "I didn't know him well, but he didn't think much of the lieutenant." He shook his head shortly. "It doesn't matter. Even if Lieutenant Markham did it, I would still be the one to hang."

America found a tree stump nearby and sat on it. "But if they discover that the lieutenant killed the colonel—"

Black Wolf shot her a harsh look. "It would never come out. The white man does not think well of the Indian. To most white men, we are lying, sneaking, murdering thieves."

America lowered her eyes and fell silent. Black Wolf stopped drawing crude pictures and walked over to her side. "I am sorry for the way my people treat you."

He stood up and stared into her face. "Don't apologize. At least you are not that way." Their eyes met.

Black Wolf's expression became inscrutable. "You have come back to the white man's world, and if this is what you want, I will understand. But I have risked coming into town to see you, and I will continue to help you get Sierra back. But I may have to disappear for a time. I need to know if I should come back."

America had pondered the question often. She and Black Wolf had become good friends over the winter. She did not love him, neither in the burning way that she had loved Jan nor in the comfortable way that she had loved Will. But she respected him and would be happy as his companion and life mate.

Her realization had come with a price—she would have to give up the idea of living in the world that she grew up in. Black Wolf could never adapt to this life, even if the army rescinded the bounty on his head.

"I don't feel comfortable here anymore," she admitted. "I've changed so much since I left the East."

A lock of hair escaped her bun and Black Wolf reached out to gently tuck it back in. "You have had to adapt to many strange circumstances. But you may have to adapt even more if you are to live with an Indian with a reward on his head."

Her answer was in her fingertips as she touched his face, gently running them down his neck to his bare chest. Black Wolf lifted her in his arms and carried her over to a mossy bed under a weeping willow. It was there that she told him with her body that she respected and appreciated him. It was there that America knew she would never be alone again.

It was well after midnight when she returned to her room. She entered quietly, assuming that her roommate would be asleep, but found Dancing Feather humming as she readied for bed.

"Am I to assume you've been with Roaring Bear?" America asked, happy that her friend had found someone special.

Dancing Feather nodded. "And how was your meeting with Black Wolf?" she asked, pulling a clump of grass from America's hair.

America blushed. "Fine."

Dancing Feather sat at their working table, suddenly serious. "Have you decided what you will do?"

America knew well that Dancing Feather was referring to Sierra and the Sanfords. She shook her head. "No. Black Wolf suggested that we take her by force."

Dancing Feather frowned. "Time is getting short for him."

"What do you mean?"

Her friend stared at her. "Did he not tell you? One of Lieutenant Markham's soldiers recognized him."

"Yes, he told me that, but I thought he had escaped them."

Dancing Feather shook her head. "There were more soldiers today in town, asking Roaring Bear and the other Indians about him."

"Then he'll be safe, won't he?" After the words left her mouth, America remembered that town Indians were not the same as the Paiutes she had lived with.

"There are some who do not look out for their brothers. Black Wolf has enemies here, and not just the white man."

"Enemies?" America asked. "I thought the Paiutes had very few enemies."

"The Shoshone have many enemies, and Black Wolf carries Shoshone blood."

"I see. Then I guess I don't have much time to find a member of the wagon train who can verify that Sierra is my daughter."

Dancing Feather walked over to her friend and put a hand on her arm. "You must ride out early tomorrow and start looking."

"I'm not even sure where to start."

"Go to the end of the trail and start from there."

It was still dark when America rode out the next morning. There was a chill in the air and the trail to Sacramento was settled with low mists. The heavy, wet air clung to America's face until she felt as if she had just stepped out of a cold spring. She pulled her Indian blanket coat closer around her shoulders, feeling the rhythm of Fanny, the dapple gray, as they alternately plodded up hills and trotted down vales. The weight of the pistol lay against her side, tucked into her skirt waistband, for lack of a holster.

She stopped at a trading post in the late afternoon for a meal, and a few questions. The owner recalled the wagon train coming through in October of last year, but he couldn't recall how many had been in the company.

"There are never too many by the time they get here," he said. "Only the ones who have Sacramento or San Francisco in mind from the get go."

"Do you remember if Mr. Terwilliger was with them?" She described him.

The trading post owner, a short, stocky man with a permanent squint, moved the cigar clamped between his teeth from one side of his mouth to the other, without using his hands. "Seems like the feller in charge, all right. I think he told me he was only goin' as far as Sacramento."

"And you haven't seen him since?" she asked, brightening with hope.

He shook his head. "Not this season. Of course, he might have gone up to Oregon."

America recalled Addie Schreck and Tal Bowen with a sinking heart. Terwilliger probably did go up that way. Captain Conway was another possibility, but she doubted that she could squeeze a character reference out of him. But maybe the Tobiases were still around.

"Do you recall a Negro couple?"

The man lit his cigar and sucked on it until the end was a glowing ember. "Don't recall them. I'd remember 'em."

She paid for a bed for the night, and in the morning, headed to Sacramento. When she got there, the town was so big, she felt lost. Philadelphia had never felt this big, and Sacramento couldn't have a tenth of its population. She felt like a foreigner, walking the streets, looking for information that was vital to her. When she was glad to come across Captain Conway staggering out of a saloon, she knew she was desperate.

"Captain Conway," America said, stepping closer to him. "Do you remember me? From the wagon train?"

He stepped back, stinking of raw whiskey and tobacco, and turned pale. "You're—you're supposed to be dead. We buried you."

"Prematurely," was the only thing she could think of to say. She stepped toward him again. "Captain, I need your help."

"I ain't got your necklace, lady," he said in a loud voice. America looked around, realizing that he was creating a scene and several passersby had slowed down.

She felt her cheeks burning, but she carried on. "No, that wasn't what I was going to ask you. Is anyone still here from the company, besides you?"

He thought for a moment. "The captain's gone. Went up north to Oregon. That nigger couple you were so friendly with went to San Francisco, I think. And a couple of the men went south to join the war against Mexico when they got to California. Don't know if they're alive or where they'd go after that."

Dismay was the only emotion America felt. But if Conway was the only choice, she would have to see where this conversation led her. "A little girl was born to me on the trail. Do you remember?"

He peered uncertainly at her. "Yes, I remember you. I remember." *Rosemary for remembrance,* she thought.

"The Reverend and Mrs. Sanford took the child in after you buried me, didn't they?"

He hesitated, swaying on his feet. America breathed in his presence only when she felt it was necessary. "Ye—es. They did, that. Mrs. Sanford said she'd always wanted a daughter."

"I have found them and my daughter. And they won't

give her to me now. Would you be willing to go back to Sutter's Fort and testify in my favor?"

He bent over, and America thought for a moment that he was going to be sick. She stepped back so he wouldn't throw up on her good boots. But he straightened up quickly and roared with laughter. When he had slowed down to a chuckle and wiped tears from his eyes, he said, "You thought you was better than me, didn't you? Back then on the trail, acting so high and mighty about them slaves."

America closed her eyes, her last vestige of hope seeping away like water absorbed by sand. She opened her eyes again when she felt his rough hands shaking her, pulling her into a nearby alley. She looked and considered calling out for help, but there wasn't a person in sight of the alley.

"Look at me, dammit, when I'm talking to you." He stuck his face close to hers and she winced, turning her face away from the stink of his breath. "So I'm your only hope, huh? I like it. Oh, how I like it."

He let her go suddenly and backed away, dancing a drunken jig. America's eyes darted around, watching the street. Two men were passing by and she was about to call out for help; then Conway was back in her face again. "But it'll cost you, lady. It'll cost you more than your pretty little pearls." He grabbed her arm roughly and pulled her close. "And it'll cost you more than what's in your purse if you want to see your daughter again."

America's heart felt like it was bound tightly to the

point of bursting. She had to make a decision, and realized in a heartbeat what that decision might cost her. Her free arm snaked around and grabbed the butt end of the pistol on her waistband. She pulled it out and stuck the gun in his neck. "Get your hands off me," she said quietly.

"You wouldn't use that thing," he said with a grin. His hand grabbed her buttock and squeezed hard enough for America to ascertain that she would have black-and-blue marks there.

She responded by shoving the gun harder against his throat. "If you don't remove your hand and back away, I will kill you." America was surprised how calm her voice sounded. "I'm sure I can get some witnesses to back up my claim of self defense. It sounds as if they are easy to hire, if you are any example."

Conway paused to consider her words, then seemed to think better of his actions and backed off.

"Now," she said, still pointing the gun at him from a safer distance, "will you come back to Sutter's Fort with me and verify that the Sanfords have my daughter?"

He scowled. "Madam, I wouldn't spit on your grave for five dollars." Conway turned around with as much dignity as a nasty drunk could muster, and started toward the street. America watched her last hope walk away.

When he got to the opening of the alley, he turned around and gave her a sweet smile. "In fact, I might just head to Sutter's Fort and testify in the Sanfords' behalf. I'm sure they will reward me well for my efforts."

As he left, America involuntarily brought the gun up with both hands and aimed it at Captain Conway's back. She had to make a conscious effort to keep her finger off the trigger.

CHAPTER 23

Without a vestige of hope left, America left Sacramento and headed back to Sutter's Fort. She traveled on, not stopping to sleep, and stopped only once to rest her horse. There was a full moon to travel by, and for that, she was grateful.

By the time she got back to the edge of town, the sun was winking at her over the horizon. Fanny hadn't once complained or acted in a stubborn manner, but America could feel how weary the dapple gray was. When she brought her into the stable to board, the horse went right to the oats and couldn't be budged.

America had also come to a conclusion: she would have to steal her own daughter from the Sanfords, and she would let Black Wolf know tonight, if he came to meet her. When America opened the door to her room, Dancing Feather wasn't there to greet her. But what did greet her was a room that had been searched. The baskets and rushes had been tossed around, as had her bedclothes and her two dresses.

She pulled the pistol out of her waistband and stepped over the threshold, wary of anything that might move in the room. A mouse scurried out the door and her gun followed it as her finger hovered nervously over the trigger. Taking a deep breath, she slumped against the wall and surveyed the damage.

America was cleaning up when Dancing Feather walked through the door. Her friend's tight expression told America that something was very wrong.

"Black Wolf has been captured. Marshal Gates has him in the jail. There is a load of new lumber arriving today and the marshal has said that he wants the scaffold to be strong." There were tears in Dancing Feather's eyes.

America sat on the mattress as if someone had pushed her down by force. "How did it happen?"

Her friend began to clean up their room. "I see that the soldiers have been here. They found out that we are friends of Black Wolf. They must have searched this room just before they found him."

"Dancing Feather, tell me, how did it happen?" America asked again.

The young Indian woman abandoned her cleaning and sat down next to her. "He tried to abduct the child."

America's hands went up to her mouth. "No." She shook her head quickly. "He did that for me?" She wasn't sure whether to love him or be angry with him for taking such a fool chance.

Dancing Feather quickly nodded her assent. "I told you before you left that someone had spotted Black Wolf here in town, and he knew it was just a matter of time before he would have to disappear. He thought if he could get Sierra for you, you could go away together."

America covered her eyes. "Of all the foolish—" She broke off and took her hand away from her face. "When did they capture him?"

"Sometime last night. Yesterday afternoon, Roaring Bear came by our room and told me that he had heard that the army would be coming by to search our room. He wanted me to go with him."

America shuddered at the thought of Dancing Feather facing soldiers alone and unarmed. They would not have treated her well. "I'm glad that you're safe. Should we leave here now?"

Dancing Feather shook her head, anger still residing in her eyes. "These men have what they came looking for— Black Wolf. We'll be safe now." She hesitated. "What do you plan to do now?"

America thought. It was time for her to do something. Black Wolf had tried, and now she had to act. "How long do I have before, well—" She couldn't bring herself to say the words "they hang him."

Dancing Feather seemed to understand. She frowned in thought. "Tomorrow morning at sunrise. That is what I have heard."

She nodded and stood up. "I will go out to the Sanfords and get my baby. Then I will come back for Black Wolf." She stopped and took her friend by the shoulders. "Will you help me?"

"I will. And so will Roaring Bear." There had been something different about Dancing Feather, something

America couldn't put her finger on. But it was when their eyes met that America realized that her friend could not help her.

"You can't go with me."

Dancing Feather blinked and stood up. "Why?"

America smiled. "You're with child."

Dancing Feather looked stricken. "Please, America, let me help."

America gave her friend a gentle hug. "You cannot endanger your child. When I carried Sierra, I had to make some decisions that I didn't necessarily want to make. Sometimes I had to think of my child first, before anyone else."

Dancing Feather closed her eyes. "Then at least let Roaring Bear go with you. I can speak for him."

America laughed. "And if we're caught, both Black Wolf and Roaring Bear will be hanged. And you would be left without a husband and a father for your child. No. This is best done by the one person who has nothing to lose and everything to gain."

After a few moments of silence, Dancing Feather began taking apart one of her deerskin dresses.

"What are you doing?" America asked, bewildered by her friend's actions. Her friend only had two dresses, and she was wearing one of them.

Without looking up, Dancing Feather replied, "Making a carrier for Sierra." She looked up, her expression serious. "You haven't thought of how you plan to carry the baby away from the Sanfords, have you?"

America realized that she would have to be on a horse, not in a buggy, for a faster escape. And it was true—she hadn't thought of how she would transport her baby. From the glimpse she had gotten of Sierra, she would need something to strap her child down.

Dancing Feather worked all afternoon and when she was finished she had a carrier that would fasten onto the front of a saddle and around America's waist. They brought it out to Fanny, saddled her up, and attached the makeshift papoose, using a bag of sugar as a substitute baby. When America sat on the horse and affixed the straps, she was assured that Sierra would be safe.

"Thank you, Dancing Feather," she said as she untrapped the carrier and dismounted. "It works just fine."

Her friend made some minor adjustments to the pack. "I do not like to leave you to do this alone, America. I wish you would accept my offer of taking Roaring Bear with you."

America sighed. "The more people involved, the more chances of getting caught."

"Black Wolf was alone, and he was captured."

America didn't answer Dancing Feather right away. Her mind was turning over possibilities. Finally, she turned to the woman, her expression grim. "There is one more thing you and Roaring Bear can do for me—"

America had only practiced with Will's flintlock a couple of times, but she found it easier to use than the pistol. When Roaring Bear provided her with a flintlock and a supply of powder and lead, she was ready to use it. By late afternoon, she had strapped it to her back, saddled her horse, and was on the road toward the Sanfords.

She studied their homestead from a hilltop, concealed by a group of horse chestnuts, and watched the comings and goings of the family. Mrs. Sanford only came outside once to take in the wash while she hummed "Bringing in the Sheaves." Sierra accompanied her, playing with a rag doll.

America was tempted to face Muriel Sanford alone and take Sierra right then, but she knew that the reverend would follow her into town. Her timing had to be right.

Mr. Sanford and his son didn't come in from the orchard until suppertime. When they did make an appearance, they carried baskets of ripe fruit. America's mouth watered at the sight and she realized she hadn't eaten all day.

It was difficult to sit and wait for the perfect opportunity. As she went over the possibilities again in her mind, it came to her in a sudden flash what she had to do. Examining her scheme from every conceivable angle, she felt comfortable with her plan of attack.

In those hours between planning the rescue and executing it, America had never felt so alone. She only hoped she could get Sierra in time to rescue Black Wolf, too. Then her life would be complete again.

America studied the layout of the cabin and where the horses were corralled. Try as she might, she couldn't remember the inside of the cabin. She had only been in the cabin for a few seconds, so she didn't know where the Sanfords kept all their guns. She would have to take a chance on finding them.

It was late in the evening when the lights were finally extinguished, and America waited an extra half hour to make sure everyone had gone to bed. Since the moon was full, she picked her way down to the homestead without much trouble. Tethering Fanny loosely to a tree nearby, she made her way to the shed, where she took the bridles.

The Sanfords' three horses were grazing down in the pasture. America had taken several pears from the baskets in front of the cabin and now she extended them as an offering. The horses willingly followed her out of the gate, not one of them making a sound to wake their owners. After fitting them with bridles and bits, America led them to the same area where her own dapple gray was tied and left them grazing peacefully.

Next, she made sure her pistol was tucked snugly inside her waistband in case she needed it fast. Approaching the cabin, she stepped on the porch and a board groaned under her weight. She stopped and waited, listening, but heard no movement inside. The door opened easily and she slipped inside. Once again, America stood in one place and listened to the sounds to make sure that she was the only one awake and to let her eyes adjust to the dark.

Lem was asleep on a straw mattress by the fireplace, and was snoring so loudly, it was difficult for America to keep herself from exploding in a fit of laughter. She realized that her nervousness was causing the giddiness, so she took a deep breath to calm herself.

She didn't see Sierra. The child wasn't with Lem, but America spied a doorway covered by a blanket. It must be a two-room cabin, she thought, then remembered that the Sanfords had been building onto it when she had visited last time.

Taking a deep breath, she moved silently across the cabin floor and through the blanket-covered opening. It was dark and stuffy inside, and she could hear the reverend muttering passages from the Bible. She thought she recognized a quote from the book of Ezekiel.

America realized that there was no window in this room, and she wouldn't have the advantage of moonlight to negotiate the room. When the reverend's voice thickly recited a Bible verse, America felt as if she were standing right next to him. And, in fact, she discovered she was.

Taking a step back, she felt her way around the form of the bed until her ankle bumped up against a low wooden frame. As she bent down, she heard the soft breathing of a baby. The newness of her smell filled America's head and tugged at her heart. Gently, she reached for Sierra.

The flare of a match and a shriek startled her. Turning her head, America looked right into Muriel's pale face. The reverend snorted and turned over. America noticed that Mrs. Sanford was groping around by her bedside.

"Tarleton! Lem! Wake up! That harlot is trying to take my baby away!"

America stood up and pulled the flintlock up. "Put

your hands in your lap, Muriel. I've come for my child, but I don't want to shoot anyone."

"You won't get her," Mrs. Sanford spat as she put her hands slowly in her lap. "We'll send the marshal after you. We told him how crazy you are."

Her husband had finally roused himself, rubbing the sleep from his eyes. His face sagging with interrupted sleep, the reverend reached out to pat his wife's hand. "Muriel, do what she says. A woman with a gun is unpredictable."

Muriel shot him a venomous look. "She's taking *our* daughter, Tarleton. Rebecca is ours."

In the middle of the night, the reverend didn't look as fearsome as he did with a Bible in his hand and a thunderous and righteous tone in his voice.

"Reverend Sanford," America began, "you know full well that this is my daughter. I tried to be reasonable. I tried to be fair, but you wouldn't listen. You think you can make pronouncements and they will be taken for gospel. But I carried this little girl for nine months, and I didn't do it just so you and your wife could have a daughter. I didn't do it just so you could scorn her real mother and tell lies about me. How righteous is it to lie to the law, or to a child, for that matter?"

There was silence. For once, the good reverend had nothing to say. But he continued to glare at her. America kept her flintlock trained on the couple while using her free arm to pick up Sierra. America had fully expected her baby to start crying because her sleep was disturbed, but

Sierra nestled into her arm as if she had always belonged there. She was about to leave the room when she remembered Lem. She gestured with the gun.

"Both of you, get out of bed."

"I'll do no such thing," the reverend sputtered.

Muriel appeared to have had the wind knocked out of her. Her back slumped against the wall and tears ran down her cheeks quietly.

"Now."

They slowly got out of their bed. Clutching their nightwear around their forms, they shuffled over to the doorway.

"You go through ahead of me," she ordered, then called out to Lem. "Your parents are coming out of here first. I will be behind them with my daughter in my arms. I have a gun and will not hesitate to shoot them if you try to stop me."

From the other room, Lem's sleepy voice replied, "Come on out, Mrs. Hollis. I don't have a gun."

Slowly, they came into the other room. America lined up the family in front of the fireplace. It was a warm night, so when Mrs. Sanford shivered, it must have been from fear.

"You won't get far," the reverend said. "We'll ride after you."

America smiled. "It might be difficult without your horses."

"You're stealing our horses?" Lem asked, his eyes widening.

America softened slightly. "I apologize, Lem. You were always kind to me. I'm borrowing them to make it inconvenient for you to get to town," she explained. "They will be in Sutter's Fort tethered to the hitching post in front of the marshal's office by tomorrow morning."

"We can walk there in a few hours," Mrs. Sanford replied. The reverend shot her a look to silence her, but it was already too late.

"Then I guess we'll have to do something with your clothes." America looked around and saw Lem's clothes hanging over the back of a chair. Then she saw a washtub filled with water in the corner by the fireplace.

"Put those clothes in the water. Mrs. Sanford, you'll go back into the bedroom and get the rest of your clothes and put them into the water as well."

"But—but—" The woman was at a loss for words, but she moved back into the bedroom as she was told.

"Remember," America called out, "we did laundry side by side on the trail, and I know you own three dresses, and the reverend has two coats, three shirts, and two pairs of pants."

She was only guessing at how many items of clothing they had, but it seemed to work because Mrs. Sanford came out with a bundle of clothes in her arms and a sour expression on her face. America made her drop the clothes in the water one by one, soak them thoroughly, and put them on the floor. Next, she told Lem to throw their pistols and flintlocks into the water.

"Aw, Mrs. Hollis, don't make me do that," Lem groaned. "It'll ruin them."

America nodded at the washtub. "Dry them out real good and use a clean cloth, then use bear grease."

Lem sighed and dropped the weapons into the water, one by one. When the last flintlock was immersed, America started to back out the door. For just a moment, she caught Lem's eye and he smiled at her. She nodded slightly to him in response.

The Sanfords' clothes would dry out by midday in the strong summer sun; then there would be the walk into town. She shouldn't have a problem with them once she left their homestead. Muriel came to the door, followed by Tarleton and Lem. They watched as she strapped Sierra into the pack that Dancing Feather had crafted.

"God will punish you," Reverend Sanford intoned in a shaky voice. "You shouldn't take what isn't meant to be yours."

"After all we did for you," Mrs. Sanford said as she choked back tears. "We took you in when you had no place to stay on the trail. Look at what our Christian charity has cost us—Rebecca is rightfully ours."

"I gave birth to her," America replied, swallowing the resentment and frustration that was eating at her, "and my daughter is not chattel to be used for payment of a debt. But if it's payment you want." America took the bag from around her neck, the bag that held the money she had saved from the baskets, and she threw it at them. "I think have paid a dear price for your Christian charity, and I owe you nothing more."

A moan escaped from Muriel as America settled herself into the saddle and took up the reins of their horses. Fanny began to move at a slow trot, the Sanford horses following in their wake.

"Don't take my baby!"

"Muriel, get ahold of yourself!" the reverend said in a stern tone. It was the last thing America heard from the Sanfords as she headed toward Sutter's Fort and the most dangerous part of her journey.

CHAPTER 24

On the way back to town, Sierra seemed to sense that something was wrong, that her world was changing. She began to cry. America crooned a lullaby that her mother had sung to her when she was a child. Rocked by Fanny's slow gait and her mother's song, Sierra finally fell asleep.

It was still dark when, halfway to town, America spied two shadowy figures on horseback up ahead. They were blocking the road. She tensed, but continued to approach them.

One of the figures raised a hand in greeting and America returned the salutation. Moonlight fell on Dancing Feather's features and she was smiling, obviously pleased by America's success. Roaring Bear nodded his approval to America and they turned their horses around, beckoning her to follow them. They all stopped by a stream, well out of the way of the trail. Black Wolf's Appaloosa was tied to a bush nearby.

When they dismounted, Dancing Feather lifted Sierra out of her pack and held her up. "She's beautiful!" Dancing Feather declared.

Awake now, Sierra gurgled and looked down in a

benevolent manner at Dancing Feather. A few tiny
bounces in the air produced a wet smile from Sierra and a
little laugh. Dancing Feather held the baby out to America, who took her and held her close, breathing in the
fresh smell, feeling the wisps of hair tickle her chin and the
tiny hands clutch convulsively at the collar of her dress.

Roaring Bear broke into America's reverie. "The gallows were finished just before the sun set today."

A jolt of fear shot through America's body, but she
took care to maintain an outward calm.

"Let me come with you," he said. "I can help Black
Wolf escape, and we can all leave together."

America shook her head. "If anything happens to me,
to us, I need someone to raise my child." She looked
meaningfully at Dancing Feather, then turned to Roaring
Bear. "She's going to need a father as well as a mother. If
we don't return to this spot by eight tomorrow morning,
I want you to disappear with Sierra. Go back to Oregon
Territory to the Klamath."

Roaring Bear looked very unhappy, but he nodded reluctantly. America handed Sierra to Dancing Feather and
kissed her daughter on the cheeks and the forehead. Without another word, she got back on Fanny, took the reins
of Black Wolf's Appaloosa and the Sanfords' horses, and
left.

The hidden sun illuminated the sky as America rode
into town. She stopped only once along the road to make
sure her flintlock and her pistol were loaded and ready in
case she needed to use them.

Although she thought she was prepared for it, the sight of the scaffold in the center of town sent a shock through her. She touched her pistol reassuringly and was relieved that only a few people were on the streets at this early hour. When she arrived at the jailhouse, it was on shaky legs that she dismounted and tied Fanny and the other horses to the hitching post.

While she was searching for the best place to ambush the marshal when he escorted Black Wolf to the gallows, the jailhouse door opened and Marshal Gates stepped out, followed by a shackled Black Wolf. The lawman paused just outside and swept the immediate area with a hawk-like gaze. He apparently didn't notice America step into the shadows around the corner of the building.

Black Wolf turned his defiant gaze on America and held her eyes for a moment before turning toward the scaffold. Two deputies were approaching, and a small crowd was gathering in the street, talking excitedly about the impending execution.

No, America thought, this wasn't the time to make her presence known. The men surrounded Black Wolf and escorted him toward the platform. The crowd parted like wood cleanly split with a new axe.

America propped the flintlock up behind a barrel that sat at the back of the building, then stepped out, the pistol concealed by the folds of her skirt. She walked toward the crowd, following the deputies. One of the lawmen was lagging behind the others, and America took advantage of his slow gait to catch up with him.

"Sir! Sir," she said in a whisper, "I wonder if you could help me out."

He was a young man with eyebrows that gave his face a serious look. "Ma'am," he replied, "this is not a good time."

"But it's my mother, sir; she wants to see the hanging and she's an invalid."

The deputy in front of him had heard most of America's fabrication. He turned around. "Go on, Frank," he said with a guffaw. "Marshal Gates and I can handle this one. Don't want the old woman to miss out on an Injun hanging."

America shuddered inwardly as she gave Frank, the young deputy, a grateful smile. She let him lead the way.

"Where is she?"

"Back here, sir," she replied. "We tried to take a less traveled path—" As she rounded the corner behind him, she brought the butt of her pistol down on the back of his head. He crumpled to the ground without a sound. For a moment, America was afraid she had killed him, and she bent over him to make sure that his heart was still beating.

"Hey, Frank, the marshal told me to come help—" The other deputy, a short, burly man, came around the corner in time to face America and her pistol. He blinked rapidly several times as realization dawned.

"Take off your gunbelt," America demanded.

The deputy held out a hand as if to calm America down. "Now, ma'am, I don't know what this is about, but—"

"Please do it now," she said in a flat tone.

The deputy's expression became patronizing and confident. "Look, miss." He began to walk toward her, his hand still out. "You don't want to pull that trigger. The marshal will hear it and—"

He lunged at her and grabbed the pistol from her. Stepping back, he eyed her weapon to see if it was loaded. America's back was up against the building and she was right next to her flintlock. Her hand strayed toward it, just a few more inches and—

"You could have hurt yourself, ma'am," the deputy was saying with a frown. "These guns, they can go off without warning—"

America hit him with the flintlock, right across the shoulders. He staggered, dropping her pistol to the ground. A second tap to the back of his skull brought him to his knees. America stepped over him and, with some effort, took his gunbelt.

She stepped over to the other deputy, who was starting to come to. After giving him another rap on the head, she relieved him of his gunbelt as well. She slung both gunbelts over her shoulders and stepped out onto the street, walking quickly to the scaffolding before anyone had a chance to stop her.

The marshal had his back to America, as did the growing crowd. All eyes were on Black Wolf, who by now was standing with the noose around his neck. He spotted her, but closed his eyes. It was the hangman, a slender man dressed in a formal black suit, who first noticed America's approach. But not until she was halfway up the steps.

"Marshal," he called out, "I think we have trouble."

America kept well down, making herself a smaller target for anyone in the crowd who might have a gun handy. She swung the flintlock up and pointed it at the lawman as he turned around.

"Let him go," she said.

Marshal Gates blinked, then seemed to recognize her. "You! What are you doing here?"

"I've come to free him," she said. "He's innocent."

The marshal made no move. America motioned for the hangman to step away from the lever and to take the noose off Black Wolf's neck. The executioner complied. As he started to step away, a shot rang out from the crowd. The hangman sank to the ground, bleeding from a bullet in the back.

Realizing that the bullet had probably been meant for Black Wolf, or herself, America began to perspire. She couldn't take her eyes off the marshal, but noticed Black Wolf's eyes sweep the gathering below.

"Innocent?" Gates asked. "He killed an army man a few months ago and we just caught him the other day trying to abduct a child." Light dawned in his eyes. "The child you claim to be yours!"

America gave him a bleak smile. "She is mine, and the Sanfords know it. He was just trying to get my daughter back to me."

"He also killed a man, missy," the marshal said. "An army man."

"Then why isn't he being tried by the army?" America asked.

"We got him first on the attempted kidnapping."

"And that warrants hanging?"

Marshal Gates shrugged. "He's an Indian." His hand hovered near his gunbelt, but Black Wolf neatly drew the pistol out of it and stepped away.

"Give him the keys to the manacles," America ordered the marshal. Reluctantly, the keys were tossed to Black Wolf.

"Of course he's guilty," the marshal replied. "The army told me to go ahead with the execution."

America may not have been a lawyer, but she had grown up with a lawyer for a father, and had spent many long hours discussing law with Will. "You mean, there was no trial?" She had assumed there would have been one.

"No. I was told by a Lieutenant Markham that they had already tried him in absentia."

Black Wolf had taken his shackles off and had moved to America's side, watching the uneasy crowd the entire time.

"Mrs. Hollis," Gates said quietly, "don't do this. You know you will be wanted."

America looked at Marshal Gates. "There has been no justice for Black Wolf, and there has been no justice for me. What difference does it make?" She backed up with Black Wolf by her side. "Ask yourself this, Marshal—

why did the army have you proceed with the hanging so quickly, with no trial?"

The lawman shrugged. "I guess because he's just an Indian."

She shook her head solemnly. "I think you know why."

America and Black Wolf backed down the steps and, back to back, made their way to their horses. Once mounted, they rode out of town amid shouts by the marshal that he wanted volunteers for a posse.

When they reached the place where they were to meet Dancing Feather and Roaring Bear, a cave a few miles outside of Sutter's Fort, Black Wolf slowed down. America followed suit.

"I haven't had a chance to thank you," he said, his eyes studying her intensely. "You saved my life."

America felt a glow inside. "I've never been so scared in my life," she admitted.

He reached out and touched her hair. "You have more courage than most Shoshone warriors I have known. Some of the fiercest warriors in our nation are women. But now we must get your daughter back".

"I already have her back," she said, quickly telling him about her midnight raid at the Sanfords'.

He smiled at her tale, then said, "I must ask you once more, knowing all you know about me. Will you be my wife?"

She was silent for a minute, enjoying the feel of being alive after what had happened over the last twelve hours. Finally, she said, "Yes."

America already felt married to Black Wolf. Any wedding ceremony—whether performed by a tribal spiritual leader or a preacher—would not make them more so.

When they arrived at the cave, Dancing Feather hurried out, carrying Sierra. America reached out to encircle her daughter in her arms.

"Where will we go?" she asked as she held her daughter close.

Black Wolf squinted at the sun. "North."

Oregon Territory, America thought, or maybe farther up.

"We can stay with my people for a short time, then decide," Roaring Bear said.

Dancing Feather brushed a strand of Sierra's hair out of her face. "She is beautiful, America."

Yes, she was. But Sierra and her mother were on the run now. America was an outlaw and an outcast from white society, and she would never be able to provide her daughter with the privileged upbringing she herself had experienced. But as long as they were with Black Wolf and their good friends, they would have a good life.